D1015728

DAUGHTER

of

BLACK LAKE

ALSO BY CATHY MARIE BUCHANAN

The Painted Girls
The Day the Falls Stood Still

DAUGHTER

of

BLACK LAKE

CATHY MARIE BUCHANAN

Riverhead Books

New York

2020

RIVERHEAD BOOKS
An imprint of Penguin Random House LLC
penguinrandomhouse.com

Copyright © 2020 by 2167549 Ontario Inc.
Penguin supports copyright. Copyright fuels creativity, encourages diverse
voices, promotes free speech, and creates a vibrant culture. Thank you for buying
an authorized edition of this book and for complying with copyright laws by
not reproducing, scanning, or distributing any part of it in any form without
permission. You are supporting writers and allowing Penguin to
continue to publish books for every reader.

Riverhead and the R colophon are registered trademarks of
Penguin Random House LLC.

LIBRARY OF CONGRESS CATALOGING-IN-PUBLICATION DATA
Names: Buchanan, Cathy Marie, author.
Title: Daughter of Black Lake / Cathy Marie Buchanan.
Description: New York : Riverhead Books, 2020.
Identifiers: LCCN 2020004065 (print) | LCCN 2020004066 (ebook) |
ISBN 9780735216167 (hardcover) | ISBN 9780735216181 (ebook)
Classification: LCC PR9199.4.B825 D38 2020 (print) |
LCC PR9199.4.B825 (ebook) | DDC 813/.6—dc23
LC record available at https://lccn.loc.gov/2020004065
LC ebook record available at https://lccn.loc.gov/2020004066

Printed in the United States of America
1   3   5   7   9   10   8   6   4   2

Book design by Amanda Dewey

This is a work of fiction. Names, characters, places, and incidents either are
the product of the author's imagination or are used fictitiously, and any
resemblance to actual persons, living or dead, businesses, companies,
events, or locales is entirely coincidental.

For Mom,
with love and gratitude

Hatred is blind as well as love.

～～～

—Plutarch

DAUGHTER

of

BLACK LAKE

1.

HOBBLE

~~~

I AM KNOWN AS HOBBLE. My mother, father, and I live among the bog dwellers settled on the peaty soil of the clearing at Black Lake. The place is peaceful, remote, far to the northwest of the regions fully occupied and subdued by our conquerors. Seventeen years have passed since our vast island fell to Roman rule and became Britannia, the newest province of the Roman Empire. Even so, we persist much as we always have—sowing wheat fields at seedtime, swinging scythes at harvest, stooping under the weight of gathered sheaves. My father has long contended that great change exists on the near horizon. "They edge closer," he says, of the warriors worming westward across Britannia. "They will bring their Roman ways." His palms turn open as he speaks, welcoming. My mother's lips press tight. Her fingers twist a fold of woolen skirt. And me? As one year rolls uneventfully into the next, I have come to think of the talk that so agonizes my mother as little more than the yearning of a discontented man. But then three days ago, I saw them on that near horizon.

Romans in our midst—a vision preceded, as always, by a flash of white light.

VISIONS ARE NOT NEW TO ME. I knew my birth from one of the earliest, a scene that had come to me even before I abandoned my mother's breast. I saw the swirl of milky curls that would one day fall to my waist, the blue eyes that remain as startling as the first violets poking through the thawing earth. I watched my mother stroke my tiny earlobe in that vision, the pads of my toes, and then gently turn me in her hands. She saw it then, the mark on the small of my back—a stain like elderberry dye slopped from a mug to form a reddish-purple crescent at its base. My father was drawing his knife through the jelly and sinew of the umbilical cord and had not seen the mark. Though she had labored hard, she possessed the wherewithal to pull me to her breast, tucking that crescent from view. What to make of the stain hidden behind her pulsing wrist?

She touched her fingers to her lips and then, with great reverence, threaded them through the covering of rushes to reach the earthen floor beneath, a spot alongside her sleeping pallet. She held them there a moment longer than was customary in honoring Mother Earth, the goddess who had blessed the seed left in her womb, same as she did the seed sowed in the fields.

MY MOTHER has not breathed a word about the mark, and yet I know to keep the small of my back hidden, even from my father. I know to protect the secret shared between only my mother and me. Always, I use two clasps at each shoulder to bind the front of my dress to its back when one would suffice. Though we do not speak of my birth, I can describe the deep blue of the veins webbing my mother's breasts, the slight tremble of my father's hand as he clenched his knife, and above all, the way she hid the crescent from his view. The finer points of the scene glinted before me with the exactness of a sharpened blade, same as they had for that vision of Romans at Black Lake.

THREE DAYS AGO, as my mother and I gathered sorrel to flavor our evening soup, my mouth flooded with the taste of metal. I stopped in my tracks and steadied myself for the vision that I knew would come. The metallic taste broadened, and I waited for light, white as the sun. It came—blinding for a flash—then vanished. I saw the clearing at Black Lake—the lone bay willow; the thick lower branches of the nearby ash, the one that swooped close enough to the earth that the children in our settlement seldom resisted the perch.

I counted eight figures riding into the clearing, figures who appeared more instrument than man. Metal plates covered their torsos and shoulders. Bronze helmets protected their heads. Flaps shielded their cheeks. Their right hips held swords; their left, daggers; their fists, spears of several lengths. Each sat abreast a horse, his well-muscled body taut, ready to strike. Then, within an instant, I was back to the pretty day, the sorrel that blazed green. "Romans," I gasped to my mother. "At Black Lake."

Her face fell.

"Mother?" I said, waiting for the consolation I had known her to weave from even the flimsiest threads.

Her fingers let loose a clutch of sorrel, and it fell to her feet.

'HOBBLE

~~~

I AM THIRTEEN YEARS OLD, just a few moons shy of my mother's fourteen years when she took her first mate. It is an age when a girl grows curious about her parents: their courtship, their happiness. I see how my father's eyes follow my mother as she grinds dried meadowsweet, preparing a remedy for an aching head. I notice the rise and fall of his chest deepen as he watches, the softness of his gaze, his hesitancy as he reaches for her, as though she might dodge his edging-closer hand. I note her uncertainty—the pause before she wraps her arms around his neck, as though she needs a moment to calculate the cost of that intimacy. I see her eyes dart away from his, like a mere girl, drawn to him but lacking the familiarity of a mate who has shared his table and sleeping pallet for fifteen years.

All this, and yet, sometimes my mother stands undetected, except by me, contemplating my father—Smith, he is called—a look of longing plain on her face. She once held her palm to her cheek and said, "Never has there been a better man."

I work to piece together my parents' story, to discover the wedge that keeps my mother distant from my father. I ask her about the moment she first knew his love. Her face turns girlish, faint lines retreating, as she looks into the far distance. "He made me an amulet once, forged from silver. To see it was to wonder whether the gods had a hand in crafting it."

"Where is it?"

"Gone."

"Gone where?"

"I'm sure you've heard the story," she says, twisting to reach for a bundled sheaf of meadowsweet hanging from the rafters.

The story every bog dweller knows is that she had long ago pitched the amulet into Black Lake's pool—an offering to Mother Earth. It is our custom in paying tribute, and always my mother has honored the goddess in the most excessive way. The bog dwellers call her Devout, and often nod to one another and say how well she earns her name. She is their healer after all, a woman adept at drawing the strong magic from Mother Earth's roots, leaves, and blooms.

Another time, heart pounding, I ask, "Did you love Arc?"

She looks at me, eyes wide, her bottom lip gripped in her teeth, both astonished and afraid that I should ask about her first mate. Of course, I know this fact and plenty more, too. Like midges, hearsay thrives at Black Lake.

"Never mind about all that," she says. And then she feels an urge to collect wood from the pile stacked outside the door.

But I want to know about Arc, the mate who preceded my father, and so I turn to Old Man, who has had the bad luck to have grown pained in both his knees and to have outlived his mate and seven sons. He sits upright but asleep on a bench. His head rests against the wall behind him.

I tap his bony shoulder, and his eyes jolt open, cloudy, blinking in confusion. "Hobble," he says eventually, pleased that I have come.

"I brought your magic." I hand him a small clay vessel of my mother's silverweed liniment, the same blend my father uses to soothe a shoulder grown stiff under the weight of the hammer he swings in his forge.

We comment on the warmth of the day, the fields that are nearly ready for seed, our desire that the weather hold until the wheat is planted, and then I prod. "Tell me what he was like, the man my mother loved first."

Old Man tells me Arc was orphaned at eight, his father departed from this world for the next after he was bitten by a cursed hound. Arc's mother railed and shook a fist, accusing the gods of forsaking her mate, and the next morning was found pale blue and rigid on her pallet. After that Arc lived in the smallest shack at Black Lake, at first with Old Gazer, a loner who spent his days wandering and plenty of warm, clear nights stretched out beneath the stars. As a young boy, Arc had walked behind him, examining the deer print or swallow nest at the tip of Old Gazer's staff. Once Old Gazer began to ail, he ambled off, perhaps desiring solitude for his final breaths, and Arc found himself alone.

I go to others. I prompt. I dig. I return to my mother, coax another fragment from her—a feat better accomplished when our hands are busy picking leaf from stem, straining herbs from draft.

I wait for my father's thoughts to come to me, too, for sometimes in this world of wonder they appear inside my own head and they are often useful in piecing together the patchwork. Those thoughts arrive indiscriminately, without a pattern that I can figure out. They enter my mind more like a scene, an impression given all at once, than a stream of words.

He had barely stepped in from his forge the first time I understood he had not spoken the thought that materialized in my mind. As he closed the door behind him, poof, it came to me that he was considering whether a bog dweller called Tanner would trade a section of deerskin for a new fleshing knife, whether the hide would please my mother, whether she minded the shabbiness of the sack she hung from her shoulder. "She doesn't mind that her sack is old," I said. She sometimes tapped a particular repair and said "From your father's old jerkin" or "From your first shoes."

My father eyed me, uncertainty hanging in his mind, a vague itch it seemed best not to scratch. Ignore the tingle, the prickling, and it would go away.

I have known to proceed with caution ever since, to keep to myself those thoughts he has not spoken aloud. Any notion that I knew his private mind would surely be as unwelcome as mealworms in the flour.

TODAY MY MOTHER keeps constant vigil from the fields. Her hoe stills, and her eyes lift to the southeast. I see her throat constrict, soften, but no amount of swallowing seems to rid her of the bitter taste of dread. She has forbidden me to wander the woodland, even to collect sweet violet for the draft that eases sleep. "But what about Walker?" I said, well knowing my mother's soft spot for the woman who, deprived of the draft, would pace through the night. Without shifting her gaze from the far horizon, my mother shook her head.

As I trudge in from the fields my father looks up from his work in the forge, fixes on my lopsided gait, and lays a hand over his heart. My deformity so pains him. And my status as a field hand, too. How far the Smith clan has fallen since the days of his youth. It is just the three of us now—my father, my mother, and me. Beyond my parents, the only kin to have welcomed my birth was my mother's mother, and even she is gone now, succumbed to an unrelenting cough soon after I had taken my first steps.

Though he works alone, the forge is expansive—some twenty paces in breadth, large enough to accommodate a dozen blacksmiths. In my father's youth, his father, brothers, uncles, and cousins all shouted over the din of iron clanking iron. Much more so than my mother and me, he feels the ruin in the unoccupied anvils, the ordinariness of our clothes, the storage vessels empty of smoked venison and salted pork, the shelves cleared of the finery traded away over the years for the iron bars that allow him to work, for the hard cheese that preserves my family those years the harvest is poor.

The forge stands roughly at the center of the clearing and is ringed on one side by the nine roundhouses where Black Lake's hundred and forty-two men, women, and children live. With its low walls, the forge is more roofed shelter than cabin. My father likes it that way. The open walls mean that the hearth's tremendous heat drifts away; that he can exchange greetings with the bog dwellers as they go about their lives; and, most of all, that he is often able to glimpse my mother and me as we work.

He calls out, "Hard day?"

"Not so bad." I pull my tired shoulders straight.

Hot iron sizzles as he drops it into the cooling trough. He unfastens the ties of his jerkin and steps from the forge. When I am within reach, he tousles my hair, and I lean into his hand.

Had I been a boy born to a tradesman—a blacksmith, in my father's case—I would have inherited my father's trade. But as a girl, I take my status from my mother and that makes me a hand, a bog dweller born into a life of sowing and reaping. As our healer, my mother leaves the fields midafternoon to prepare the remedies that keep us well. It is our hope that one day special dispensation will be extended to me, too. For now, though, I remain unrecognized as apprentice healer and raise my hoe daybreak to nightfall, bringing it down on clods of clumped earth.

Though my days are hard, after I am through in the fields, my father and I make a daily sojourn to the bog, where I run the length of the causeway—a platform of rough timbers that reaches across wet earth and then out over Black Lake's shallow pool. My mother says the running lessons—as she likes to call them—began as soon as I first stood on two feet. She had already explained the nature of my imperfection to my father—how the thighbone of one leg was not fully nestled in the hip socket, how I would always limp. I have imagined his head in his hands as he wept. Who would love his child? What would become of a cripple hand? My lame leg made me a runt. I expect that, even as tears rolled over his cheeks, he had made up his mind: I would learn to run.

My speed has improved, and each year at the games that accompany the Harvest Feast, I race the other youths and show the entire settlement my strength. I have seen a sparrow knock a hatchling with a bent wing out of its nest, a ewe prod a runt away from a milk-laden teat. I remember the deformed hoof of the boar, the cleft palate of the lamb—both slain on the stone altar, offerings to the gods, each a runt, as tradition holds. I know the importance of never appearing weak.

"Let's go," I say.

He unthreads his fingers from my hair.

"It's so peaceful at the bog," I say, pushing merriment into my voice. "I like the mist and the way the mud smells. I like how it gets dark there first."

He thinks a minute, then nods his agreement that, yes, it is true. Any given evening, it is darker at the bog than in the clearing. "You notice so much," he says. "Always have."

I take his hand as we cut across the clearing and leave behind his forge and the thatched roofs and wattle-and-daub walls of the round-houses clustered there. I grip it tightly in the woodland, reach across my ribs with my free hand to clutch his wrist.

His pace slackens, and we still. "You okay?"

"It's nothing," I say. "A little jumpy. That's all."

"The Romans?" His brow furrows. "Your mother told me what you saw."

Though she does not share, with my father, the secret of the crescent on the small of my back, she speaks freely to him about my visions, and he has witnessed their truth: a strayed ewe returned with a torn ear, for example, or a vixen birthing her kits in the forge, both instances I had foreseen.

"Changing wind brings new weather," he says.

Or storms, I think but do not say.

"The southeastern tribes have grown rich trading with the Romans," he says.

I know the history, his opinion. I have heard him tell it before. As far back as anyone can remember, the tribes in Britannia's southeast traded salt, wheat, timber, cattle, silver, and lead for the indulgences brought from distant lands inhabited by the Romans. Yes, he admits, the Romans eventually grew disgruntled with their lot as simple traders and came bearing swords. But the tribesmen, he continues, they hardly resisted. Why? Because they saw futility in battling the Romans. And they saw the advantage of expanded trade.

I force lightness in my voice. "They say more and more Romans settle in the southeast. Mother says we'll lose our way in the world. She says the Romans are our conquerors, that we shouldn't forget."

So far we have been spared their intrusion; Black Lake is on the far side of the island. But I saw the will and might destined to arrive—men with armor and rigid faces, men with tense limbs and glinting blades.

He glances toward me, takes in the slight tremble that has come to my lips. "I know," he says. "I know."

I hurl myself against his chest and only then realize the full burden of my fear. He wraps his strong arms around me. His heart beats steady as a drum.

I have seen his legs coil, at the ready, when a stranger appears at Black Lake—a trader come to hawk his wares, a wanderer arrived to beg table scraps. I watched as he leapt the low wall of his forge, hooting and hollering and raising his hammer, when the grass at the fringes of the clearing parted to reveal, a few strides from me, a snorting, pawing wild boar.

He holds me tight, and sheltered in his mighty arms, my heart slows to match the beat of his. The Romans will bring no harm to so beloved a daughter, not so long as my father presides from his forge.

3.

'HOBBLE

~~~

A CLOUD OF DUST appears beyond the fields, at first so faint that I squint and peer across the freshly furrowed earth. I straighten from squatting. My mother and I have spent the morning with the rest of the hands in the field closest to the clearing—seed wheat falling from our fingers, disappearing beneath the black earth. The cloud swells and at its center a dark speck emerges—a horse galloping at tremendous speed. I feel my knees weaken as I wait for seven more horses, for glinting armor and swords. Soon the mount grows recognizable—not a Roman but a druid with a gleaming white robe fanned out behind him like spread wings. But something is amiss.

Druids—our high priests—come to Black Lake to bless the feasts at festivals and to carry out our most sacred rites—the sacrifices undertaken to appease the gods. They rule the settlements as our lawmakers, our judges, emissaries who tell us the gods' will. It was the druids who stirred up the early resistance to our Roman invaders; and my father says the Romans have not forgotten the power the druids hold, their ability to provoke, even coerce rebellion against Roman rule. As a consequence, whenever one of our druid leaders comes, he rides under the cloak of night. Not this druid though. He rides by daylight, and I have never known a druid to be so careless as that.

When I was a child, a druid's raised arms stirred feelings of consolation and hope in me. But as I grew, I began to notice how the adults spoke of the druids in hushed whispers, and afterward touched their lips, the earth. I had gone to my mother. "Are you afraid of druids?" I had said.

I remember the answer she gave. I even remember her lacing her fingers together in her lap as she still does when deciding what to say. She said that in her youth, the wheat rotted in the fields one harvest. I nodded because I already knew about the rain and the ruined wheat and the bog dwellers who starved. It was an old story, one I had heard many times, a story passed down with solemn faces and then fingers to lips, to the earth.

My mother took my hand then—I remember that—and said, "That harvest, Hobble, a druid commanded a sacrifice."

Sacrifices were how we regained Mother Earth's favor. During a plague of moths, we offered a dozen laying hens. Another time—a drought—we sacrificed a pair of partridges. It was ordinary for us to make an offering, even a ewe, to secure a good harvest.

This is the point where my recollection grows blurred. Sometimes I remember her voice turning raspy, like the edges of the words caught her throat, as she said, "He commanded that a blind boy be slain."

Sometimes I remember saying, "A runt?" and then my mother cupping my hand with both of hers as she whispered *yes*.

Other times, though, I am uncertain any such revelation took place.

I have imagined a blind boy heaved onto the stone altar, the hands that must have held him still as his throat was slit, as he was drained of his blood. Having imagined it time and again, it has hardened into something like memory. Might the same be true of that moment when my mother spoke of a runt slain? Most often I lean toward believing that my recollection of that conversation is corrupted. Never has she repeated the story, and never has any bog dweller, when recalling the bleak aftermath of the rotted wheat, suggested that anything other than the customary laying hens or ewe was offered to the gods. And if a blind boy lived at Black Lake in my mother's youth, how strange that no mention of him enters the bog dwellers' talk. How inconceivable.

The druid racing toward us rides by the light of day and does not hide his flowing robe. I look toward the clearing for my father and see he has already stepped outside his forge. All around him, bog dwellers hush. Looms stop weaving cloth and quern stones cease milling grain. Fingers still from mending, from stringing bows with gut. As I scan those distant bog dwellers—now filing toward the center of the clearing—I spot Feeble in a sling on his father's back.

Feeble was born four years after I was, a fifth child for Tanner, who heads the clan that tans the hides at Black Lake. The newborn's brow stretched twice the normal size and a soft, membranous lump protruded from his lower back. Such a brow was a sign of pressure beneath, an aching head. My mother was called to the Tanner roundhouse, and for the newborn she left willow tea to be sucked from a scrap of cloth.

I think of her returning home from that call, her head hanging low, and explaining to my father that there was nothing to be done for an improperly formed spine. Had my father's heart fluttered, a flicker of lightness, as he digested her words? Had he counted his good fortune that I had been replaced as the most imperfect at Black Lake?

Feeble did not take his first steps until he was four, but he was not like the usual toddlers—teetering two steps one day and six the next. He never progressed much beyond a dozen, before he collapsed to the ground. Nowadays he spends most of his time cradled on his father's back, or slouched against a wall, moaning and holding the aching head that no amount of willow tea can soothe.

Why has the druid come? The eldest of the Carpenters—that Black Lake clan respected for their sturdy wheels—had recently taken his last breath, collapsing even before he loosened the harness he used to haul logs. But we knew how to proceed without a druid's guiding hand, and days had passed since we took the body to Bone Meadow—that place where flesh decays, where maggots and carrion pick bones clean. Could the druid only mean to lay offered loaves in the fields once they are fully planted? But then why the rush when only half the fields are sowed? And why ride by day?

My mother positions herself between me and the druid very nearly upon us, but I peek around her thin frame, straining to see any evidence of eight mounted Roman warriors in quick pursuit.

His horse still at a gallop, the druid skirts the field where we stand. As he passes, I take in his ridged brow and deeply grooved cheeks—a face made lean by unrelenting effort, I think; by accomplishment.

"He isn't old," says Sliver, my steadfast friend, born when the moon shone a thin slice in the sky. "Druids are supposed to be old."

"Usually, my sweet. Hush." Sliver's mother touches her lips, the earth.

"His beard is short," says Sliver's younger sister Pocks, whose skin is pitted around her mouth.

"It isn't white," adds Mole, his eyes beadier than usual as he squints to see.

The color has not yet drained from the druid's hair or beard. Both are trimmed and still reddish brown. He rides erect on his horse, rather than with a humped back. The whispered consensus among the hands is that this particular druid has never before come to Black Lake, that his face promises severity, and that his youth suggests recklessness, impatience.

"Don't like the looks of him," Old Man says.

Sliver tugs her mother's arm in the direction of the clearing. "Let's go. Let's see what he wants."

The hand children begin to plead.

"The horse. I want to see the horse."

"He might bless us."

"He might leave."

"It isn't fair, missing out."

The hand mothers shush their children, pull them close; and for a moment, I breathe in the comfort of shared fear.

"Why has he come?" Sliver asks.

"He's come to lay the loaves," her mother says, her weak smile as unconvincing as an early thaw. "That's all."

"Your Romans," my mother murmurs just loud enough for me to hear and lifts her fingers to her lips.

The druid's horse halts a step shy of my father and those bog dwellers gathered in the clearing. As the druid dismounts, all of us—in the fields and the clearing—touch our lips, then the earth. We remain crouched on one knee. Eventually Hunter, who is First Man at Black Lake, rises to address the druid. As our settlement's leader, he has no choice. My father briefly held that role, before the distinction passed from the Smith clan to the Hunter clan. Though that loss pains him as keenly as an open wound, today I do not feel a scrap of remorse.

Hunter and the druid speak—Hunter, with his head bowed. I try but can hear nothing other than the shrill cries of a caged partridge fretting outside the Hunters' roundhouse door.

The druid beckons those of us kneeling in the fields, his arm cutting through the air, a gesture he must repeat a second time when, for a moment, our knees remain rooted to furrowed earth.

Old Man steps first toward the clearing, then Sliver and Pocks. Sliver teeters on the edge of skipping farther ahead, then glances over her shoulder, seeking permission, but her mother clasps her daughter's shoulder, tethering her to the group. My mother and I hesitate, putting off that moment when my lame leg will reveal me as a runt. I seek courage in the idea that the druid has already seen the misshapen boy bundled on Tanner's back but find it in a nobler thought: Soon I will show the druid how I can run.

When my mother and I reach my father, we drop to our knees on either side of him. He rests a hand against my shoulder blade, wraps his free arm around my mother, who does not shy away but rather leans into the heft of him.

"I'm called Fox," the druid says.

I try to keep the quickness of foxes from my mind, their known cunning. My eyes lift to his reddish-brown beard. It is bushy. Yes, like a fox's tail.

He moves among us, his fingertips grazing our shoulders, the backs of our necks. He approaches the three of us. I hold my breath as he shifts to squatting, as he lifts my chin with two fingers so that we are face-to-face. "A runt," he says.

My eyes flicker to Feeble, a lowly effort to redirect the druid's attention to Black Lake's true runt. But Fox's two fingers press against the fleshy underside of my chin, and I cannot manage even to turn my head. Then my mother touches the druid's sleeve, lifts her face. She is fine featured, lithe, pale, ethereal in her beauty. Just now, though, she looks as frail as a sigh. "A seer," she says, timid as dew.

She bows her head again. The cords in her neck appear, withdraw, a slow laborious pulse.

Fox huffs. "And what is it the runt sees?"

"Romans," my father says, his voice low yet laced with authority.

My parents gamble, then, to shift me from runt to seer, from unworthy to worthy in the druid's mind.

Fox's eyes light with interest, and he leans close enough that I feel the wet of his breath. "Romans?"

I blink, make a slow wisp of a nod.

The horse paws the earth, and Fox's fingers drop from my chin. He pats the beast's hindquarters, strokes the hollow running the length of its neck. He turns back to the gathered crowd. "Rise," he commands.

I watch as bog dwellers straighten, brush the dust from their knees. My father hoists me to my feet. He holds me steady as Hunter steps forward and touches Fox's sleeve. "Come," Hunter says. "Come eat, rest with us." As First Man he is obliged to provide the druid respite from a hard ride.

"You," Fox says to Hunter. "See that the horse is watered and fed."

He turns to me. "What am I to call you?"

"Hobble," I say, a tremor exhaled. A maiden who walks with a limp.

He juts his chin toward my father. "Your maiden?"

"Yes."

"I'll reside with your clan, then. Your prophetess."

My mother quiets the hand reaching for her lips, returns it to her side. My father nods slowly, evenly. As Hunter takes up the horse's reins, I notice the hard set of his face—irritation that Fox has chosen my father's household over his, over that of Black Lake's First Man.

"Come, Devout, Hobble," my father beckons, and the crowd parts, clearing passage for my small family.

4.

DEVOUT

≈≈≈

EVOUT WAS ONCE A MAIDEN of thirteen, wandering the woodland at the northern boundary of the clearing at Black Lake. She felt the sun reaching through her skin cape and her woolen dress as she walked, gaze sweeping the curled leaves, twigs, and fallen branches of the woodland floor. She bristled with anticipation. Now that she had begun to bleed, that very evening she would join the rest of the youths eligible to take mates in celebrating the Feast of Purification. Together they would mark the advent of a new season, and in doing so leave behind the cold, bitter season called Fallow and welcome the slow thaw of the season called Hope. At such a promising juncture, Black Lake's boys offered trinkets to the maidens. With a polished stone or an opalescent shell, a boy made known his desire to take a particular maiden as his mate, and with that gift accepted and then a witnessed declaration, a maiden cast her lot.

Devout told herself not to be selfish, not to set her heart on holding in her cupped palms evidence of a boy's yearning. It was her first

Feast of Purification, and the possibility of a mate remained as un-fathomable as the distant sea. Still, the idea of a trinket, of being singled out, of wide eyes and maidens gushing that she had drawn affection—all of it glinted like a lure before a fish.

She stooped to peer beneath a bush, looking for the bluish-purple petals of the sweet violet she had come into the woodland to collect. The flower held strong magic: A draft strained from a stew of its boiled flowers brought sleep to those who lay awake. A syrup of that draft mixed with honey soothed a sore throat. A poultice of the leaves relieved swellings and drew the redness from an eye. She touched her lips, then the earth. "Blessings of Mother Earth," she said.

Mother Earth would come that night, and in Devout's mind's eye, she pictured her arrival, imagining it much like the mist rolling in from the bog. Mother Earth would glide into the clearing, permeate the clutch of roundhouses, and in doing so chase away vermin, dis-ease, wickedness. The cleansing put the bog dwellers at ease. Though the Feast of Purification came at a time when the days were growing longer, still night ruled. After a day that was too short for the bog dwellers to have grown tired, they tossed amid tangles of woven blan-kets, furs, and skins, worry creeping into their minds. Would the stores of salted meat, hard cheese, and grain last? Was there enough fodder left for the sheep? Had slaughtering all but a single cock been a mistake? Were the ewes' bellies hanging sufficiently low? Were their teats adequately plump? But with Mother Earth's visit, the ewes would lamb well, perhaps even produce a set of twins. Their milk would come in. Stinging nettle leaves would unfurl, ready for the cauldron, while the stores still held enough oats to thicken the broth. The cough that had plagued a newborn for two moons would disap-pear. The bog dwellers would begin Hope—that season of birthing, sowing, and anticipation—free of worry and disease. Purified.

As she searched for sweet violet, Devout thought of the wild boar that a bog dweller called Young Hunter had slain. He had been so arrogant on his return to Black Lake, calling out for men to help haul the carcass, recounting how he had tracked the boar three days, but never once pausing his story to give Mother Earth the praise she was due. Even so, Devout salivated. This Fallow, like most every other, bellies had seldom been full.

In preparation for the evening, Devout and the other maidens would bathe and comb out their hair and leave it unbound to show their purity and youth, and clasp over their shoulders woolen dresses that smelled of the breeze rather than unwashed flesh. Then they would call at each roundhouse in the clearing, collecting offerings of honey and wheaten beer and bread still warm from the griddle. Last, they would stop at the largest of the roundhouses and find, above the firepit's lapping flames, the expertly roasted boar. The girls would set aside part of their haul—an old custom, staunchly followed by the bog dwellers, and not only on so hallowed a night. Of all they reaped, they returned a third to Mother Earth, payment for taking what belonged to her. And then, fingers slick with grease, they would swallow pork and bread and wheaten beer until their bellies grew taut. Eventually the boys would come, rattle the barred door, and demand to be let in for the dancing and merrymaking that would last until daybreak.

She heard the snap of a branch behind her and whipped around to see a boy a year older than she was. "Young Smith?" she said.

Of course she knew him. Only three dozen of the bog dwellers were youths, and he was a tradesman, one of the high-ranking Smith clan—thirty-four strong, and easily the largest and most prosperous at Black Lake. He was the youngest of six brothers, born after a gap of six years, and the only brother not yet joined in union with a mate. His clan's roundhouse, where they would celebrate that night, measured twice the breadth of any other. Inside, the low benches and sleeping pallets were heaped in skins and furs, and the shelves teemed with flagons and serving platters. His father—Old Smith—supplied the bulk of the accompaniments for the bog dwellers' feasts. He fed and clothed a pair of orphan hands, an old woman without kin, and the family of a man crushed when an elm was felled. His wealth and generosity had established him as the uncontested First Man at Black Lake, and as such, he decided when the fields would be sowed and reaped, when the stores of grain and roots would be rationed, when an ox would be replaced or a ewe slaughtered and offered to the gods.

Young Smith was already the tallest among the brothers, and though his bulk had yet to catch his height, his broad shoulders foretold the strength that would one day assist him in his clan's forge. There was talk, too, that his father entrusted him alone with the most delicate bits of ironwork, that he accompanied his father, more so than his brothers, as he inspected the fields or adjudicated the bog dwellers' grievances. He was a boy much discussed among Black Lake's maidens—his assured future, also his muscled shoulders and forearms, his pleasing face.

Devout took in his tentative mouth, his uncertain eyes, thick lashed as a doe's. She could not claim friendship. She was a hand, and the hands and the tradesmen clans held themselves apart at Black Lake. Young Smith seldom spoke to her more than a few words called from the low-walled forge where he worked alongside his kin. Usually "fine day" or "the wheat looks promising," though once she had wondered if he had said "the hearth is ablaze here, if you're . . ." before his voice trailed away. She had given little thought to him as other than a blacksmith of burgeoning skill. He ranked far above her, beyond her reach—a circumstance that was perhaps unfair given her usefulness as apprentice healer at Black Lake. And there was her piety, too. She bit her lip as she sometimes did at those moments when she recognized herself as prideful. Mother Earth expected humility.

"I made something for you," he said now. He held out his hand, and she saw a packet of folded leather about the size of a walnut.

A blacksmith, a tradesman such as he, was offering a gift to a hand on this particular day? She took the packet.

She unfolded the leather and into the bowl of her palm slipped a gleaming silver amulet strung through with a loop of gut. She drew a finger over the raised detail of the arms of the Mother Earth's cross at the amulet's center. She touched the outer ring. How had he accomplished the detail—swirled tendrils as delicate and intricate as a fern, a spider's web, a damselfly's gossamer wings? Not in nature, not in all the clearing, woodland, or bog had she seen the handiwork surpassed. Never had she conceived that other than Mother Earth was capable of such beauty. Though it was small, the amulet weighed mightily on her palm. "Young Smith," she whispered and raised her lit face to his. "It's magnificent."

He held her gaze and heat rose through her.

She put her fingers to her lips and then to the earth, that familiar gesture, giving herself time. He had followed her to the woodland to give the amulet to her. But why not wait until the feast? Was he wary of how the gift might be received? Could so regarded a tradesman be as unsure of himself as that? She teetered on the edge of telling him that she had never imagined such perfection, and truthfully, the amulet did bring grace to mind, otherworldliness. But then it occurred to her that perhaps he was ashamed of his fondness for a hand and could not bear the thought of an audience. But if that was so, why give her the amulet at all? Why not give it to Reddish—who was the prize of the Hunter clan, the tradesmen clan that ranked second only to the Smiths at Black Lake. Reddish, who had milky skin and hair that glinted sunshine as spellbinding as fire. Reddish, who possessed a full belly and a doting father, an endless ability to attract the favor of the gods. Reddish, who last Feast of Purification was given a comb carved from ash and etched with prettily arched ferns by one of the Carpenter brothers. She had returned the comb and made a habit of lingering at Young Smith's forge, her neck arched in laughter, her throat exposed.

Devout closed her fingers over the gleaming bit of silver. She deserved the cross more than Reddish. Reddish did not care about the magic of Mother Earth's roots and leaves and blooms. More than once, Devout had watched as Reddish stooped in tribute, her fingertips not quite grazing the earth at her feet, no look of reverence on her face.

Devout brought the fist clutching the amulet to her lips. With that gesture, Young Smith grew bold and said, "I thought you could wear it tonight while you collect for the feast."

She held the amulet against the hollow at the base of her neck.

"Let me show you," he said.

The loop of gut was doubled in such a way that by sliding the knots, it could be expanded to twice its size. He slipped the loop over her head and adjusted the knots so that the amulet hung at her throat.

She imagined going from roundhouse to roundhouse as she collected for the evening's feast, the amulet in plain view on her neck. At each door, eyes would fall to the gleaming silver, and then a little smile would show what the matriarch handing over a clay flagon of wheaten beer had figured out. Devout—a hand—had drawn the attentions of Young Smith. He had recognized her piety, her skill, her place as apprentice healer and chosen her above any other maiden at Black Lake.

As Devout and Young Smith intruded on the woodland's quiet with idle talk—the feast, the boar Young Hunter had speared, the late-night merriment to come—she felt moisture collect at her hairline. This, when in his absence, she had pulled her skin cape tighter against the woodland's chill. When he wiped his brow, she saw that it glistened, no different from her own, and her heart fluttered. Oh, but he was humble as stone. And handsome, too—warm eyed, full lipped, broad shouldered—this boy she had never dared consider, this boy who had singled her out.

Eventually he said, "I should go," but his feet remained rooted.

"It'll be my first Feast of Purification."

"Yes," he said.

"Your second," she said and thought herself daft. Boys attended the feast from the age of thirteen, and girls only after they began to bleed with the new moon.

He nodded, and her eyes fell to the woodland floor.

"Tonight, then?" he said.

She forced herself to look up, but his warm eyes were on her and her gaze flitted to beyond his shoulder. "Tonight," she said and lifted a hand to touch his arm, but too late. He had turned away.

When she could no longer make out his retreating back, she again put her fingertips to her lips and then the woodland floor. Before she had fully straightened, she heard the song of a bullfinch—a string of quick chirps broken by a longer, lower one. It was Arc—a boy, just her age, whom she had sowed and reaped alongside since childhood—calling to her. Should she answer, repeating the song, as was their custom? She shook debris from the lower edge of her dress. No, not with Young Smith's amulet hanging on her neck. But Arc, who took in the world around him, would follow her trail of disturbed underbrush and stones, and in no time, he would approach laughing, holding out a thread from her dress, a lump of dried mud fallen from her shoe, and so she worked the knots, loosening the amulet. She lifted it over her head and slipped it into the pocket of her cape. Then she answered his call, though what she really wanted was solitude, time to ponder Young Smith, his gift.

Arc appeared before Devout, wrists extending well past the rim of his skin cape and his toes poking from the scraps of hide laced around his feet. He plucked a twig from her hair and said, "I have a gift for you." A teasing smile came to his mouth. "Guess what it is."

She lifted a shoulder.

"It isn't something I can give you at the feast," he said.

Despite the amulet settled in her pocket and a looming sense that keeping it hidden there was somehow deceitful, she smiled. She liked this game. She liked Arc, too, his lankiness; his flaxen hair; his quiet voice and pale, watchful eyes. She liked that he meant to give her a gift—nothing too precious, for, same as she, he was a hand. "Not a stone, then. Not a shell."

"It's something begun before Fallow."

She again lifted a shoulder.

"It's something you want," he said.

What was it she wanted? A fertile Hope? A quiet moment to consider the amulet that weighed in her pocket? To sort through all that had just taken place with Young Smith?

"You've kept to the edges of the woodland," he said. "I like knowing my gift is something you've been looking for today."

"Sweet violets!" she exclaimed.

"Come."

He led her across a dell of dormant ferns, up a wooded embankment, and along the high, bald ridge of red gritstone and thin soil called Edge. Here the wind blew in gusts, but they traveled at a brisk pace. Growing warm, Devout pushed her cape behind her shoulders so that it hung at her back.

She took in the plain of fields nestled below; the abutting clearing and nine roundhouses; and then farther to the north, the woodland they had just left; and farther still, the bog. At its center, she could make out the dark pool of Black Lake. She marveled that the world stretched on and on, that all she knew of it was so small. She had been told she lived on a vast island but even from her high perch, she could see no evidence of the surrounding sea. She had been told, too, that the island was divided into territories, each ruled by a chieftain and inhabited by a particular tribe, perhaps fifteen territories in total, though an exact count was difficult to make with borders always shifting as old feuds erupted, as new alliances were struck.

She looked to the west, could just make out the purple-gray shadow of the distant highlands. Those highlands formed a different territory and were settled by a different tribe and chieftain. Her tribe occupied the territory abutting the highlands, a sprawling lowland plain dotted with settlements much like Black Lake.

The druids traveled the island, setting down roots in a particular settlement for a moon or two before moving on to the next. No chieftain knew the land, the history, the laws, the intricacies of the tribes the way the druids did. Nor was any chieftain able to divine the will of the gods. She thought of her tribe's chieftain, whom they simply called Chieftain. He was mighty, wealthy, yes, yet even he would drop to bended knee in the presence of a druid, a true overlord.

She would like to have lingered, gazing toward those high-lands, imagining the sea that lay beyond. Today, though, her mind churned. The silver in her pocket. Arc's promised gift. She galloped a few steps, fell again in line with him. Eventually they came to a stand of beech and, in their shadow, a bed of bluish-purple sweet violets, more than she had ever seen. Her breath caught at the sight, the idea that he had planted them for her.

On their knees, as the sun fell lower in the sky, Devout and Arc gathered blooms and leaves, careful not to take too much, careful not to pinch off stems holding unopened flowers. Before that evening's festivities, she would scrub herself with dried moss on the timber causeway that extended out over the bog's pool, lather her hair, and rinse it with the brew of chamomile so that it would glint in the firelight. Most of all, though, she needed to think about how beholden she had made herself to Arc by gathering his sweet violets, to decide whether she should return Young Smith's amulet or wear it for all to see. It seemed as momentous a decision as she would ever make.

"I've still got to prepare for tonight," she said. As the words left her mouth, her eyes fell to her laden sack. Arc would always bring her sweet violets. He would always bring her joy. At that moment, he laid his hand on her cheek, and she leaned her head slightly, putting weight on his palm. She took three breaths, strange breaths, and felt jittery, light-headed.

"I'll go, then," he said, smiling.

Once he was gone, she slumped onto the trunk of a fallen beech. Had Young Smith set her reeling in quite the same way? Was that reasonable to ask when, as far back as she could remember, she had toiled in the fields with Arc? She knew she was prideful, aspiring. With the amulet on her palm, she had been uncharitable toward

Reddish, jealous in truth. Was it only pride that had driven her to so recklessly want the amulet, to desire Young Smith? She sat there, stroking leaf litter and decay. She whispered to Mother Earth, promising humility and the amulet returned to Young Smith until she better understood her mind.

She turned her thoughts to the words she would speak to Young Smith and reached into the pocket of her cape, anticipating the craftsmanship, the grace. Her fingers felt only hide, the threads holding the pocket in place. She probed each corner, the emptiness. She held open the pocket and looked, but the amulet was not there.

She fell to her hands and knees, hunting among leaf litter as the sun fell lower still, and then grazed the horizon. She galloped down the steep slope of Edge—feet flying, stumbling, catching herself. At the place where Young Smith had given her the amulet, she dropped again to her knees and searched until the sun was gone, until there was scarcely time to make it back to the clearing and begin the collection rounds with the other maidens—her hair dull and tangled, her skin ripe with the odor of panic and toil.

She wept, face in her hands, but only for a moment. Then she wept as she ran through the woodland and then across the clearing to her roundhouse and the fresh, sweet scent of the rushes newly laid over the earthen floor, spread there in deference to Mother Earth.

What would Devout say to Young Smith? How would she explain the cross that did not rest against her throat, that she had not returned to him? Oh, how he would despise her, she who had lost his prize.

5.

DEVOUT

～～～

NINE MAIDENS CLUSTERED OUTSIDE Devout's round-house, chatting excitedly as they awaited the start of the Feast of Purification. She hung back at the pack's rear, her cape tightly bound at her neck. She counted as she breathed, work-ing to slow a heart not yet settled from riffling through brush and debris and stumbling homeward from the heights of Edge. The col-lection began, as always, with the lowliest roundhouses, and, quite truthfully, Devout's household was lowly. Unlike the others at Black Lake, it was not a clan united by blood but rather a ragtag group of eleven that had come together piecemeal. Her mother had taken a hand with a single brother as her mate. That brother was poisoned by the same pottage of mushrooms, barley, and venison that had caused Devout's father to grip his belly and shit and vomit, and then grow yellow and convulse, until breath came no more. By similar misfortune, each member of the household—Devout, her mother, Old Man, an orphan called Sullen, another widow called Second

Hand Widow, and her brood of six—lacked the net of kin with whom they would otherwise reside.

Reddish counted to three, and the maidens called out, "Mother Earth is coming." Devout's mother appeared in the doorway and, as was their custom, said, "Welcome, Mother Earth. Abide with us." She held out a small loaf. The maidens accepted the offering toward their feast, and in return filed through the doorway. They walked sunwise around the blazing firepit at the center of the round-house, a solemn procession that prepared a household to receive Mother Earth. As she paraded, Devout glanced toward her mother and saw her bewilderment that Devout trailed, bedraggled, at the pack's rear.

The next household was again small in number, and the maidens were neither surprised nor disappointed when they left with a se-cond meager loaf. The two remaining hand households promised more. Each had been blessed with fertility and was large enough that the clan could weather misfortune come to a few. The first household, for instance, bore the burden of a twelve-year-old blind boy called Lark without hesitation, perhaps because he sang sweetly, perhaps because he prepared the clan's meals with surpris-ing expertise. From that household, the maidens gleefully collected a cauldron of Lark's barley flavored with sorrel, and from the next, a sizable vessel of the butter the hands had mostly gone without for the final moon of Fallow. They made their parade, then moved on to the five roundhouses belonging to the tradesmen clans, first to the Tanners, where they knew to keep their hopes in check. While any tradesman had more to spare than a hand, the Tanners were known misers. And more, Old Tanner had not a single brother, and of the seven children his mate had birthed only two survived. The woman produced a flagon and, with chin tipped high, handed it to

Sullen. This, when the maidens rightly knew it would hold mead rather than the preferred wheaten beer.

"No doubt, only half-full," Sullen said.

"We'll fare better with the rest of the tradesmen clans," Reddish said.

True to her words, at the Carpenter roundhouse, Old Carpenter's mate held out not one but two rounds of hard cheese, proving her clan's generosity and wealth, underscoring the success they had trading the wheels they crafted. The maidens went next to the Shepherd roundhouse and were given two flagons of wheaten beer when one was sufficient; surely Old Shepherd's mate had witnessed the generosity of the Carpenters. Brimming now with expectation, the maidens moved on to the Hunters, an even more prosperous clan headed by Reddish's father, Old Hunter, and grown in number in recent years to twenty-two. What might Old Hunter's mate provide to outdo the Shepherds' two flagons? The maidens departed the Hunter roundhouse, weighted with two more flagons of beer. This, when Young Hunter had already speared the boar the maidens would eat. As they approached their final stop, Reddish settled a flagon in the crook of her arm and said, "Wait and see. We'll get at least the same from the Smiths."

As far back as Devout could remember, when stores outlasted Fallow, they sat on the Smiths' burdened shelves. The maidens called out, and Young Smith's mother opened the door, her eyes roving from one scrubbed face to the next. It would not matter that the girls were lit only by the moon and the blazing fire within. Devout's foulness, her dishevelment, would be apparent to Young Smith's mother, that is if she so much as bothered glancing at the hand maidens.

Young Smith appeared behind his mother in the doorway.

Devout gripped the neck of her cape, though it was not possible to hold it more snugly closed than it was. It pleased him, that infinitesimal shift of her hand, the whitening knuckles, and his face broke into a wide smile. His mother turned to him, turned back to the maidens, and said, "A boy besotted with a shabby lot of maidens begging at the door."

Her eyes were on Reddish as she spoke, and it was plain that his mother was not wise to her son's gift, that so far as she was concerned, Young Smith would have Reddish as his mate. His mother had concocted the insult so that Reddish would know to come into the household with her head bowed.

The maiden smiled slyly, as though certain that her life would unfold much as she had planned.

Devout swallowed hard at the thought of the woman's eyes on the glinting Mother Earth's cross. Even if Devout were washed, even if her hair gleamed with chamomile, to Young Smith's mother she would always be a hand. The woman's blindness caused something to harden in Devout's chest, and any ambivalence about wanting the lost amulet at her throat collapsed. She imagined herself alongside Young Smith, cape pushed back from her shoulders, amulet exposed as he told his mother that he had made his choice. Devout's hair shone in the scene. Her cheeks gleamed. Her dress was not creased or stained with sweat.

When finally Young Smith's mother said, "Welcome, Mother Earth. Abide with us," the words were flat, and it sent a chill along Devout's spine that anyone should call so indifferently to Mother Earth. The woman handed over two flagons of wheaten beer, also a round of hard cheese, a sack of hazelnuts, and a vessel of honey, then drew back from the doorway, and the maidens entered, Devout with her head bowed under the weight of Young Smith's gaze.

Young Hunter's boar hung over the firepit, sizzling and crackling and dripping grease into the flames. Smoke curled upward and disappeared through the roof's thatch, a sweet, smoldering reminder of the feast to come.

Though they were meant to parade solemnly, Devout looked up from the hands clasped together at her waist. She took in the great rectangles of woven wool partitioning the alcoves where Young Smith and his kin slept from the bulk of the space. Each alcove contained a sleeping pallet thick with rushes and heaped furs, and neatly enclosed by four planks. She counted ten alcoves, observed that not a single partition was the yellow gray of undyed wool but rather the blue of woad, the green of nettle, the purple of elderberry, the yellow of goldenrod. It made her think of her own home as wearisome even though the wattle-and-daub wall was well patched and the floor spread with a thick covering of new rushes. In the dim light, she noticed the hoard of swords, one for each clansman, leaning against the wall; the trio of low wooden tables; the dozen low benches ringing the firepit, each draped in furs; the shelves laden with bowls and plates and every kind of serving vessel and more flagons than even so large a clan could use.

She looked at her clasped hands, tried to focus on Mother Earth, who would come freely that very night to rid the clearing of fleas and rats and wheat-felling moths and those dark fairies—imps too small and too fast to be seen—who stole milk from ewes' teats, who snatched sprouting seed from blessed women's wombs. But she could not shut her mind to the infrequency with which Young Smith's mother trudged beyond the clearing to collect wood, certainly not to the base of Edge to draw water at the spring. Nor did she hunch for long hours over the quern stones milling wheat. She spent her days with the matriarchs of the other tradesmen clans, women with sons apprenticed to their fathers from whom they would inherit their trades. She spun wool to yarn and idly chatted about the superiority of rowan over meadowsweet in creating black dye, the usefulness of urine in making a color fast.

Was Young Smith eyeing Devout in the procession just now, seeking a wink of silver at the front opening of her cape? She would not be found out, not just yet. All the girls wore their skin capes as they paraded sunwise, their arms heavy with bread and cheese and wheaten beer. Still the moment would come when maidens slid capes from shoulders. She picked at the dirt beneath her fingernails, wondered if she might abandon the procession, slip away, and then later quietly rejoin the maidens. Might she return to her round-house, rub a handful of crushed sweet violet into her skin, masking her ripeness? She could tidy her hair. She did not want Young Smith to find her repellent as they stood face-to-face, could not bear his disapproval, though it would surely come. It was a slight like no other, her carelessness with his gift. Yet still she wanted his good opinion. She wanted the unassuming boy, who had made her an amulet and who had flagons to spare and rafters hung with every color, to favor her still. She wanted Reddish to know.

Such thoughts! And at the very moment when Mother Earth should be uppermost in Devout's mind. Her sack, at home on her pallet, brimmed with sweet violet, the full haul, even the third that belonged to Mother Earth. This, on the Feast of Purification, the very night she would come, the very day Devout had been so heed-less as to lose the cross that paid homage to her. And yet she paraded sunwise, mind ablaze rather than steadfast on Mother Earth.

Her eyes lit on Mother Earth's cross hanging from the rafters, same as it did in each roundhouse at Black Lake. Twelve rushes woven together formed the central square and four extending arms of the cross, a configuration meant to remind the bog dwellers of the goddess's limbs reaching outward to all the world. Devout went to her knees beneath it, touched her lips, the covering of new rushes spread over the earthen floor. She closed her eyes to pottery vessels and woven partitions, opened her mind to Mother Earth, to ewes lambing well, to the blush of green soon to unfurl. Devout's chest expanded, became a waiting cave. She breathed deeply, filling that hollow place with a spreading warmth, not unlike hot soup during the coldest, hungriest days of Fallow. Mother Earth had come. They called, and she had come to Devout.

She had earned her name early, after a long stint beneath Mother Earth's cross even before she had turned four. In truth she could not remember the episode, but the bog dwellers had supplied her with enough detail that it was almost as if she could: an egg, bluer than the sky, alone in the mud. The egg rescued, carried home in cupped hands, and then held in the valley where her thighs met as she knelt beneath the cross, asking for the egg to hatch. Finally, a crack appeared in the perfect shell and then a pink-yellow beak emerged, an orange-red throat, slick feathers, matted and black.

Afterward, hardly a moon passed without the girl spending an extended stretch beneath the cross. She asked for meat, and Old Smith appeared, arms heavy with a joint of salted pork for her household. She asked for the itchy pustules that had come up on her abdomen to vanish, and they dried to brown crusts. She asked for some gift to make her mother smile; and Arc, who knew the ways of bees even as a child, produced a dripping slab of honeycomb. She asked not to be afraid, and daybreak broke; for rain, and the heavens burst. She asked reverently, and exulted Mother Earth fervently in return for the gifts bestowed. It had been easy; easy to notice, too, the way Mother Earth heard her, the favor shown to so devoted a girl, the way she and her mother were spared the worst hardship when others were often not.

By the time the procession ended, Devout felt reassured, ready for the evening, as though her woolen dress were fresh, as though her hair reflected the gold and silver of the flames. Had she really considered abandoning the procession? For what? To perfume her arms? She would face Young Smith, ignore his flitting eyes as they leapt from dirt-lined fingernail to tangled lock of hair. She would say it plainly, that she had lost the amulet. And as he took in her tousled, unkempt state, he would feel relief that he was not beholden to her. No mother's fury to bear. No perplexed looks from the other young tradesmen. It struck her that Arc would not appraise her now, wondering what had possessed him to unearth sweet violets and haul them to the summit of Edge so that he might plant a glorious bed for her. Day in, day out, he toiled alongside her in the fields belonging to Chieftain, ruler of their territory. They had tilled the earth together in cold, relentless drizzle, and he had seen her nose red and running, her face set and grim.

The maidens sat on the low benches circling the firepit, passing a goblet of wheaten beer, always sunwise, each solemnly swallowing a mouthful when it was her turn. They ate the tenderloin first, slowly, pondering the sweet juice in their mouths. Devout swallowed her share of the meat and barley but hardly tasted it. She had forgotten the filth under her fingernails, and the moment when she took off her cape to reveal a dress as filthy as it had ever been passed with little anxiety. Young Smith and his clan had left so that the maidens might feast in private, but he would return to see her throat bare. Never mind, though. Mother Earth resided within her now.

What Devout felt was goodness, benevolence, peace. She wanted to clear away the new rushes, lie on the ground, and put her cheek, her heart, her hands against Mother Earth; but it seemed she should remain still, that if she were quiet, she might preserve the moment, that Mother Earth might stay.

Then the boys were pounding on the barred door, as the maidens knew they would. They smoothed their dresses, laughed, and called out, "We have more to eat," for, according to tradition, the maidens must finish the feast before opening the door to the boys. The maidens began milling and speaking loudly enough to taunt the boys waiting outside. "You'll have more loin?" Reddish called out. On such a night, Sullen answered back, "Can't bear another bite." Her usually slackened cheeks lifted. "I'm as full as a ewe's ripe teat."

Eventually the door was opened, and the boys came in with more flagons of mead and, carried in the arms of a hand called Singer, a large circular frame covered with a pulled-tight skin. It was a tool for tossing wheat into the air, for catching the grain that remained after the chaff was carried away by the breeze. But from the frame against Singer's hips, the skin beneath his tapping, patting hands, the rhythm of a song would swell.

The boys' voices boomed, and there was mead in their laughter—too easy, too loud, falsely low, mimicking the men they would become. As Devout turned toward the din, she caught Arc's eyes. He smiled, and she tumbled back to the reality of an afternoon searching the underbrush.

She glanced away from Arc, who was good, who made her heart flutter, who would favor her still, who need never know she was given an amulet. Certainly, Young Smith would tell no one, would not admit he had once felt affection for a hand. With his smile unreturned, Arc would not approach but stand bewildered. With a bed of sweet violets, he had made his feelings clear. As he stood peering over the rim of the goblet passed to him, he would wonder whether he had declared a kinship stronger than what she felt, and it made her heart ache. By now, Young Smith would have looked, seen her naked neck and felt the insult of a lowly hand's rejection. She would not go to Arc, not tonight, would not further offend Young Smith.

Her elbow was nudged, and she took the goblet Reddish held out to her. She drank a long swallow and watched Young Smith step around Young Hunter and then walk toward her in a straight line. Reddish nudged her a second time. "He comes." She and Devout stood with three other maidens, and each stirred taller as he approached. Reddish took the mead from Devout and held it to her mouth, moistening her lips, though it broke the rule of passing sunwise. And then Young Smith was close, among the cluster of maidens, saying, almost too quietly to make out, "The amulet?"

Her fingers moved to the hollow at the base of her neck. She did not wear it, and he could not pretend it was hidden by her clothing or otherwise made invisible. He focused on the spot on her neck where the amulet should have hung, his brow a web of questions.

"Amulet?" Reddish said, her face as expectant and immaculate as Devout's was unsure and unclean. "You gave her an amulet?"

Eyes leveled on Devout, he nodded.

Tiny gasps escaped the clustered maidens.

"To her?"

It was like a slap, Reddish's disbelief. Devout willed her voice to steady and said, "An amulet such as you have never seen."

Reddish turned to her. "Where is it, then?"

Devout opened her mouth to say she had lost the gift in the woodland, but under Reddish's blistering gaze, she found her tongue, her lips, her teeth forming different words: "I made an of-fering of it to Mother Earth at the bog."

Young Smith's hand clapped his chest, and all eyes on him, he worked to keep his face still, but the firmness of his jaw, the tight-ness of his lips gave away an inner storm. He had spent days. Taken great care. He had suffered risks, perhaps, even lied to his mother, saying he had stayed late in the forge perfecting his barrel hoops.

Devout's fingers went to her lips, the rushes. As she crouched there, inspecting his shoes—the laces crisscrossing his instep, the leather snugly drawn into place—it occurred to her that a hundred times over she had earned her name. Might he believe a maiden of such sure devotion would have taken what was most precious and cast it into Black Lake's pool, as was the bog dwellers' custom in honoring the gods?

His fingers lifted her face.

In his soft eyes, his relaxed jaw, she saw that he had swallowed the lie.

6.

HOBBLE

≈

FROM JUST INSIDE THE DOORWAY, Fox takes in the breadth of our roundhouse and the jumble of flora hanging from the rafters. His nose wrinkles as he spies the bundled roots, some like oversize slugs, others like wrongly formed fetuses sent too early from the womb.

My mother, father, and I hover near the door, uncertain about entering our own home, afraid to speak, to disturb. Is this how we are to live until we rid ourselves of our unwanted guest? He begins to slowly circle the roundhouse sunwise, palms open, arms splayed from his hips, lips moving in silent blessing. His thoroughness is unrelenting, and I look to my mother, whose eyes stay put on Fox, and then to my father, whose jaw is set, whose fingers are curled into fists.

Eventually, Fox clasps his hands, and they disappear inside his sleeves. "I'm famished," he says.

In silence, Mother makes a stew of greens and barley, humble fare meant for our evening meal. The silence continues as I lay a low table with four spoons and four bowls, as we take our seats, as my mother ladles stew into bowls. We do not touch our spoons until Fox lifts his and begins to scoop his meal into his mouth.

In between swallows, he peppers my father with questions: How many hands? Forty-nine. How many tradesmen? Ninety-three. Which clans trade most successfully? The Hunters, the Carpenters. Which have abandoned our old customs? None. As the interrogation continues, I await his expectant face turned to mine. That claim made by my parents—he will ask about the Romans I have seen. But he proceeds as before, without engaging me, until his bowl is emptied and refilled and emptied a second time of more stew than the complete share allotted my mother, father, and me. Fox sits afterward with fingers threaded together over a sated belly, but still his lips purse. "The Romans have built a fortress just west of Hill Fort."

Neither my mother nor I doubt my vision, and yet with Fox's news, her mouth drops open and my back stiffens. Fox's lips curve into a satisfied grin.

"I didn't know," my father says. "Hill Fort is a full three days' walk from here."

Hill Fort is the closest market town to Black Lake and takes its name from the high mound at the town's northern border. Chieftain and his kin live at the summit, their roundhouses protected by a wooden palisade.

"The Romans call their fortress Viriconium," Fox says. "It's permanent, made of stone."

He pauses, awaiting some response, but my father only turns the spoon, held between his fingers, end over end.

"They used that fortress to push into the western highlands and snuff out the last of the rebel tribes," Fox continues. "They've been as thorough as blight."

Traders come to Black Lake to take away Shepherd's wool or my father's ironware. Sometimes they bring news of rebel tribesmen swooping from the highlands—those same highlands we can see from Edge—and wreaking havoc on the Roman encampments far to the east. I sat among the bog dwellers, gathered around a blazing bonfire, listening to accounts of raided Roman camps and watchmen slain in defensive ditches and granaries set aflame and torches hurled onto the roofs of tents. Though that rumored defiance existed so far outside Black Lake that it hardly seemed real, quiet pride stirred within me. "To the rebels," the traders said and lifted their mead toward the highlands. In return, we held up our mugs and repeated the tribute.

Fox pauses again, eyes on my father, but he keeps his face blank. My mother, on the other hand, looks as mournful as the wailing wind that the last holdouts from Roman rule are defeated.

"They say warriors from that fortress take their leave at Hill Fort, drinking and eating and playing dice in the marketplace stalls." Fox raises his eyebrows. "Ever heard such talk?"

My father lifts his shoulders, opens upturned palms. "Only Hunter ever makes the trek, and it's been a long while."

"Think of it, serving mead to a Roman." Fox slaps his palms against the tabletop, startling both my mother and me. "Have they ever set foot in Black Lake, the Romans?"

My father shakes his head.

Fox nods knowingly. "No reason to stick their noses into so remote a place."

Silence throbs as I wait for my father to correct the druid, to explain that my vision foretold a band of Romans at Black Lake. Sweat collects at my neck, trickles between my shoulder blades.

When I cannot stand a moment more, I say, quiet as a lamb,

"Hunter is expecting me and Walker, too." For a low moment, I am thankful that Hunter's mother ails, that she insists only I correctly rub liniment into her limbs, also that Walker will pace the night through without the sweet violet draft that eases her to sleep. "I should go."

Fox says, "I'll accompany you. You can point out the cesspit."

"I'll show you." My father begins to rise to his feet, but Fox's hand lands on his shoulder.

"You'll sit."

No man denies a druid. To deny a druid is to offend the gods. It is a truth I have always known, and yet in such close proximity to Fox, who swallows stew and feels an urge to empty his bowels, no different from anyone else, I wonder about the perfection of druid rule. Might a druid, like any man, fall prey to his own ambitions, his own needs? Such thoughts! Dangerous thoughts. Useless thoughts, when druids have the power to banish, to condemn a man to live out his days away from his kin and the only life he has ever known.

My father sits down, and my mother's wariness washes over me like the cold shadow of a cloud.

Fox and I are not three steps from the roundhouse when he says, "You're a seer? It's true?"

I focus on the moon, shining feebly, a thin slice against a starless sky, as I nod.

"And what do you see?"

Where to start? How to start? And is it firmly in my best interest to convince this druid that I am a true prophetess? My parents seem to think so, seem to think it might overshadow that I am a runt. "Storms before they come."

"Plenty of folks predict storms."

I lick my lips. "Whether a ewe will birth twins."

"A ewe's belly would hang lower."

I point a trembling finger in the direction of the cesspit. "That way," I say. "Past the sheep pen."

"What else?" Fox says.

I take deep breath. "Spots to find honeycomb or a certain plant, white bryony most recently."

He huffs, as if to say there is nothing extraordinary in my claims.

"I caught a hawfinch fledgling. It fell from the treetops, from a nest."

He throws his palms wide.

"I hadn't looked up, but I knew—I knew to lift the bottom edge of my dress, to catch it there."

Fox halts, knocks a curled finger against his lips. "You saw Romans?"

"Yes."

"Men have had their tongues cut out, their lips sewn shut for speaking lies."

I think of the bard who came to Black Lake and sung a history of our people to the bog dwellers. I was only nine and the song was long and complicated, full of warriors and maidens and druids, places and battles with unfamiliar names. Still, much stayed with me, and even now I recall the lines that recount druids, by waves of holy hands, turning a warrior into stone, a maiden into a deer, crops into blighted, shriveled waste. "I'm not a liar."

"Tell me what you saw."

I describe the band of warriors in the clearing, their mounts. I give him details—the metal plates of their armor, the bronze helmets. Still, Fox appears unconvinced, as though anyone might know Roman armor, as though I had been told the intricacies by a trader who had come to Black Lake. My desire to be believed takes me by surprise, and for a brief moment, I consider saying I will describe the vision in front of the four witnesses our traditions require to establish a claim as fact. But then, I have a better idea: I trace the contours of a helmet's protective cheek flap over my cheekbone. Fox settles his weight into a hip, ready to consider, and I continue talking, reckless, determined to impress.

I should have remembered my father's mouth sealed shut as he turned his spoon end over end, should have remembered the way he kept his thoughts private when he did not know a druid's mind. Instead, I set loose dangerous words.

Though I have called on neither Hunter's mother nor Walker, I return to my roundhouse, I push open the door to see my mother kneeling beneath Mother Earth's cross and my father squatting at the firepit. Both are quick to their feet and then are at my side, swallowing me with squeezing arms. "I'm all right," I say. "I am."

As I pull away, I glimpse the flicker of my mother's tongue and a dab of blood licked clean from her bitten lip.

"What happened?" My mother grips my shoulders. "What was said?"

I fold an arm across my ribs, clutch the opposite elbow. "I described the Romans, here at Black Lake, same as I described them to you."

"Start at the beginning," my father says.

I bring a touch of irritation to my voice and say, "I told him what I saw."

More softly than warm rain, my mother says, "Did he believe you?"

"I wouldn't know."

"Come," she says. Her eyes flicker to my father—a tiny gesture to say that she will try alone to find out what she can—and we make our way to the sleeping alcove long ago occupied by my father's parents. "Fox will need somewhere to store his things."

She takes a pair of worn-out breeches, a ragged dress, two threadbare blankets, an old oil lantern, and then a tiny hide cap—prettily decorated with rows of embroidery—from the chest at the foot of the bed. "Yours," she says. "I embroidered it before you were born. Your father's mother taught me." She turns the cap, touches two places where the stitches stretch too long. "I was rushed." She looks up from the cap, smiles a weary smile. "You deserved better."

She folds the cap in half and pats it into place on the blankets taken from the chest. Her face glints hope as she says, "Fox won't harm a seer."

I do not say that liars have their tongues cut out, their mouths sewn shut.

"Did he ask questions?" she says.

"No."

She lifts a nest of unspun wool from the chest. She handles the mass gingerly and then peels back a layer to reveal a silver goblet, a relic from that earlier time when the Smith clan reigned at Black Lake.

I run my fingers over the band of leaping roe deer circling the rim. I had once seen my father hold that goblet and then afterward put his face in his hands. It had been a kindness, hiding an object that stirred his longing, that tipped him toward despair—the meager sort of kindness my mother is able to offer him. A different woman might have cradled his head against her chest, might have whispered, "Oh, Smith, you're a good man. We have enough."

"You can wash it for me when we're through," she says.

"You're leaving it out?"

"Fox is a druid."

"But—"

"Your father asked me to fetch it. All of us need to earn Fox's respect. Your father and I agree on that." She puts a hand on my thigh. "You've done your part."

But I have not told my parents everything. I left out what I said to Fox after he settled his weight, ready to listen. "The season was Hope," I said to him. "The leaves were in early bloom."

Fox had dropped his curled finger from his lips and sneered. "Hope?" he said. "That gives you eighteen days to produce these Romans."

I had opened my mouth to protest that I did not know the year and had never claimed to, but Fox had turned toward the cesspit.

My knees weakened as I watched after him, disappearing into the night.

7.

DEVOUT

~~~

THE EWES LAMBED WELL during the Hope that followed Devout's lie. Not a single runt. Two pairs of twins. Milk came into teats in abundance and flowed generously into the mouths of the suckling lambs. The last of the storage pits was unsealed, and the bog dwellers found that the seed wheat entombed there had come through Fallow without damage from mice or beetles or damp. The sun warmed the earth swiftly and the ox drew the plow through the fields. The weather held, and the work of breaking up the clods with hoes and mattocks proceeded without delay. The bog dwellers touched their lips and then the earth with extra care. With the seed sowed early, might it mean higher yields at harvesttime? Yes, Chieftain's men would come from Hill Fort with their oxcarts and haul away the two-thirds share due to him each year, but ample wheat would be left behind to sustain the bog dwellers through Fallow.

Oftentimes Devout's fingers found their way to the base of her neck, to the amulet that was not there. It seemed ominous, the lie she had told Young Smith. It was a poor way to begin a friendship, as though she had thrown open the door to deception, a weighty door not easily shut tight. She pictured herself dangling the amulet above the still waters of Black Lake, imagined loosening her hold on the gut loop. She watched it slide from her fingers into the murk of the lake. It was a comfort, this scene, where she truly made the offering to Mother Earth. She called it to her mind again and again, until it began to feel more like a memory than a lie. Sometimes she was able to recall certain details, the way the amulet glinted in the moonlight, the way the gut loop was the last bit to be swallowed by the black pool.

ARC TRUDGED THE length of a fresh furrow, hoisting his mattock, bringing it down on the larger clods of earth. As Devout followed, she thrust her hoe over and over, severing the smaller clods left in his wake. She watched the height to which he lifted the mattock, the force with which it met the earth, and it seemed to her that he did more than his share, that by his hard labor he intended to spare her what toil he could. "I'm stronger than you think," she said.

"I have little else to give," he said and went back to breaking up the clods.

A small ripple of what felt like hopefulness rose in her chest. She did not wish him heartache, but perhaps he missed her the way she missed him. Since the Feast of Purification, there had been no long, easy walks, no bullfinch call to answer. Like everyone else, he had heard about Young Smith's amulet.

The sun beat down, and Arc removed his tunic. She took in his chest glistening with sweat, the line of golden curls on his belly that disappeared beneath the cord holding his breeches in place. A strange ache came to her loins. She wanted to touch the ridge of muscle that ran the length of his forearm, arising close to his elbow, tapering as it approached his wrist. She put her eyes back on her hoe, breathed in and out. Was such an ache best heeded? Or better ignored? How she dreaded either boy prodding, asking if she might announce her intention to join with him in union when she felt as unsettled as a hive of bees. Surely the bog dwellers waited for Devout to hold herself tall and say, "I declare my intention to receive Young Smith as my mate." Any one of them would think her—a hand—a fool to let one day slip into the next without securing Old Smith's treasured son as her mate. Arc offered kindness, familiarity, gifts of sweet violets, that pleasant ache; but when she thought carefully, clearheadedly, all she knew with certainty was that once it would have been enough.

But then came Young Smith's attention, and now her growing confidence that he did not loathe her for making an offering of his gift as she had claimed. In the moons since, he seemed to watch for her to appear in the clearing so that he might smile and take up his hammer, perhaps too vigorously. Sometimes he fell in line beside her as she came in from the fields. He said he hoped preparing the fields was less grueling with the sun so strong in the sky and, another time, that he had woken to the rain and been thankful it meant a day of rest for the hands.

One day, he asked quite plainly if she would follow him. He said he had something he wanted to show her in the old mine. Quiet tunnels and caverns riddled the base of Edge, a maze hacked from the red gritstone by those seeking the copper ore long since hauled away. She had seldom been to the mine, which was meandering and black as night and forbidden by her mother. He carried two rushlights, as though she had emboldened him those other times they had spoken, as though he had not considered that she might refuse him. Even so, she hesitated. Might he mean to ask her about the declaration she had not made? Might he mean to push? But then, how was she ever to know her mind if she dodged Young Smith's every advance?

"It's safe," he said. "I know the mines better than just about anyone. I've gone looking for ore there for years."

Anxious that he had interpreted her hesitation as fear, she quickly said, "Show me your mine, Young Smith."

The sun was low in the sky, the light gentle, the shadows muted, softer than at midday. The world glowed rosy, warm, and his beauty was golden, like late wheat in a gentle breeze. She held still in that pleasing sunlight a moment. She let him look, let him take in her pale, open face; the small depression at the base of her chin. She knew her hair gleamed like polished bronze and held a pretty curve when she untucked it from behind her ear. It was her eyes—blue as a jaybird's back—that most often drew comment. Her mother had once said it was a shame, the way those eyes held the bog dwellers transfixed, unaware of the straight nose and dainty chin contributing to her beauty.

They walked side by side in the woodland, him slowing at those places where the path narrowed so that she might step ahead. They stayed quiet amid the birdsong and rustling leaves. And then, once the quiet gaped awkward, he asked about a yellow flower blooming alongside the path.

"Lesser celandine," she said. "A salve made from its leaves heals abscesses."

They continued like that, with him questioning and her reciting bits of what she knew. At one point, he stopped and shook his head. "It's incredible," he said, "what you know."

"It's Mother Earth who deserves the praise."

Eventually they came to the soaring gritstone wall of Edge and the yawning mouth of the entryway to the old mine. He struck his flint with practiced hands. Tinder smoldered, caught as he blew. He tipped a rushlight into the flame and handed it to Devout.

"You'll hear from me next time I need a fire lit," she said.

He smiled, touched his rushlight to hers, setting it aflame. "Hope so."

In that moment, she liked the idea that she would call him to her roundhouse to set tinder ablaze, or better yet that they would sit in some secluded place gazing into the fire he had lit.

He led her along a snaking passageway, taking this fork and then that. She could no more untangle their route than see into the impenetrable blackness beyond the halo of their lights, yet she felt not a flicker of distress. With Young Smith at her side, she felt light. She thought of dandelion seeds drifting upward, tethered by the smallest threads to fans of narrow wings.

Young Smith swept his rushlight over a large swath of gritstone wall that blazed orange, golden, and red. "Come," he said. He led her a few paces farther and then knelt before the wall. She joined him, and he held his rushlight in a way that showed a simple etching scraped into the gritstone.

"Do you remember?" he asked.

The etching showed three stick figures inside a circle. Devout shook her head. "I don't."

"One Harvest Feast—you would have been five—we came here." "Oh?"

"A pack of boys snuck away. Of the girls, only you and Reddish followed us."

Something flickered in her mind—boys whooping in a black

tunnel, herself amid the pack, her heart pounding, joyful, the guiding halo of light. "I remember," she said, filling with the pleasure, the glory of that old day.

"We drew this," he said.

She looked again at the etching, the chalky, ginger lines scraped into the gritstone. Did she remember a sharp rock? A knife, some tool for etching gripped in her fist? Perhaps, perhaps. Another flicker—her five-year-old self squatted at this very spot. She recalled the first thin lines, then the repetition that had made them thick.

"You drew the people," he said. "The three of them."

"And you drew the circle."

"A roundhouse."

She remembered Young Smith beside her making the picture complete, a vague sense of uplift, security. "It's strange," she said, "remembering something I didn't know I knew. It's strange to see our past."

He put his fingers on the circle, traced its arc. He looked at her, and she at him. "Maybe it's not our past," he said, and she thought that he might kiss her, that she would open her mouth to his.

She waited for his touch, wanted his touch—a kiss, a hand running the length of her spine, even an arm wrapping her waist—but it did not come.

Eventually his fingers fell from the gritstone, and he stood up. She regretted that she had not responded, had not said, "Our future, then?" as he had surely hoped she would.

On their return, she slowed as they reached the clearing, put her hand on his arm. "That picture," she said, "I'd like to see it again."

She left him without looking to see the expression on his face and continued into the clearing. Next time she would not be so closefisted. He had given her an amulet, called to her from his forge, asked her to accompany him to the old mine, and all but said their old etching foretold the family they would one day form. She had been as miserly as dirt.

SHE RETURNED HER attention to the field just as Arc's mattock fell on another clod. "Should we go to Edge?" he said, his voice luke-warm, as though it were only a passing thought.

She wanted to climb Edge with Arc, to see what she could from that only place where she had ever glimpsed what lay beyond Black Lake, but her mother would be making cheese and she should help. There was wheat to be milled to flour and thatch to be cut for a weak spot in the roof. All this, and she needed to gather comfrey root so that it might be ground to a paste, and stirred into warmed beeswax to form an ointment useful in healing the lesions blistering on a dozen of the bog dweller children's hands and mouths. The pain was mild, but she would not neglect her obligations as Black Lake's apprentice healer.

She knew the bog dwellers' ailments—Old Carpenter's gums, Old Tanner's bound bowels, Old Hunter's strained heart, one hand's menstrual cramps, another's wakefulness at night. She cured and mended and sometimes wept when all she could offer was the com-fort of sweet violet draft. For her generosity and skill in preparing Mother Earth's magic, she was praised, sometimes rewarded. When she tended a Black Lake tradesman, she might be given a scrap of hide, a handful of oily wool. From the hands, she received only blessings, bowed heads, astonishment.

"I've got to dig up some comfrey," she said to Arc, hoping he heard her sincere regret.

"A large, hairy leaf. A purple bloom."

"Like a goblet," she said, curious that he knew the flower. But then, why would he not with his habit of observing the world?

"I know a good spot," he said.

As they made their way along the path that led to the bog, he stepped lightly. It pleased her, the way he hardly disturbed the woodland floor and touched the tall grasses edging the track, their furred tips skimming his palm, the calluses left behind by the mattock. She thought of his gentle hands sliding from her cheeks to her neck.

What would she answer if asked whether she preferred Young Smith over Arc, or Arc over Young Smith? It depended on the day, who was closest, which particular moment she had most recently rehashed in her mind. Arc, when she thought of the sweet violets or the thrill that rippled through her when she heard his bullfinch call. Young Smith, when she thought of the amulet or the pair of them kneeling in the old mine. Arc, when she thought of the golden curls on his belly. Young Smith, when she thought of his thick-lashed eyes. Oh, the hours she spent pondering.

She turned her mind to silently naming the flora rooted alongside the path. Her knowledge of the riches all around had blossomed three years ago, when she was just ten. She had slipped into an apprenticeship with the ancient bog dweller who birthed the babies and cured the warts at Black Lake, who knew that a menstruous woman should not take the honey from a hive. Their familiarity began with Crone standing firmly, blocking small Devout's passage on the path between clearing and bog. "What do you seek, child?" Crone had said. Her voice was like stone sliding over stone. Her face was wizened, her eyes thinly lashed.

"Stinging nettle," Devout said, stepping backward from so ancient a woman.

"Won't be finding any so close to the path. Already been picked."

Crone pinched a handful of yellow blooms from a slender stalk and tucked them into the sack looped over her shoulder. "Bloodroot," she said and began clawing the ground with fingernails as thick and curled as talons. "Good for a nervous gut."

She teased a thick root from the earth and snapped it in half. Red sap oozed from the flesh. "I'm making dye for Old Hunter's firstborn girl," Crone said. "That buck Tanner skinned, she's got it in her mind she wants a red cape."

Few at Black Lake dyed their wool, and none their skins. It added nothing to strength or warmth, and it meant collecting and preparing the dye and then extra wood gathered and water hauled so that a cauldron could be set to boil. Still, a red cape was the sort of indulgence Reddish liked, and Old Hunter was inclined to spoil his brood.

"The scraps from the hide will come to me as payment," Crone said.

She raised a leg, stretched her ankle, rocking her foot from side to side as though showing off a foot wrapped in fine leather rather than an assortment of scraps. "I'll lace red shoes around my feet."

Crone would wear red shoes, and Reddish would cross her arms and huff. Devout dared not smile, though. The old woman was leaning close and saying, "Your name came to you because of your devotion to Mother Earth."

Devout bobbed her chin, liking how even this old woman knew her piety.

"Mother Earth's magic is a useful thing to know. The bog dwellers will need someone to prepare the magic when I'm gone."

"You're going somewhere?"

"Not just yet," Crone said. "First you have much to learn."

Devout liked the idea of being more than a hand who sowed and reaped and did not know a single thing more of the world. She liked the idea, too, of the bog dwellers one day calling her generous and wise. And would knowing Mother Earth's magic not help her in some way? Might she at some point trade bloodroot dye for leather just like Crone? Devout dipped her chin, the tiniest bit.

"I'm old," Crone said. "We'll begin today."

DEVOUT AND ARC continued through the woodland, the path beneath them well trodden by those heading to the causeway, the pool at its farthest reach. They went to scrub bodies or linens, or sometimes to find comfort in so hallowed a place. At the bog, the peat and rushes of their earthly lives touched the mist and mystery of the gods, the shadows and whispers of those already departed to Otherworld—that place without hunger and want, free of every kind of unease. The barren went to the bog, the anxious, the brokenhearted, the ill. Along with tears, they dropped offerings into Black Lake's pool—pretty stones and pottery vessels, clay roughly shaped into the tiny newborn who had not come or the eye that saw no more than dusk.

As Devout and Arc approached the causeway, he pointed to comfrey in the distance, the fallen log, and stepping-stones that would spare their feet the most sodden of the ground. He held out his hand—all strength and sparseness, all muscle, sinew, and bone. It was not unusual; many times he had steadied her as they descended slopes slick with rain or climbed patches of sheer terrain. Yet his hand had been absent since the feast, for she had not declared an intention to take him as mate. True, from that evening onward, they had been together only in the fields, but still, he used to haul her up from a low stone where they had sat drinking water and wiping the sweat from their brows. Why deliberate now, when a hundred times before she had taken his hand? She took it, because still he held it out. His fingers closed. His grip was firm, as though he would not risk her hand slipping away.

The route was tricky, and possibly his hand was only a guide. But when they came to a dry, level patch of hard-packed earth, his grip did not loosen. Her palm grew damp, but still he did not let go. He gripped infinitesimally tighter. Then his fingers threaded hers, and she gave in to an urge to rub her thumb along the ridge of his.

The comfrey consisted of a dense patch of a dozen plants as high as a man's knee. The stalks bowed under the weight of the flowers, purple and fully open at the apex of the arch, and still encased in sepal husks farther along toward the tip. In between were flowers in every stage of bloom, and it felt like a miracle, the way they were lined up in perfect order from green and unripe to purple and fully formed. "It's like seeing a lifetime all at once," Arc said, and she thought how he was her kindred spirit in appreciating the natural world.

"It's the roots we're after." She reached into her sack for a small trowel. "The taproot needs to be severed. Some are as long as a man's leg." It was what made the comfrey potent, the way it reached so deeply into the earth.

Arc took his knife from the loop of cord where it hung at his waist, and together they began to dig the circular trough that exposed the roots around the tallest of the comfrey. Their elbows, their knuckles knocked several times and they said "I'm sorry" or laughed timidly, but neither shifted to the plant's opposite side. The peat was rich and black and under their fingernails. A smear ran from Devout's cheek to her earlobe until Arc rubbed it away with his thumb, no different than he once would have in the fields. She thought of his thumb on her cheek again. She imagined turning her head so that her parted lips brushed his fingers. And it was so pleasant, that ache in her loins. How could that be when the sensation teetered on raw? Then again rams mounted ewes, and the ewes bleated and bleated yet stayed put. Her skin awakened. She felt her nipples taut against the rough wool of her dress. How strange that she could so distinctly feel the woolen folds grazing her thigh, the seam that ran over her hip. The ache between her legs widened, not unlike the pang that sometimes spread through her jaw as she raised a first heaped spoonful to her mouth after a long day in the fields.

She stood up urgently, too urgently, skittish of her mind, and she felt light-headed.

Though she was only watching now, he continued to dig. In time he angled his knife deep into the trough, working to sever the taproot. "You can tug a little from the top," he said.

She snapped from pondering to wrapping her fingers around the plant's stalk. She pulled gently and, when the comfrey did not budge, with more strength. Arc worked his knife and then she was tumbling onto her backside. She came to rest with purple flowers and hairy leaves quivering in her face.

He did not laugh, not immediately, but she could see the effort it took. "You're not hurt?" he said. And then he smiled, because she was not hurt, and it was funny, pitching backward onto boggy soil. It was the sort of thing that had brought laughter all their lives.

"I see you're not to be trusted," she said. With Arc returned to the boy she had tilled alongside in the fields, the strangeness that had come over her faded, though still her skin remained acutely awake.

They harvested the rest of the comfrey root, chatting as they worked—the fair weather, their hopes for a bountiful harvest, all she was learning from Crone. Once Devout's sack was full, Arc slung it over his shoulder and said they should walk along the causeway, that the mist had grown dense. It would feel like passing through a cloud.

A thick post reached upward from the start of the causeway to the height of a man's waist and held the large wooden wheel that symbolized the god Begetter. The causeway belonged to him, their creator, as did the bog and pool, the muck and mire from which he had drawn their earliest forefathers.

As was the custom of the bog dwellers stepping onto the causeway, she and Arc traced their fingers sunwise around the wheel. Without beginning, without end. Begetter brought the bog dwellers into this world and to him they would return. She placed her palm on her expanding chest, dwelling place of the breath he gave. Arc did the same—the wheel, his chest.

They walked side by side, bumping each other as they went. They each put one foot in front of the other, and Arc said, "Like stepping into an abyss." It was true that she could see the spot on the timbers where her next step would land but not the one after that. She liked bumping into Arc, the ease of it, the way neither of them made an effort to move apart. They took another step, and a farther timber shifted from hazy and gray to distinct and black.

Except for their breaths and footsteps, and somewhere in the distance the faint tapping of a woodpecker, the world around them was muffled to silence by the heavy mist. When a new sound came, it was Arc who heard it first. He went still, and she strained to hear what he did. From the mist farther along the causeway came a sound like someone rushing toward them over the timbers. The lightness of the footsteps told her it was a child, though the quickness suggested otherwise. The footsteps became louder and then, just when Devout expected a hurtling child to burst from the mist, the footsteps stopped, and the bog became as it had been.

She turned to Arc and he pulled her close. They stayed like that, bound together. She could feel his heart beating, his breath on her hair. How like those first warm breezes after Fallow, those first rays of sunshine potent enough to penetrate her cape. She pressed against him, wanted him closer still and yet it was not possible to be more tightly bound than they were.

Restlessness came to her, a creeping desire to investigate the source of the footsteps. As she lifted her face to Arc's, he said, "Let's take a look." They walked more quickly, though still the mist was an opaque gray mantle. Eventually they came to the causeway's end, the open water beyond.

"But there was a child?" Devout said. Our child, she thought.

"Yes."

"So strange." The vanished child, the heaviness of the mist.

She could make out his pale eyes, his slender jaw, his flaxen hair hanging in loose waves. His slight eyebrows and delicate lashes had disappeared.

"It could be last Hope or one still to come," he said.

It was true. The sights and sounds that might have tethered them to this particular day, this particular season—the one when the ewes lambed so well—were all lost in the mist.

8.

HOBBLE

~~~~~

FLEA BITES RIDDLE SECONDS—who is second son to Carpenter, the clan's head—most severely on his legs. He sits bare chested on a bench with his breeches hiked up past his knees. I apply the chickweed balm that dulls the itch on legs as strong and sturdy as a man's. He is thirteen, same as I am, and his copper hair is streaked through with red and swoops across his forehead, almost hiding eyes of the same gray blue as the morning sky. I take my time, glance up to see those eyes closed and the corners of his mouth lifted.

"All done," I say.

He opens his eyes but does not get up from the bench. "Maybe you'll go for a walk with me?" he says.

The question takes me by surprise, and I blurt, "Honey will help the bites you've already scratched."

"You're ignoring my question?"

"No."

"We're to look for honey as we walk, then?" He finally gets up from the bench.

I turn bashful and lower my gaze. He stands a head taller than I, but he ducks low and peeks upward so that I cannot avoid his face. His smile is as wide as land, and I think that a walk in the company of this boy might relieve me from scanning the southeastern horizon for the kicked-up dust of mounted Roman warriors. "Let's go," I say.

I know a half-dozen hives and lead him to one hanging from a low branch of a sprawling beech. "That's new," he says.

"Yes."

"You've seen it before?"

I understand what he is questioning. Had I come upon the hive another day through the usual means? Or had the site been revealed in some more mysterious way?

Seconds is among the group I foraged with as a child. For the most part, the children proceeded haphazardly and squatted to peer beneath any old bush, as though they had no idea where they might dig up earthnut's round tubers or pluck bilberry's purple fruit. When we returned to the clearing, my sack always hung heaviest. I had overheard Sliver's mother, Sullen, comment that I was industrious and Old Man say I knew earthnut's preference for sunlight. While both claims were true, the children knew better. They had seen me wave a hand over a hollow that held no hint of the tan, pitted mushrooms that would soon sprout at the spot and say, "We'll find morel here another day." They had watched as I stood beneath the twiggy nest of a jackdaw and predicted the six eggs we would find rather than the more usual four. The children did not probe how I knew what I did, did not adopt an adult's flawed reasoning and decide I had come that way before and inexplicably left a nest full of eggs undisturbed. The children simply accepted that I could make an accurate count of unseen eggs. Seconds had been no different from the others, but we had grown up since and for plenty of Black Lake youths, the mystery and magic so easily embraced in childhood had slipped beyond their reach.

"I'M THINKING ABOUT that game we sometimes played as children," Seconds says. "I liked that game."

It had been ages, but there were occasions when the children gathered around, and I shut my eyes. Sometimes I would open them, able to reveal the location of a particular stone. "At the spring, in the pool there," I would say to my friends, "a stone almost like ice." And off they would go, scrambling over one another to find the divined stone awaiting in the spring's pool—a stone as smooth and milky as the surface of Black Lake during the harshest days of Fallow. I was not consistently able to name a location, and when I was not, I felt the weight of having let everyone down.

I had decided to improve. To divine the location of a stone, I pinched my eyes shut and pictured a place I knew well—the spring, for instance. In my mind's eye, I scanned the smooth gritstone basin, probed the shallow pool, and sometimes—just sometimes—I would find a stone to describe. I spent more time pinching my eyes shut—in the fields or as I lay on my pallet, even as I carried a slopping bucket of water into the clearing. As I labored or rested, my mind went to the mossy floor shaded by the stone altar, to the trampled earth alongside the sheep pen, to any place I could precisely recall. I made an inventory of divined stones: at the stone altar, an oval stone flecked with gold; at the sheep pen, a jagged stone cut through with a band of white. Later, with Sliver, Pocks, Seconds, and the others waiting with laced fingers tucked beneath their chins, I opened my eyes and reported a stone, not always one I had just that moment divined. With my mind blank of a newly discovered stone, I pulled from my inventory. "A stone flecked with gold," I would say, "at the stone altar."

It meant the children came to my door, waited until I had finished milling the day's allotment of wheat to flour. It meant no one minded my limp. I was unique, yes, not because I was lame but because I possessed a gift.

Had I improved with those intensified efforts? Within a few moons, I was able to divine a stone once out of every eight or so attempts. Years would pass before we wearied of the game. By then, though, Sliver and I were inseparable, and we had turned to spending our spare time speculating whether this maiden or that bled with the new moon or deciding that sprouting Minion's name would one day shift to Stretch. Twice Sliver asked me to tell her future: Would she make the collection rounds with the other maidens at the next Feast of Purification? Who would she take as her mate?

The first time I had said, "It doesn't work like that. I don't decide what I know."

"But the stones?"

I shrugged.

The second time, I knew the answer. She would take Minion. I had seen it in a vision, plain as day—the pair of them kneeling on the causeway as they joined in union, the nettle they fed into each other's mouths to attract fertility. But to reveal this great unknown seemed almost certain to spoil the thrill of the coming years. I wagged my head without committing to whether I was unwilling or unable to name her mate. She did not push, and it made me think, same as me, she sensed the downside in denying the speculation, the longing, the discovery that would come.

As SECONDS and I stand in dappled sunlight, the buzz of the hive filling our ears, excitement ripples through me and I know I was right not to have named Sliver's mate.

"You see more than stones," Seconds says.

I nod, because I understand that Seconds wants mystery and magic. I can tell this boy is open to the astonishing.

He breaks into his wide smile.

AT LONG LAST, the work of seeding the wheat is complete and Hunter dismisses the hands from the fields midday. "Enjoy your afternoon," he says, daring to sound generous when he is not, when he is only upholding tradition because a druid lurks at Black Lake. Even the hands too young to have toiled under Old Smith know Hunter's tightfistedness. "Miser," they say and, "stingy coot." When my father's father was First Man, he suspended fieldwork three days and allotted each hand a cask of mead from his private store once Mother Earth held the seed. Still, with our storage vessels near empty and the extra mouth of a greedy druid to feed, my mother and I need the afternoon.

We roam from the clearing in pursuit of sorrel, dandelion, and nettle, even ramsons—if Mother Earth wills it—so delicious stirred into soup, mixed into hard cheese. I think of how I want the Romans to descend, how I count each passing day. I wonder, has it occurred to Fox that, with his threat, he planted in me a fierce longing for the very men he so loathes? Just this morning, he leaned close, as though I might have forgotten I have only until the end of Hope. He knew to keep his voice low as he said, "Another day come and gone, Hobble. That leaves seven." I hate how well he deciphers me, how he knows I have not breathed a word to my parents about his threat of eighteen days.

As the distance between Fox and my mother and me lengthens, I breathe in sunshine, breathe out worry. I lighten, loosen among the waking earth—shoots just poking through leaf litter, leaves unfurling tender and yellow green.

"Hunter doesn't like Fox staying with us," I say.

"Hunter clings to his position, his wealth," my mother says. "It makes him unwell, the way he clings."

"You can see it in his flushed face. Sign of a strained heart."

She nods, and then a few steps farther, she says, "Always striving, always fraught, always scheming. It's the way of ambitious men."

At the border of the woodland, I spy a span of ramsons—white, starlike flowers and elongated greenery. I crouch, touch my lips, the earth, and then ease a narrow bulb from moist soil. My mother rests a hand on my back a moment, and I know she seeks the warmth of me, the life of me—her daughter, both her worry and her joy.

She squats beside me, and as we unearth the bulbs, I feel an urge to say Seconds's name, even to hear it said, and that urge nudges me to say, "Did you hear that the Carpenters have fleas?"

"I saw Carpenter this morning. He said that without your help, Seconds would've been up half the night."

"I'll bring him more balm."

My mother hesitates in her gathering, and I await some comment about Seconds, but she says, "You'll outdo me as a healer."

Though she has dropped the topic of Seconds, I feel a warm glow.

"When I was your age, Crone had only been teaching me for three years." She puts her palm on my cheek. "And you have your gift."

According to my father, her eyes—blue and just now as steady as a hive's hum—exactly match my own.

"Come," she says. "We'll climb Edge. I want to show you something there."

AT EDGE'S SUMMIT, I scan the purple-gray highlands in the distance. The wind gusts, and I spread my arms wide, trapping the burst of air with my skin cape, and feel as though I might be lifted from Edge. I leap, glance back over my shoulder, wondering if my mother feels it, too. She opens her own cape, lets it billow. She shuts her eyes, tilts her face into rushing wind.

Eventually we move on and come to a stand of beech shadowing a tremendous bed of sweet violets. We sit on our heels, my hands drifting through the heart-shaped leaves and lobed, purple blooms, the miracle of so large a bed. And then suddenly I grow aware of a shallow sort of pulse on the small of my back, almost like the crescent there contains a heart beating out the passing moments of a life. Then the pulse retreats.

"Arc planted them for me," she says.

I twist on my haunches so that I am facing her. She does not speak of Arc. That time I dared to prod, she said, "Never mind," and left to collect wood from under the eaves.

"It was the Feast of Purification," she says. "It was a gift."

If ever I am to solve the riddle of her—the way she holds herself distant from my father—I must wade carefully. "Everyone says he was nice."

She nods.

"What was he like?"

"Observant. Humble, too, like your father." She grows quiet.

"What else?"

"He liked long walks and quiet nights beneath the stars."

She smiles, and I feel uneasy, as if by encouraging her I am being disloyal to my father. "Were the sweet violets from the same year as the amulet?"

She nods.

She chose Arc over my father, then. I suppose it is hurt on his behalf that drives me to say, "You made an offering of it at the bog," and, in doing so, remind her of the lie she lets me and everyone else believe.

How do I know the truth? It came to me in a vision when I was a small child, so long ago that it seems something I have always known.

In the scene that had opened before me, a boy on the cusp of manhood—my father—stirred the debris of the woodland floor with the toe of his shoe. The red gritstone of Edge soared behind him, also the black, yawning mouth of the old mine. His gaze was downcast, scrutinizing the leaf litter and twigs he overturned. He and I have often searched for the nuggets of blue-green ore left behind by the old people who mined Edge. And so it was with good reason that I knew the boy was looking for the ore. He searched, without diversion, until a small patch of light glinting from a low branch of an elm caught his eye. He took a few steps and saw the light was reflected sunshine, that it shone from a magpie nest. He walked closer and reached into the nest. By feel alone he knew what he had found. Even as he freed the glinting thing from yellow grass, twigs, and mud, he collapsed inward, surrendering to the belly wallop of having found the amulet. My mother had not thought the amulet precious and offered it to Mother Earth. No, she had tossed a worthless trinket to the rot of the woodland floor for a magpie to find. He raised an arm to hurl the bit of silver, then lowered it and put the amulet inside his pocket where the silver would no more glint in the sun.

MY MOTHER KEEPS HER focus on the sweet violets, her lips a thin line. I teeter on pressing, on telling her what I know, but she tents her fingers on the earth as though feeling faint. In the end, I say, "Mole gave me a dragonfly last Feast of Purification." It was not unusual—a youth not yet old enough for the feast giving a token to a maiden.

"Practice," my mother says, "for the years to come."

"Moon gave me a feather."

"Oh."

"Seconds gave me a spoon for measuring, just yesterday though, in return for the chickweed balm." I slip a small wooden spoon with a deep bowl from my pocket.

She takes it, turns it over in her hands. "You have admirers."

I smile. "Seconds is the fastest."

"He was close behind you at the Harvest Feast games."

"He slowed down at the end." Seconds and I had finished well ahead of the pack, a near tie.

"On purpose?"

I had wondered myself, at least until we had walked together to the honeycomb. "Yes."

"It's sweet, really, letting you win."

"He's nice." I run a finger along a violet stem, keep my gaze lowered. "He said I should be called 'Swift.'"

"You'd like that?"

I look up, shake my head. "I like being Hobble."

"I like you being Hobble, too."

That pretty day among the purple blooms, I had momentarily forgotten the uneven gait that decided my name, also that a druid called Fox waited at home. But neither the glory of the waking earth, nor the uplift of caught wind, not even the promise of a wooden spoon can obscure the fast approach of Hope for very long. "I have this memory," I say, "or maybe I made it up. I don't know. I have this idea that you told me something once."

She nods slowly, carefully.

"It's about the harvest when the wheat rotted, when you were a girl."

Her whole face stills, then falls.

"It's true, then." I feel my skin prickle and my heart begin to race. "A druid sacrificed a blind boy to the gods."

"We called him Lark," she whispers and the pain in her face is like a hundred sighs. "He was Walker's son."

"It's why she walks," I say, "why she doesn't sleep."

"We used to call her Willow."

"No one says a word?"

"We made a pledge afterward—each of us. We would not dwell on it, would not speak of it."

My shoulders lift that this story stays in darkness. How can no one have made the smallest mention of Lark to me?

At Black Lake we do not say *human sacrifice*. Instead we use the phrase *old ways*, as in, "Those old ways are long gone from our traditions." And I had found comfort in that phrase—proof that such brutality belonged to a distant time, proof that my mother had never claimed a blind boy's throat was slit. But the phrase, it now seems, was preferred because it helped the bog dwellers pretend.

"Hobble—" She takes my hands.

I make the smallest nod, sparing her the heartache of having to explain what I have just now figured out: Only a cruel person would needlessly divulge to me the slit throat of a runt. It is why I do not know the story of Lark and Willow, who became Walker after the slaughter that would keep her restless until the end of time.

I had said, "I like being Hobble," and I want it to be true. Just now, though, I feel only the terror of being Hobble—a prophetess yet to produce Romans, a maiden who clip-clops unevenly through the fields.

9.

HOBBLE

~~~~

A S NIGHT FALLS my mother and I attend to remedies and my father to ironwork. We grind and mix and sharpen in silence while Fox remains on his knees beneath Mother Earth's cross, his eyes pressed shut. But then suddenly they flick open and he cocks an ear. I hear it, too—the distant rumble of hooves thwacking earth. He leaps to his feet. "The Romans!" Then, eyes lit on me, he commands, "Hide my horse."

When I do not immediately budge, he says, "Now!" and I drop my pestle. He conceals his robe with a skin cape and dashes through the doorway. I follow, a step behind, intent on preventing the easy discovery of so fine a horse—evidence of a druid nearby. He heads for the cover of the woodland, and I to the sheep pen out back of the Shepherd roundhouse, where the horse is lashed. As I run, I hear a new sound in the approaching rumble—the clang of metal on metal. Swords clapped against shields, I think. An effort to raise alarm.

The beast's ears are pricked. He whinnies, paws the earth. As he sniffs the air, he pulls the slack from the reins securing him to the pen. I unlash him, and he eagerly keeps pace as I sprint the several hundred strides to Sacred Grove, that secluded place where we carry out the sacrifices that appease the gods. I knot the horse to a rowan there, pat his hindquarters twice, before racing back to the clearing.

I count eight Roman warriors, just as my vision foretold. My eyes dart from bronze helmet to chest armor to the hobnailed sole of a leather-encased foot, all of it appearing exactly as I had seen that day the sorrel blazed green.

I skim the bog dwellers filing into the clearing and dropping to bended knee as though they consider the Romans emissaries of the gods. I find my parents at the same moment my father sees me. He pats the earth beside him, and I skitter to the spot.

The warriors speak to each other in a gentle language at odds with their rigid faces and limbs. One of them—swarthy like the rest, except that a fresh scar extends from behind his ear to the base of his neck—bellows orders in our language: "Keep your hands in front. Stay on your knees."

He circles the kneeling bog dwellers on his horse and calls out, "First Man, show yourself."

Hunter continues kneeling, head bowed, until the Roman bellows, "First Man!"

As Hunter rises, I look away from his quaking knees.

"A pair of prisoners escaped from Viriconium last night," the Roman barks.

I wonder if those escaped prisoners might have been rebel tribesmen rounded up in the western highlands. If they are, I hope they have slipped far beyond the Romans' reach.

"We are loyal," Hunter says. "We send the wheat we owe your emperor."

"My emperor?" The Roman raises a spear. "Not yours?"

Hunter shuffles backward. "My emperor."

"Name him!"

Hunter's mouth gapes open.

The Roman touches the point of a spear to Hunter's chest.

My father lifts his face. "Our emperor is Emperor Nero," he says.

The crack of a smile appears on the Roman's mouth.

"We harbor no rebels here," my father continues. "We have no quarrel with the Romans. We live in isolation, content to harvest wheat for our emperor."

Hunter puffs up his chest and blurts, "I am First Man." He glares at my father. "He does not speak on our behalf."

With that, the Roman's eyes narrow, sweep the breadth of us. "Return to your homes!" he commands, and then, as we scurry toward our roundhouses, "Search them!"

Warriors dismount, head first to the Tanner roundhouse, which stands at the far edge of the roundhouses from my own.

As my father pulls the door nearly shut behind the three of us, I hurl myself against his chest, but he eases me away. "There's no time," he says.

My mother glances around the room, indicates Fox's spare white robe, hanging just inside the entryway of the alcove where he sleeps, and I understand that we must hide the evidence of our unwanted guest. I pause mid-reach, hesitant to touch a druid's robe, then lift it from the peg. She opens the chest at the foot of the sleeping pallet, then thinks better than to stash the robe in a place large enough to entice a warrior to look inside. We stuff the bundle into a small cauldron instead. My father peeks around the door into the clearing. "They'll be a while yet," he says.

I hear pottery shatter.

"They're leaving the Hunters," my father says. "They've helped themselves to a pair of pheasants, set nothing aflame."

My mother puts the heel of her palm against her forehead, says, "Hear me, Protector," as is our tradition in beseeching the god.

"Devout," my father snaps.

She lowers her hand.

"Build up the fire," he says. "Hobble, fill eight mugs with wheaten beer."

As my mother tops embers with kindling and blows, I assemble mugs and pour beer. My father slides the dagger from his belt, runs his thumb across the blade, returns it to his hip. I hear a rhythmic sort of whooshing. I strain, trying to hear more, to decipher what the source might be. But the sound is only fear—my pounding heart, the rush of blood.

The clamor of eight warriors grows near, and my father shifts to our open door. They push past him, oblivious to the extended arm ushering them inside, twice circle the roundhouse, peering behind faded partitions and, in two instances, yanking them from the rafters. My father gestures toward the benches around the fire, and my mother brings the men the mugs I filled. Their comfort as they settle suggests that sitting around a tribesman's fire and drinking his beer is nothing new. They speak in their strange tongue, laugh, drain the mugs, hold them aloft as my mother pours a second round, and I am struck that they seem little different from the men I have known all my life.

In time, the scarred Roman notices the herb-hung rafters and indicates that my mother should inspect the festering abscess tucked behind his ear at the far reach of the scar. He keeps his gaze on her as she prepares the purple loosestrife poultice that will draw the pus from the wound. In her small movements and rolled-forward shoulders, I see her uneasiness with the way he watches. Suddenly, my father lifts his dagger from his belt. He thrusts it into a tabletop with such force that it remains erect, quivering over the lodged tip. Dark eyes flicker to the knife. Hands flit to sword hilts. The scarred Roman makes as if to get up.

"Sit," my father says, with a gentle smile. "The poultice is nearly ready. My mate will tend to you. Then you will leave us in peace."

The men remain tense, at the ready, until the scarred Roman sits fully on the bench and lifts his mug to his lips.

My mother holds the warm poultice behind his ear until the skin grows soft, then touches the sharp point of a bone needle to the abscess. Pus shoots from the wound, and stink fills the air. The Roman sighs with relief and relaxes back onto the bench. The mood in the roundhouse calms.

My father's eyes linger on the Roman's chest armor. His intrigue is plain, and the Roman sees it, too. He unfastens the ties at the front of the armor and holds it open so that my father might inspect the inner workings. Eventually he crouches before the Roman, investigating the ingenuity of the design—some thirty segmented plates, all of them held together with connecting leather straps. "A marvel," my father says, eyes shining.

The Roman appears pleased and touches the hilt of the sword at his hip. He lifts his eyebrows, asking if my father wants to see the sword. He is a man as transfixed by ironwork as any man can be, and I hold my breath as the Roman slides his sword from the scabbard.

The hilt is plain, without the enamel inlay or raised detail that might impress my father. Even so, as the Roman touches the sword's tip to the earth and leans his weight into the hilt, the blade arcs, as though it were made of a material other than iron. My father's brow lifts that the blade does not snap. "Tempered," the Roman says.

Clearly he is pleased to show his Roman cleverness, to use a word we do not know.

"You know to plunge a finished blade into a cold bath?" he says.

My father nods, without hinting at insult that he might not know such a thing.

"A blade needs to be reheated afterward—tempered. With tempering," he says, "you can alter the hardness of iron." He continues, explaining that the more extreme the reheating, the suppler the iron becomes. A sword should be removed from the embers during the reheating once the blade warms to the color of straw. At that point, the iron remains durable but not so brittle as before that second dose of heat.

My father leans close, taking in every word. I tuck purple loosestrife into a dozen small linen pouches—a task assigned by my mother—and sew the open edges shut. While I work, my father gently taps his knuckles against his chin, and I know his mind is ablaze. Might he temper the saw blades he makes for Carpenter, add a bit of springiness to the iron? And what about the crooks he crafts for Shepherd? With the brittleness of iron, more than one had snapped, and the same could be said of the fleshing knives Tanner uses to scrape his hides. I cannot help but recall that when we first spoke about the Romans' arrival, my father had said, "Changing wind brings new weather," with all the optimism of a fruit tree in blossom.

Once the Romans stand to leave, my mother hands the one she assisted the linen-wrapped purple loosestrife and instructs him in caring for the drained wound. In the doorway, he turns to my father. "Your mate," the Roman says, "she reminds me of a girl I once knew. The same grace."

As they depart into crisp night air, my father stands in the doorway, his weight shifting toward the disappearing men, retreating, and then shifting again, caught between action and inaction, between endeavor and fear. In the end he follows the Romans into the clearing, and I look to my mother, whose palm shifts to her forehead as she beseeches Protector.

I sit on my hands at the firepit, silently count to one hundred, count a second time. When he finally returns, he looks as crestfallen as a wilted bloom.

"You followed the Romans?" my mother asks.

"Leave me be," he says.

"But, Smith—"

"Enough," he says with a sharpness he seldom uses, never with my mother.

She gathers the mugs in awkward silence, tilts the dregs into the fire, and I work up my nerve. "So dark," I say, "so short, the lot of them. Do you think the claim about reheating iron is true?" I ask this even though I saw with my own eyes a blade bend under the Roman's weight.

"Not now, Hobble," my father says.

Fox strides into the roundhouse, his eyes bright, alive. "You"—he points at me—"over there."

I shift to the spot alongside the firepit. Fox seats himself on the bench directly opposite me. Thighs splayed, elbows on his knees, he leans forward. "You'll divine for me," he says.

I say nothing.

"You'll divine the outcome of a rebellion."

"I can't just . . . It doesn't work like that." Sweat rolls down the nape of my neck.

"Tell me, then, how it works?"

"I don't know. I see things. They just come."

"You'll divine for me." He rises.

My head wags right, left. I cannot.

He steps closer, puts his face near enough to mine that I feel the wet as he spits, "Seer or runt?"

I cannot deny a druid. I know this and yet my head continues— right, left. I am not able to lure a vision of whatever rebellion he contemplates.

His fingers coil into a tight fist. I brace for the blow that will come. But then he yanks my father's dagger from the tabletop and touches it to my throat.

A cry escapes my mouth as I jerk back from the blade. Fox throws down the dagger. A warning, then: I am a runt and only a runt if I am unable to divine on command.

10.

HOBBLE

~~~~

SIX DAYS HAVE PASSED. I lie on my pallet unable to sleep, gaze fixed on the threadbare partition separating me from the firepit. The wool writhes with the light of the lapping flames, also the shadows of my parents, sitting on a bench in the glow. My father clears his throat—not his habit—and my ears prick.

"Another day without the iron trader," he says.

The iron trader who usually takes my father's wares to Hill Fort has not come in more than three moons. This, when the forge shelves buckle with the weight of the stockpiled ladles and small cauldrons, the three large bins of nails no trader has hauled away in his cart. This, when the stack of iron, from which my father crafts the wares, has dwindled to a measly three bars. This, when our household harbors a druid—one accustomed to plenty, an overlord who, in his oblivion, fishes the barley from the soup and snatches three of the four slices severed from a loaf.

"He'll come," my mother says. I cannot tell whether she believes it.

"Why come when wealth rains from the sky at Hill Fort? Why leave a marketplace full of traders supplying Viriconium?" He huffs. "I should speak to Hunter again."

As First Man, only Hunter undertakes the trek to Hill Fort. It is his right, and he likes it that way. I have watched my father pace, after returning from the Hunter roundhouse, yet again denied permission to trade his own wares at Hill Fort's marketplace.

"Hunter won't allow it," my mother says.

"Now, more than ever, he knows the advantage of keeping the tradesmen pinned to Black Lake." I know by the shadows that my father's shoulders rise, fall. Then his voice brims, full of promise, as he says, "I'll petition Fox."

"Smith," my mother pleads, "it's too dangerous. The Romans—"

"We're to live on seven onions and a bit of barley?" My father, it appears, had found our storage vessel just as empty as I had when I lifted the lid.

We are desperate, yes, and that desperation propels my father to seek new opportunities. But I know it is also true that he longs to hammer something less mundane than ladles from iron and feels the frustration of living in a settlement that does not participate in Roman ways and the new prosperity brought to Britannia.

Her shadow palms open to the room. "You heard Fox say Roman warriors are in the marketplace," she whispers.

"He said it was hearsay. And if they do squander their wages there, all the better for trade."

"You know my feelings," she says coolly.

They sit silent in their private furies a good while, until my father says, "You're thinking of Arc, aren't you?" and waves a shadow hand through the air. "Always on your mind."

I imagine her pretty eyes losing their light.

"Smith"—her voice is tender now, soft—"you're wrong."

"You used to disappear in the evenings," he continues, "make some excuse, and come back well past nightfall, always with red eyes and mud-caked shoes."

I have heard the rumors—how my mother once wept and pounded her fists against the causeway's timbers, grieving her first mate. How my heart aches that still my father feels the bruise of that earlier time.

"It's been years—"

"You sigh in your dreams." His voice cracks.

It makes me think poorly of my mother—that she should allow so good a man to feel as unloved as this.

"Oh, Smith."

On the partition, I watch in silhouette as she puts a hand over his heart, as they move to the rushes of the earthen floor.

I close my eyes to their shadows. I hear breath deepening, quickening. I hear the rustle of rushes. In that unexpected tenderness, I hear an apology of sorts. An apology for the comfort too often withheld. For the aloofness that keeps my father uncertain. But I hear pleasure and love and hearts cracking open, too, a cradle song that lulls me gently into sleep.

As I APPROACH THE FORGE, my father straightens from stooping over his anvil and rolls the stiffness from his bad shoulder. His fingers prod a knot of hard muscle as Hunter comes into view with the scruff of a hare's neck in his fist. "Smith," he calls out, lifting the hare. "Bring home one of the these and you might have better luck expanding your brood."

Hunter's ridicule is without effect when just the evening before my mother had enticed my father to the rushes. Another time, though, spotting my father yawning, Hunter had called out, "You're worn out like my mate," and thrust his hips lewdly. Poof, and suddenly I glimpsed my father's mind—a mind mired in thinking how there was always meat for Hunter's mate's cauldron, a wedge of wild boar to roast on the tip of a knife, how even Hunter's fingers tracing his mate's spine would be enough to entice her onto her back, her legs apart, her belly full of meat. My father pined for the same, with my mother. It was what he desired as he lay back on their pallet, her back often turned.

Should a maiden of thirteen be exposed to her father's private longing? Might it disturb her in some way? Make her think poorly of him? I suppose I might think differently if my father yearned after someone other than my mother, but he does not. Besides, that glimpse had not corrupted me or even put ideas in my mind that I was incapable of imagining before it appeared. Buds swell behind my nipples, hair coarsens between my legs; I know without prophecy that I will soon bleed with a new moon. And like most any youth at Black Lake, with only a square of wool partitioning my sleeping alcove from my parents', I have seen enough, have heard enough to have an idea of the act that binds woman and man as mates. I have known the sound of lovemaking, and its absence, too, all my life.

"Ready?" I call to my father. Even more so than before Fox, I anticipate our daily trek to the bog—a private interlude, a chance to learn his opinions of Fox and the Romans, to hear reassuring words. I have been reluctant to coax, but today as we cut through the woodland, he takes my hand and I find my voice. "Why has Fox come?"

My father slows, searches my face, which I make firm, insistent.

"Remember Fox saying the Romans were as thorough as blight in snuffing out the rebels?" he finally says.

"Those last holdouts against Roman rule."

"That defeat might have made the druids desperate."

The druids had incited the tribesmen to resist the Roman invasion; once that resistance failed, fear blossomed among the high priests. They fled the settlements and, rather than living among us, had ever since taken refuge on Sacred Isle. That small island sits beyond the highlands, just off the western coast of Britannia—the far extreme from the areas most fully inhabited by the Romans.

"First, Viriconium put Sacred Isle within easier reach of the Romans than ever before," my father says. "And now, the conquered highlands leave it even more exposed."

"The druids are desperate?" I say. "That's why Fox is here?"

His lips press tight, and I know he is deliberating how much to say to a thirteen-year-old maiden.

"Tell me."

"Look," he says, "the other night Fox commanded you to tell him the outcome of a rebellion." He pauses, and I force a nod. "It makes me think the druids are back in the settlements with the intention of inciting the tribesmen to rise up once again."

I think how no tribesman is fool enough to raise steel against the Romans, how during the invasion we were throttled in two days. "Nothing will come of it," I say and wait, expecting confirmation, but he does not respond.

"I'm setting out for Hill Fort in the morning," he finally says. "It's decided. I've got a glut of ironware and, now, another mouth to feed."

Does desperation impair my father's judgment? He will leave me to fend for myself?

"I petitioned Fox."

"He agreed?"

"He wants to know about Romans at Hill Fort. I said I'd find out what I could."

The beech and ash bordering the path have given way to the willow and alder that prefer moister earth, and I stand still, breathless, balanced on two stones, an effort to avoid soggy peat. I am to brave six days—three to walk to Hill Fort and another three to return—without my father's watchful eyes? "But—"

"My father made the trek a hundred times," he says. "He had commissions to deliver."

He tells me how Chieftain once preferred the Smith forge above any other, how his father's father's father was trained by a long-ago chieftain's blacksmith. It is a story I know well. Once that apprentice matched his master's skill, he was dispatched to Black Lake to continue his trade in a place so remote that no raiding tribe would bother looting it. The Black Lake Smiths rose in stature with each brooch, each goblet, each sword produced, evermore securing the forge as the reigning chieftain's sure choice.

My father's face shines with ambition as he speaks—ambition that I know extends beyond trading the ironware bloating his shelves.

"Father?"

"I'll bring along the bronze serving platter," he says, "call on Chieftain while I'm there."

Years ago my father showed me the platter he had crafted in his youth. As I traced my fingers over the raised swirls and inlaid red glass wreathing the rim, I asked why he had not traded it. He answered that he had not given up on Chieftain one day coming to Black Lake and, once he had seen the platter, ordering a commission.

No longer will my father stand idle, looking toward the horizon, awaiting fate. He will show his handiwork to the traders at Hill Fort. The platter he will reserve for Chieftain, who will take so impressive a piece in both hands and, full of desire, order a dozen goblets with adorned rims.

And then, on my father's return, might the bog dwellers recall his father's evenhanded counsel, the distinction of the Smith clan? The shift toward returned status, toward reestablishing himself as First Man, would happen simply—one day, my father would give an urn of thick soup to an ailing family; and another, parade an ox around the clearing and announce it as replacement for the ancient one. His opinion would be requested on the best day to harvest the wheat, whether the hawthorn berries were ready to be picked. He would find such satisfaction in the rise, in honoring his father, his clan, in providing amply for my mother and me, in ensuring Hunter never again dared say, "You're worn out like my mate."

My father wants more, and that want stirs the dread already roiling in my gut.

"At the very least," he says, "I'll trade the ironware clogging my shelves."

"But Fox—" I blurt out.

He combs his fingers through my hair, slides his hand to the back of my head, pulls me to his ribs. And I feel his heartache—as palpable as that embrace.

"When will he leave?" I let my shoulders slump, my face hang. I know my childishness—the feeling that I want my world set right, to get my way. And yet I do not care. I want my father to stay put. "That night I showed him the cesspit—" I say, truly on the edge of tears.

He pulls back, looks at me with such intensity.

"I said the Romans would come in Hope"—I sputter out the

words—"and he said liars have their tongues cut out and their mouths sewn shut."

"Hobble?"

"He said I had eighteen days."

His eyebrows draw inward. His lips compress.

"I know about the blind boy who was sacrificed," I say. "Walker's son. Lark."

He takes hold of my shoulders. "You'll go with me."

I want to make the trek and fear Fox so much more than the Romans, who seemed almost like bog dwellers in their camaraderie at the firepit. I am certain, and yet I am only able to smile meekly. "But Mother?"

"The worst Roman is a lamb compared to Fox," he says. "She'll see that you're better off with me."

"And Fox? He'll let me go with you?"

"I'll tell him that you can follow the stars better than I." He smiles. "It's true enough."

I throw my arms around his neck, and my feet leave the stones. They skitter over the slick surfaces on the way to settling into wet peat, but I am indifferent to soaked shoes.

"We'll show him your strength, your endurance." My father laughs sincerely. "We'll show Hunter, too."

"Think of it," I say, "a lame maiden undertaking a trek he thinks only he can make."

My father laughs again. "We'll set out before the cock crows."

We continue our journey, chatting excitedly about all we will find at Hill Fort—a marketplace bursting with wares; the high, palisaded mound where Chieftain lives among his kin. "We'll make the last bit of the trek on a Roman road," my father says.

A trader had come to Black Lake to collect the Carpenters'

inventory of wheels and insisted the Romans had done us all a great service with their roads. During their rule, the entire length of an old trackway, reaching from the southeast coast clear across Britannia, has been improved to a stone-paved Roman road. No more carts sinking to the axle in mud, he said, not on that road.

Anticipation swells that I should see a marketplace, a Roman road. I feel near to bursting as I think of having my father all to myself for six days. Away from Black Lake, I expect he will speak more openly than he would otherwise.

We arrive at the spot where the waterlogged path meets the causeway. Though the woodland opens onto a brush of meadow-sweet, nettle, and willow herb, the setting sun's golden light does not penetrate the mist hanging low over the bog. The world here is black and gray. We trace our fingers sunwise around the Begetter's wheel and place our palms on our chests.

As we walk the causeway, the shoreline transitions to marsh thick with yellow iris, water dock, and rushes and then, as the water grows deeper, purple loosestrife and cowbane. We stop, as we always do, at the spot where the lake bed falls away and the plant life—tendrils of water starwort, heart-shaped pads of frogbit—float, no longer rooted in muck.

I crouch low, my lame leg stretched behind, my good one bent in front, my fingertips alongside it, lightly touching the causeway's timbers. He counts to three as he does each day, and then I am off, a sight to behold. A lame maiden hurtling down the causeway—clip-clop, clip-clop—my gait hardly uneven at all.

11

DEVOUT

$\approx$

EVOUT AND ARC KNELT AMID the bog dwellers gathered in the clearing. A druid stood before them. Though he bore the customary robe and streaming yellow-white beard, the strain and dust of a hard ride lined his wizened face, dried spittle crusted his beard, and dirt caked his robe. He appeared as inglorious a druid as she had ever seen.

"Water," he commanded, his voice as dry as tinder.

Old Smith nodded to his mate, who stood and strode toward the Smith roundhouse. He then nodded to Young Smith, who knew to take the reins of the horse. As he led the beast to the sheep trough around back of the Shepherd roundhouse, Devout thought how he shared his father's composure, never mind that the druid had yet to announce why he had come.

Young Smith's mother returned with a silver goblet. The druid gulped, wiped his mouth. "Time is of the essence," he said, "and so I will speak plainly. I do so not to fill you with fear, but so that we might act quickly and decisively." He cleared his throat. "Thirty thousand Roman warriors are encamped at the place where the channel separating our island from Gaul is narrowest. The shoreline is clogged with some three hundred ships. They intend to conquer our island and claim it for the Roman Empire, just as they did Gaul."

Faces were blank. The bog dwellers had heard tell of Roman warriors, had listened to them described as gleaming contrivances from another world, combatants who moved in unison, more like a flock of starlings than like individual men. All this was hearsay, rumor brought to Black Lake from Hill Fort by way of Old Smith. He had been doubtful, had waved a hand dismissively as he spoke. "Too much time traipsing the woods alone," he said of the traders who blathered of faraway lands in the food stalls at Hill Fort. "Imaginations like wind on a plain. Tongues like lapping flame."

The bog dwellers knew of Julius Caesar and his army invading their island nearly a century ago: The vast flocks of Roman warriors. The hundreds of ships. Those warriors marching inland, and then the druids conferring and taking to sacred groves all across the island to lead the tribesmen in slaying beasts. With those offerings, they had conjured a tempest, and that tempest wrecked most of the ships. Even so, Caesar's warriors marched inland a second time. The druids ordered another round of sacrifices—this time, men rather than beasts. The Roman warriors retreated from the tribesmen's island, and ever since the tribesmen have continued without Roman intrusion.

But what, Devout wondered, was an empire? A channel? What was Gaul?

The druid held up a palm to the bog dwellers' blank faces, as if to say *wait* and then began again. He explained and explained until they understood that the Roman Empire was most of the known world, incomprehensibly immense. It consisted of Gaul and a swath of lands extending south and east from there. A channel was a narrow ribbon of sea, and just such a narrow ribbon was all that separated Gaul—the empire's farthest western reach—from the vast island where the tribesmen lived. "We must prepare to battle the Romans," he said, "even as they step ashore."

Messengers had come to Black Lake to rally the men before, sent by Chieftain to relay some slight to be avenged: a river fished or cattle snatched by a neighboring territory's tribesmen. Other times, a messenger brought news of a chance for plunder: a flock of sheep strayed close to Chieftain's territory; rumor of an unguarded stockpile of harvested parsnips or onions. Devout could count three occasions when Black Lake's tradesmen sharpened their steel and followed Chieftain and his warriors, seeking revenge or the glory of a raid.

This was different. Thirty thousand was not a number she, or any bog dweller, knew. It was more than a thousand. And she supposed it made sense that thirty groups of a thousand was the same as thirty thousand. But even if every man, woman, and child inhabiting Chieftain's territory were counted, she could not fathom that it would amount to such a sum. And more, if a glimmer of all Old Smith had relayed about Roman warriors were true, even an equal number of Chieftain's tribesmen would not put the Romans in retreat.

Old Smith lifted his bowed head, and the druid nodded so that he might know to speak. "Have any ships left Gaul?" Old Smith asked.

"No."

It seemed Old Smith wanted evidence that the Romans intended to cross the channel and invade, but the druid did not like this and turned his gaze from Old Smith.

Young Smith raised his head, held his gaze steady—oh, but he was brave—as he awaited permission to speak. The druid dipped his chin, and Young Smith said, "How do we know their plan?"

"You question the Romans' intention to invade our island?" The druid's voice remained steady, but his flared nostrils gave away his ire.

"I do not doubt a druid's word."

The druid drew himself taller. "For those of you who doubt, I tell you this: The encamped Romans spend their days rehearsing embarking and disembarking their ships and wading to the shore."

Devout dared a sideways glance. In Arc's face she saw forbearance that men should be rallied when the fields were green with wheat. The hands would stay put, as they always did, but with the tradesmen off marauding and their women left without a man's brute strength, the hands picked up the slack, hauling water, splitting wood, repairing thatch. In Young Smith's face she saw pragmatism—questions forming, order brought to disarray. Her eyes flitted to Young Smith's oldest brother. She saw a face lit with fire, certainty that adventure lay ahead. She touched her lips, the earth, held her fingers there a moment. Then she returned her hand to her knee and clutched the folds of her dress.

"Even as I speak to you," the druid continued, "my druid brethren pass from settlement to settlement across our island. We tribesmen are one people—and I refer to all tribesmen, whether residing in Chieftain's territory or a different one. We are brethren joined by our shared tongue, our traditions, our gods, our island. We must rise as one against the Romans, who are our common enemy."

She understood, then, that the druid did not mean for Chieftain's tribe to face the Romans alone. He meant for tribes all across the island to unite as one people, rather than persist as they always had, as some fifteen feuding nations. He spoke with assurance, as though the valley dweller tribe to the south were their brothers, as though the uplander tribe to the north was not the sworn enemy of Chieftain's tribe. They were to forget, then, the history they learned as children—how the uplanders had captured two of Chieftain's father's father's nephews while they were on a hunting expedition, how the nephews went unreturned, never mind that a ransom of fifty cattle was paid. Those times bog dwellers had followed Chieftain and his gathered warriors, not every man had returned. No news spread more gleefully at Black Lake than a report of uplander heads skewered on stakes at the gate of Hill Fort.

Young Smith again tilted his face to the druid. "You ask us to accept the uplander and the valley dweller tribes as our brothers?"

"It is the Romans who are different, who will take what is ours."

She saw that Young Smith wanted to continue, to point out that the long-warring tribes would not easily forget their old grudges, but the druid turned his eyes away.

He promised the bog dwellers a future of plunder and killing and all manner of violence if they did not act. He spoke of crops burned to the ground and looms and water buckets turned to tinder; vessels smashed; of sacred traditions outlawed, exacted from their lives. He described a system where one man owned another, like Old Hunter owned a hound, and where that owned man was bound to a lifetime of servitude. If they needed proof, they should look to Gaul, he said, where all he promised had come about since being conquered by the Romans.

The druid's eyes narrowed. His lip curled to a sneer. "Do not forget the Romans' mighty Julius Caesar failing in the same quest a hundred years ago."

Still, fingers wrung folds of wool.

The druid raised his arms overhead, looked to the heavens. "War Master will protect."

The god's favor—crucial to triumph on the battlefield—would be sought before any tradesmen headed out, same as it had been those other times Chieftain had recruited men to join him in a raid. They had gone to Sacred Grove, stepped into the ancient oak's shadow there with chickens and partridges and ewes. As fowl or beast was held still on the stone altar—a chiseled slab of cold gritstone—its neck was looped with braided sinew, the sinew knotted into place and pulled tighter by rotating a stick slid between sinew and neck. Devout had closed her eyes to the twitching feet, to the still-throbbing hearts. But some put their hands on the stone altar and cried "Heed War Master. Heed him well." And those who had swallowed black henbane—especially those—danced wildly, leaping and calling out to War Master, who had given his devotees— as they afterward described—the sensation of soaring above the earth. The Smiths took black henbane, all but Young Smith. And the Hunters, too. Always they danced until they dropped. Their eyes glinted pride afterward, as they said how they had woken to the black of night, their limbs stiff as wood, their mouths dry as winnowed wheat.

The druid clasped his hands over his ribs, paused so that the bog dwellers would know the severity of the words to come. "Any man among you who prefers freedom to servitude will present himself to the fearsome band of united tribes already gathered in the southeast."

He eyed the bog dwellers knelt before him, his gaze as fierce as a god's.

12.

DEVOUT

~~~

ONCE THE DRUID WAS GONE and the household fed, Devout made the excuse of going to collect kindling for the bonfire Old Smith had ordered lit. It was easier than saying she was going to meet Arc when even mentioning his name led to brows lifted in curiosity.

Any confusion, any ardent thoughts of Young Smith had come to an abrupt end the evening she and Arc clung to one another in the thick mist and heard the footsteps of the child who was surely theirs. Two moons had passed since, and while she still felt a tenderness toward Young Smith, more than anything she felt shame that she had stood quiet in the golden sunlight, letting him look at her. She had encouraged him and then, after those footsteps, abruptly altered her ways, giving wide berth to his forge as she came in from the fields, ducking and dodging, rather than facing what she must. After a handful of such days, she had seen him catch sight of her in the distance. She watched as he shed his leather jerkin and trooped from the forge. She thought of the gulf between them, of how she lacked the mettle that spurred him toward her, toward the conversation from which she shrank. She slowed so that Sullen and the other maiden hands with whom she had been walking might pass ahead of her.

"Young Smith," she had said when he was near.

"You saw the picture we made in the mine." His brow pulled to a knot. "You said you wanted to see it again."

She hung her head.

"Devout?"

"I'm sorry."

"I don't understand." His head wagged softly.

"I have an old friendship with Arc," she said.

She had chosen an orphaned hand, who lived in a shack, over Young Smith, a tradesman, youngest son of Black Lake's First Man. Such insult. And yet Young Smith said nothing, just looked as forlorn as frost-singed blooms, until he backed away.

She had stood at the fringes of the clearing afterward, shoulders slumped, but then she breathed in the relief of having done what she needed to do. She felt the tingle of mounting excitement, the lightness of good cheer. Surely it was shameful, the ease with which her happiness rose. She looked over her shoulder, hoping to catch sight of Arc making his way in from the fields.

AT THE GATE leading from the clearing to the woodland, she whistled the call of the bullfinch—that string of quick chirps followed by a longer, lower one. Then she went into the woodland a dozen strides and settled herself on a low stump to wait for Arc. All the while, her mind buzzed with the druid's words—*thirty thousand warriors, invade, conquer, crops burned to the ground.* She touched her lips, lowered herself from the stump, and put her fingers to the debris of the woodland floor. When she looked up, Arc stood in front of her, and she thought how no one stepped as carefully as he.

"I told them I was gathering kindling for the bonfire," she said.

"The floor here's picked clean."

They walked farther along the path. Then, he veered into the underbrush and emerged a moment later hauling a pair of fair-sized branches fallen from an oak. "Enough?"

She nodded. "That story about Julius Cesar getting turned back, you think it's true?"

What she meant was did he believe the part where the druids ordered a round of sacrifices where men were slain. No bog dweller, not even Old Man, with his long life, had witnessed such savagery, and she had moments of wondering whether the old ways might be more rumor than fact.

He nodded.

"All of it?"

"You know the old words Singer sings. Everyone does." He cleared his throat, crooned the song she had heard all her life:

The half-witted, the lame
Came on two feet,
Offered on stone altars,
Their destinies complete.

Gooseflesh rose on her arms.

"You're shivering," Arc said and pulled her close, but the shivering did not cease. Voice brimming with certainty, he said, "The old ways have been gone for a hundred years, and they aren't coming back."

———

ONCE NIGHT HAD FALLEN and the bonfire was lit, the Smith clan, carrying flagons of mead, came into the clearing. They took their places on the benches circling the blaze, and the bog dwellers assembled in the halo of warm light extending beyond them. Arc stood beside Devout, his knuckles knocking hers now and then, their fingertips meeting on the flagons passed sunwise through the gathered crowd. Mead spilled into the mugs that would be drained and refilled as the Smith men debated, as bog dwellers listened, as Old Smith made up his mind.

He sat with his thighs parted, forearms resting on his knees, hands loosely holding a mug of mead. He rubbed his whiskers more often than was usual, and it made her wonder if he was more bothered by the ruling to be made than he let on. He lifted a hand, and a hush spread over the group like mist rolling in from the bog. "The tribes taking up arms against the Romans are more than twelve days' walk from here," he said.

"On uncertain trackways," added Young Smith's oldest uncle. He was Old Smith's trusted adviser in all things, whether it was naming the day to sow the fields or selecting the beast to be slaughtered in Sacred Grove.

"Or on no trackway at all," said Old Smith.

"Who's to say we'd make it in time," said the uncle.

A slew of younger tradesmen listened with their arms folded over their chests. Some had yet to accompany Chieftain on a raid and knew the affront of sitting silent as the others laughed and slapped their thighs and recounted the time they hurled firebrands onto thatched roofs or the time they were forced to hide in a ditch for three days.

"Would we even find the place?" said a second uncle. "How did the druid instruct us? Walk exactly southeast for eight days?" He shared Old Smith's opinion, then, this uncle who was usually inclined to speak dissent.

"We have little experience navigating beyond Hill Fort," said Old Smith.

The uncle threw his hands in the air. "When we meet a river larger than any we've ever seen, we are to discover how to ford it? What sort of instruction is that?"

The oldest Smith brother took a long slug of mead. "What the druid said was once we meet the river—a river impossible to miss—we walk east to the place where the river meets the sea and then—"

"He said we were to wait there until the water grows shallow, to cross once the mud flats are exposed." The oldest uncle lifted his gaze from the flames and met the oldest brother's. "I have yet to see a river grow shallow twice each day as the druid claimed."

"Do not doubt a druid," the oldest brother snapped. He gestured, indicating that a flagon should be passed to him. He refilled his mug, set the flagon at his feet.

Young Smith pulled himself taller on the bench, glanced toward Devout a moment and then quickly away. "A trader once told me about the regular rise and fall of the water in the sea," he said. "The tide, he called it."

Had he piped up, in part, to impress her? Ever since revealing Arc as her choice, Devout had been careful to offer nothing more than a nod when they met at the spring or on the path to the bog. She averted her eyes when he looked up from his anvil, following her as she came in from the fields.

The oldest uncle flicked his wrist, dismissing Young Smith's idea of an undulating sea.

She saw how the evening would continue, with Old Smith and his brothers wary, unreceptive, and the younger contingent—Young Smith's brothers and cousins—cajoling, pushing for battle. Why not, when in the end it was Old Smith's decision, and he had already made up his mind? None of the younger Smiths would be called on to prove the courage they so easily voiced.

"And if we find ourselves lost?" Old Smith said, directing the question to Young Smith. His father had noticed, then, that Young Smith's words about the rising and falling sea had been flicked away.

"You know the route to Hill Fort," Young Smith said. "We'd be with the others leaving from there."

"And if they've already set out?"

"We could hire a trader to guide us."

Again, Young Smith glanced toward her, and she grew heavy with the idea that she made him blind to the seriousness of the decision being made.

Old Smith ran his thumb over the rim of his mug. "Have none of you considered that we would be crossing enemy territories?"

"The druid promised safe passage," said the oldest brother. "The chieftains have given their words."

"Are we to believe that word has reached every settlement? Would we not slay any valley dweller who set foot in Black Lake?"

"I'd put a spear through his heart," said the brother closest in age to Young Smith. That brother was a known braggart, one bent on compensating for his clumsiness in the forge, if Old Man were to be believed.

Old Smith opened his palms, as if to say his point was proven.

The flaming logs crackled and hissed as the Smith men grew quiet around the firepit. Devout felt the blaze's heat on her cheeks, Arc's heat on the length of her arm. She moved her hand so that it brushed his. His thumb traced her wrist, and her skin awakened. That pleasant ache she had first felt the day they harvested the comfrey came to her loins. She put her attention on Old Smith—the dark hollows of his eyes, the reflected firelight brightening his brow, his cheeks.

"They say the Roman warriors—" he began.

"They say they're short," said the braggart.

"They say they act in unison, as if their gods whisper in their ears," Old Smith continued.

"Our gods are mightier than theirs," said the oldest brother. "That was proven a long time ago."

The younger Smiths nodded, surely recalling Julius Caesar's retreat, and then the uncles, too, slow, careful bobs. Old Smith joined in with a single drawn-out lowering of his chin.

"To defy a druid—" Old Smith said and shook his head.

"Would be to anger the gods," said the oldest uncle.

"When have we ever submitted to nuisance invaders?" said the oldest brother.

"When have we ever lain down to a marauding tribe?" said the braggart.

He leapt to his feet, swiped the air as though with a blade. "We'll come back with a dozen Roman heads."

Had jealousy, as much as courage, formed the words? A skull hung over the Hunter roundhouse door. That skull had been struck though by Old Hunter's spear during a raid against the uplander tribe. The Smith clan had no such prize to attest to their bravery.

The oldest brother was next on his feet. He pumped his fist overhead. "We'll nail the skulls up over the forge's gate."

A bronze serving platter—Young Smith's handiwork—occupied the spot. Devout had watched as Old Smith positioned it there during an earlier bonfire. First, though, it was passed among the bog dwellers so that they might admire the raised swirls and inlaid red glass. "You'll see," he had said as he clapped Young Smith on the back. "One day he'll surpass me in skill."

One of the brothers, then the next, got to his feet, Young Smith last of all.

"Glory will be ours."

"More skulls than we can count."

"Hail, War Master!"

Devout grew chilled among the blustering brothers, troubled that they—blacksmiths, all—should want to replace the platter, evidence of the clan's skill, with the skulls of felled men.

Old Smith stood, then the uncles. The uncles raised their fists overhead. Old Smith lifted a palm, held it out in front. Once the din had settled, he walked the inner perimeter of the benches, his attention passing from one face to the next. "The Smiths will join the united tribes," he said. "As for the rest of the tradesmen, the head of each clan must decide what is right for his kin."

By DAYLIGHT, the bog dwellers offered a runt lamb to War Master in Sacred Grove and learned that, from Black Lake, only the Smith clan would pursue the Romans. The clearing was a hive of activity, with the Smith women spreading skins, heaping one with salted pork, another with dried fish, another with smoked venison. They filled drinking skins; shook dust from woolen blankets, rolled them into tight cylinders, bound them with sinew braids. The men tested the readiness of spears, the security of the joints between the heads and shafts. They polished swords, sharpened blades, yelped, and swiped them through the air.

Devout milled about the clearing in her field dress, uncertain on so uncertain a day. Were the hands expected in the fields? Old Smith had not hesitated long enough in his preparations to instruct that, yet again, the farthest field needed to be cleared of creeping thistle, ragwort, and dock. She tried to make herself useful, taking up the stray end of a blanket being folded, straightening a toppled stack of dried fish.

Midmorning, Young Smith emerged from his roundhouse carrying a dozen spears. As he unburdened himself, tilting one spear and then the next against the roundhouse wall, it struck her that this morning could be the last that he traipsed Black Lake. Conviction washed over her that she must speak to him, must say she knew not what, but it seemed that he should know her respect, her good wishes, before he set out. What was their last exchange? He had said, "Weather's holding," and she had said, "The wheat grows well." Pleasantries that would not do as parting words.

She was emptying a vessel of the Smiths' hazelnuts into a linen sack and watching for a private moment to speak to him when Young Hunter brushed by Young Smith's oldest brother. Loudly enough for a handful of bog dwellers to hear, the Smith brother said, "Your clan are cowards, staying behind, spineless worms." Then the braggart brother spat toward the skull over the Hunters' door. Old Smith bellowed, calling his sons close. Wearing his harshest scowl, he told them to keep their needling to themselves. "Undignified," he said, not minding that Devout—a hand—remained within earshot. "Unbefitting a Smith. Imprudent, too, when our women and children stay behind."

He locked his gaze on his oldest son, kept it there until the son's head bowed. Old Smith looked from one son to the next, summoning obedience in much the same way. When his eyes lit on Young

Smith, he did not glower but rather touched his son's forearm with all the tenderness of a newly sprouted leaf. "Walk with me," Old Smith said.

Devout watched as they passed the forge, as Old Smith ran his fingers along the rough timbers of the low wall. She saw reverence in that touch, a sort of longing for the place he had not yet left. They stood still once they were out of Devout's range, and Old Smith clasped his son's upper arm. He spoke and maneuvered to keep his grip when Young Smith tried to shrug the hand away. Eventually he ducked, releasing his shoulder from his father's hold, and strode toward the gate leading to the woodland.

She set down the sack of hazelnuts and caught up with him in the woodland, where he was kicking stones and thwacking the underbrush with a stick. "Young Smith?"

When he turned toward her, his eyes shone damp. "I'm to live among women and children," he said, "and haul the wood and water once hauled by a dozen men."

"You're staying behind?"

"You must think I'm a shirker, that my own father sees me as a burden." He kicked the earth.

"I don't."

"And once they're back"—he shook his head—"there'll be endless nights at the firepit. Backslapping. Tales of the battle, of bravery. Talk of the southeast, the sea I'll never glimpse."

He sniffed, wiped his nose with the back of his hand. How much she wanted to console him. How much she wanted to touch his cheek.

"I told him I'm ready, nearly a man," he muttered. "He said it's why he was entrusting me with the forge, the women, their broods."

"It's a lot of responsibility. You shouldn't feel—"

"I'm already stronger than two of my brothers." He thwacked the ferns edging the path. "I told him that. You know what he said? He said, 'And a better blacksmith, too.'"

"Everyone says so." She nodded.

"How is it fair? For hard work, for skill, I'm made to stay be-hind?"

"He's seen how capable you are."

He cocked his head toward a lifted shoulder.

"I'm happy you're not going."

She had meant it sincerely, but as he stilled from wielding his stick, she feared she had said the wrong thing. How might a boy who had shown her affection, who wore his anguish when she said "I have an old friendship with Arc," interpret those hasty words?

"We should get back," she said. "They mean to set out before the sun crests."

At the clearing, they found the provisions divided, bundled, and secured with sinew braids, and Old Smith inspecting the spears Young Smith had tilted against the roundhouse wall. Old Smith separated three spears from the lot, said, "These ones need atten-tion before we go." He held them out to Young Smith. "Waste no more time."

The sun crested and the Smith men, already weighted with swords and shields and bedrolls and drinking skins, hoisted the rush baskets holding their bundled provisions onto their backs. Devout stood wringing her hands amid the bog dwellers waiting for the mighty Smith men to lumber away. Young Smith's kin went to him one by one, spoke in hushed voices. He nodded, no doubt promising that, yes, he would keep close eye on a brother's thin-skinned son or heed a brother's ripe-with-child mate. Last of all, Old Smith narrowed his eyes and leveled his gaze at the bog dwellers. "I leave my son as First Man," he said in a loud clear voice. "He will lead as I have led until I return."

Those departing words surely met Young Smith's ears like rain come to parched earth. No one would think him a pitiable, left-behind boy but rather a man chosen by his father for the safekeeping of his clan and an entire settlement until his return.

Then Old Smith, his brothers, his nephews, and sons—all but Young Smith—lifted their swords overhead, let out great yelps, and turned away.

13.

'HOBBLE

≈

E SET OUT for Hill Fort, walking in a southwest-erly direction for the better part of the first morn-ing. My father hauls a laden handcart—borrowed from the Carpenters—over roots and around hollows in the middle of the trackway. I want to feel light away from the burden of Fox, as though I could gleefully clip-clop the full distance to Hill Fort, but I do not.

The evening before, Fox had calmly slit the throat of the Hunter clan's hound pup. This, because Hunter griped that my father had no right to go to Hill Fort. Fox had raised a silencing hand and said he would not hear another word, but Hunter could not keep his mouth shut and blurted out that my father did not even know the route. I am breathless as I recall that sweet pup swept from his paws in the clearing and locked under Fox's arm. He put out his hand and, his face daring objection, demanded Hunter's dagger, no matter that the pup was favored by the Hunter brood. The pup writhed and squealed as blood spurted, as the sleeve of Fox's robe bloomed red, as mothers pulled wailing children into their skirts.

I LOOK OVER my shoulder on the path, take in the glum set of my father's face, the strain that shows in the way his hand clenches the cart's handle. I turn to face him, trot backward. "You know what Old Man told me?" I say, thinking of my father's pleasure when he speaks of his youth.

"I can't imagine."

"He told me the Smith clan was once thirty-four strong." I knew the clan had dwindled after my father's kin set out to meet the Romans but had not imagined so large a clan, so steep a fall. I went to Sliver, who, because we are like sisters, confirmed the number with her mother when I asked her if she would.

"A long time ago." My father nods. "It was a druid who cajoled my kin into a battle the tribesmen could never win."

For him, the moons following the Roman invasion form a chasm, cutting through his life, severing a whole into two parts—before Roman rule and afterward. In the early days, our clan had number, stature, wealth. Now we endure, diminished—at least, in my father's mind. And yet he does not despise or fear the Romans, not like my mother does. I have found his receptivity curious. Yes, he is forward thinking, secure in the skill he has to offer, but until this moment, I had not fully understood. My father does not hold the Romans solely accountable for our clan's fall—not when it was the urgings of a druid that prompted his kin to join a slaughter that was over and done within two days, not when Fox just the night before reminded us of druid mercilessness.

Trying a second time, I say, "Old Man said the forge was more industrious than any hive."

He nods, and one corner of his mouth lifts. My heel snags a root. I stumble, catch myself.

"Careful," he says. "Better turn around."

"I should know my family's history." I continue my backward trot.

He draws a circle in the air, instructing me to face forward on the trackway.

I stumble again, maybe a little on purpose. "You'll tell me?"

He nods, and I do as I have been told.

"I was fourteen when my kin left," he says. "I managed well enough for a while, making a steady stream of swords and scabbards and spears, all delivered to Chieftain at Hill Fort."

"By the traders?"

"That's right," he says. "But within six moons, the traders were telling me my wares were required in lesser quantities. I thought I only had to be a better blacksmith, and the commissions would return."

I picture the boy I had seen reaching for a shiny object in a magpie nest. I think of him at his anvil scrutinizing a spearhead, shoulders slumping at the flawed symmetry. "Old Man says you're more skilled than even your father was."

"Not early on."

"He says you're the clan's great talent," I say.

"It made no difference to the traders," he says. "When they came back, it was only to tell me Chieftain had little use for flawless blades and intricate hilts. Blame the Romans, they said."

He nudges the drinking skin against my arm, continues. "From the start, the Romans insisted on civility between the tribes and punished any chieftain unprepared to set aside the old grudges and live in peace."

I have grown up with old tales of raids against the uplander and valley dweller tribes. In my time, though, I know of no such incident. "No more arming Chieftain's warriors."

"I told the traders I'd make up for the loss with housewares and spent a moon forging a pewter flagon." His voice grows distant, hushed. "A thing of beauty: a convex body tapering to a base rung with scrolls and vines twisting through rosettes." He clears his throat. "But the traders hardly looked. Half Chieftain's wheat goes to the Romans now, they said. Even he must economize."

It is not like my father to speak so openly, and it makes me think Fox's presence has stirred a sort of reckoning. "Where's that flagon now?" I say.

"Long gone," he says, and then, after a pause, "like so much."

This is the part of my clan's decline—the disappeared possessions—that I know. Old Man has described the past lavishness of my roundhouse—the vibrant woolen partitions, the multitude of low tables and benches, the furs, the laden shelves. He has said, too, that my father's mother clung to extravagance far too long. She kept a cook in the household, ordered meat served at every meal, wore dresses cut from the best wool. It cost her the household's finery—the pewter flagons. When a trader trundled off to Hill Fort, his cart was almost always loaded with a number of items she had selected for trade. Within a few years, the household's shelves were bare, and unable to face a meatless pottage, unable to muster the humility to stir that pottage herself, she succumbed to a fever that every other afflicted bog dweller had survived. She took her last breath and departed for Otherworld the moon before I took my first.

"Gone, like your kin." I speak quietly, tenderly.

"Yes."

I place my palm on my chest. "Blessed be Begetter." The god dwells among our ancestors, the spirits he shepherds to Otherworld. "Blessed be his flock."

I wait as he quietly echoes my tribute.

Then I say, "I know about the men."

"But not the women?"

"I've heard rumors."

"Rumors that my mother was thorny," he says, "that without her servants, she was a brute to my brothers' mates?"

"Something like that." Old Man said she prodded and snapped at those women—those extra mouths to feed.

"My brothers' mates saw me—just a little older than you—alone in the forge. They saw traders indifferent to a pewter flagon, the pittance—a few iron bars, a length of wool—handed over in return. One after another, the women struck out for Hill Fort with their broods."

The uncertainty of that distant place held more appeal, it seems, than the certainty of what would happen at Black Lake.

He sighs. "All of them were gone by the time my mother departed."

We walk in silence after that, and though he is at my back, I know he agonizes. I am aware of this even before his thoughts appear, poof, in my mind, and I learn for the first time the burden of his mother's parting words: Do not insult your father further. Reclaim your clan's position.

The quiet is thick between us. I drag my feet, rustle leaf litter. I pick up a stick, thwack the underbrush alongside the trackway. The path widens, and as I slow to walk beside him, he finally says, "I started making the plain cauldrons and cooking knives that the traders could hawk at Hill Fort. I made the nails my father had told Old Carpenter to acquire from a lesser forge."

He pats a linen sack lashed to a crate of nails on the handcart. The linen pulls taut against the smooth curve of the bronze serving platter that he had tucked inside. "It used to hang over the forge's gate."

I think of him removing the platter, running his thumb over the raised swirls and inlaid glass a final time before tucking it away, out of sight, where it could no longer mock a blacksmith who forged cooking knives and nails.

It occurs to me that the sack could well hold a second prize, one too delicate to imprint the linen with its shape. Now is not the right moment, but I will keep an eye out for a chance to confirm my hunch. "Father," I will say. "I'd like to hold the platter."

He will oblige. Only then, with the platter in my hands, might the linen divulge the smaller prize—a silver amulet crafted to win my mother, brought along to ensure Chieftain's restored patronage.

I put my hand over my father's on the handcart's grip, and he says, "My father fussed over that platter."

He smiles. I smile back, and we carry on.

ON THE SECOND DAY of our journey, the trackway disappears and reappears; or maybe it is only a trail the roe deer take to drink from the river we are to locate farther to the south. My father pulls the cart's handle, squints to glimpse some break in the foliage. And then finally, as the sun slips low in the sky, the woodland opens up to reveal a meandering river and timber bridge, and beyond, a massive field of newly planted wheat and a large settlement—Timber

Bridge—ringed with a wattle fence. A stone ribbon bisects the land like a gash. "The Roman road!" I say, scanning its length.

The wheel trader, who had spoken so favorably about Roman roads, had scratched a drawing of one, cut right through, into the dirt. They dig a ditch first, he had said; fill that dug ditch with rubble and then gravel; and after that add a slurry of water, gravel, sand, and a white powder called lime that hardens the mixture to stone. Last of all, he explained, they cap those sturdy underpinnings with paving stones.

"The wheel trader was right," my father says. "A Roman road will last for all time."

That trader had said, too, that the Romans had done us all a great service with their roads, and I see quite plainly how the absence of a road has kept Black Lake almost impervious to Roman influence. But am I uncertain I want quick access, the great wheel of Roman influence rolling to Britannia's farthest reaches, delivering I know not what.

In the far distance—still another day's walk—I make out the vast mound of Hill Fort. I touch my lips, the faint trackway, all the while transfixed by the paving stones reaching before me, one fitted tight as teeth against the next.

WE STRETCH OUT THAT NIGHT, a bed of clover beneath us, the nighttime sky overhead. No more midge-infested underbrush such as we endured the previous night. No more oppressive canopy. No more uncertainty about the route. And most of all, no more Fox. With distance, the druid—his blade at my throat, his mercilessness with the hound pup—has drifted from the forefront of my mind and my father's, too. He laces his fingers at the base of his head, yawns contentedly.

"Father," I say, "I'd like to hold the platter."

I am prepared to argue that it could be my last chance if Chieftain wants it for his own. But without further persuasion, my father pulls the linen sack from beneath the skin cape bundled around our food. My eyes are wide, ready to scrutinize the contours of the linen for the amulet after he removes the platter. But he lifts the sack and, without even loosening the drawstring, slides it to me.

I pat linen, feel the faces of the platter, both front and back, each without protuberance. My fingers slide to the sack's corners, to emptiness.

"What is it?" he says.

"Nothing."

"Let me help," he says, reaching.

I do not budge.

"You look disappointed," he says.

"I thought—" I bite my lip.

"Go on.

"I thought the amulet was inside."

His face retreats—his chin tucking, his eyebrows knitting. "The amulet?"

"I thought you'd show it to Chieftain. Mother told me that to see the amulet was to wonder whether the gods had a hand in crafting it."

His bewilderment continues. "She did?"

I nod.

"What else did she say?"

I badly want to say more, to say she called the amulet a marvel, a miracle, to say she had said no finer blacksmith existed in the land, but she had not.

"Did she say she offered it to Mother Earth?" He rolls from his back to his side, props his head with the flat of his hand.

"I know that story, same as everyone."

He opens a palm to the stars. "And yet you expected to find it inside the sack?"

He knows my gift, accepts my gift, but still I would rather not say I have seen him as a youth, reaching into a magpie nest. And so, I tell a lie that is almost true. "I doubt that story."

I count the rise and fall of his chest, three drawn-out breaths. "Regardless," he says, "I don't have the amulet."

"Why not?"

This time I count six breaths before he returns to his back and, eyes on the stars, says, "I was a fool the night the Romans came to Black Lake."

I burrow my fingers deep into the clover, say to my father, "You were brave."

"You remember the Roman who showed me his armor?"

"Yes." The stars above shine, each glint like sunshine glanced off a distant blade.

He stays quiet, and I fear I have lost him to the intricacies of that armor, but then he says, "It made me bold, his willingness. He seemed indebted—your mother's poultice. He said she reminded him of a girl he knew. 'The same grace,' he said."

I wait.

"I followed him outside to show him the amulet. I said he should take it to his chieftain, that he might want to commission a sword, a shield boss."

I remember my father standing uncertainly in the doorway, peering after the Romans. Had he recalled his mother's final words—Do not insult your father further. Reclaim your clan's position—as he stepped into black night? I had sat on my hands afterward, desperate for his return, and when finally he did, his face was crestfallen.

"He snapped, that Roman. Said his commander was not a chieftain but a legate, that he'd piss on work crafted by anyone other than a Roman." My father pushes breath through closed lips. "He snatched the amulet, drew his dagger when I told him to give it back."

I think of that Roman striding into the night, his step light, as though he did not hold the yearnings of a man in his fist.

"Your mother doesn't know any of that."

He shrugs a sheepish shrug, and I am struck that he keeps this secret, when I thought secrets were solely my mother's domain. I understand his silence, though. She claimed to have pitched the amulet into the bog, and he could not admit he found it and gave it to a Roman without exposing her lie.

"Best not to wake a sleeping babe," I say, and he nods, the glass of his eyes reflecting the shine of the stars.

We breathe in the sweetness of the clover all around, listen to the hoot of a distant owl.

"Wanderers' star," I say, pointing to a star shining bright in the northern sky.

"Remember?"

"Yes." Same as he, I am remembering our small family lapping up just such a night.

My mother lay on a woolen blanket, my head resting on her belly as she taught me how to locate wanderers' star. She explained how it stayed put in the swirling sky, always showing the way north. My father squatted, poking at the fire, not bothered in the least on that perfect night that it was Arc who had taught her about the stars.

14.

HOBBLE

～～～

THE NEXT MORNING my father and I are skeptical that Hill Fort remains a further day's walk, but even as the sun crests, our destination stays in the distance. Eventually I can make out the earthen ramparts ringing the high mound and the wooden palisade at the summit. "This road," my father says for the third time. "You've noticed the slight arc of it? It stops the rain from puddling."

I laugh that still he marvels, though, in truth, the road is wondrous—straight as a shooting star, even as an anvil's face, and, yes, dry as salt.

In late afternoon, we skirt massive pens of sheep and cattle, too many to count. "Chieftain's?" I say, and my father nods. The road widens, and then we are amid a jumble of shacks and ramshackle stalls with traders hawking lamb and pork already butchered, spears and axes already made, clay vessels already shaped, even wheaten beer already poured into mugs.

I feel assaulted by the bustle—the scampering children and

skittering hounds, the braying hawkers and bartering women, the creaking carts and clattering wares. I steady my roving eyes on a single stall but remain overwhelmed. "So many eggs," I say, hands flitting from my sides. An assortment—at least fiftyfold more than I have ever seen gathered in one place—fills the shallow bins laid out on the counter spanning the stall's front opening.

"Look at the partridges." My father points to rafters thickly hung with fowl.

My eyes drift from the partridges to a flat square of wood nailed to the stall's rear wall. The wood's face is etched with segments of line—sometimes curved, sometimes straight, sometimes diagonal, other times vertical or horizontal. "What is it?" I say.

"Words, I think."

"Pictures of words?" I frown.

"Symbols, each representing a sound, strung together to form words. A trader explained it to me once. He claimed the Romans have been etching words into wood and stone for hundreds of years."

I am no less puzzled, and he sees it in my face.

"Give me a word," he says.

"Bird."

"*Buh. Er. Duh.* Each of those sounds has a symbol. You join each symbol's sound to the next until you've linked *buh*, *er*, and *duh* to get *bird*."

We walk in silence while I consider what those etched symbols might say. Perhaps *partridges*, but it seems a wasted effort when anyone need only open his eyes. Perhaps *fresh* or some other enticement, but would not anyone sniff a bird even if such a claim were made? But then I remember my father telling me about the Romans using small metal disks—coins, they are called—for trade. Those words instruct any Roman warrior come to Hill Fort from Viriconium that three coins or perhaps six can be traded for a partridge. How ignorant I am, and my father, too, all tribesmen, really, except perhaps those few who have learned to decipher Roman symbols, who know the worth of coins.

"They say the Romans use those symbols to set down their history for all time," my father says.

The druids lack such a system of symbols. They hold our history in their memories, along with our laws and any gained understanding of the world. It occurs to me how very fragile that knowledge must be, how susceptible to alteration, to loss. How much better to have all of it etched into wood. I imagine a great collection of wooden slabs holding Britannia's history. I imagine deciphering that history, speaking it aloud. No more waiting for a bard to come. No more wondering if the old words he sings are invention or fact.

"The Romans know so much."

"Nothing we can't learn," my father says. "Maybe you'll make a record of Mother Earth's magic someday."

"Imagine that!" The idea would irk my mother. My father had recently managed to successfully temper a blade and, afterward, commented how much he would appreciate a day in a Roman forge. Fury had come to her face as she pounded her pestle, turning root to paste.

By the third time my father is beckoned, he has grown wise and does not approach the merchant's stall and hold in his hand a bone comb or shaving blade. I know he intends to examine the ironwork on display, perhaps even show one of his small cauldrons, but he says, "Chieftain first," and we walk on.

"Look," I say, pointing to a stall lined three deep with men.

They hoot and jostle, drain mugs, and hold them out to the merchant to be refilled. Today their armor is absent. Only their swarthy skin and the swords belted at their hips mark them as Roman war-riors on leave from Viriconium.

My father steers me to his opposite side, away from the carousing men. I watch transfixed as one of those men snatches an egg from the neighboring stall. He knocks the egg against the rim of his mug, arches his neck, and positions the hand holding the cracked egg over his wide-open mouth. The yolk and trailing white slide from shell, drop into the waiting cavern. He swallows, and his brethren war-riors slap their thighs, guffaw as though they have never seen a more hilarious stunt. He snatches a second egg, then another and another. Each is passed among the men, eventually swallowed to a chorus of encouragement.

The egg merchant folds his arms. Lines of worry crease his face. He loses a dozen eggs before he begins edging the shallow egg bins away from the warrior. Eventually the warrior extends an arm and discovers the eggs out of reach. He shifts so that he stands opposite the merchant. Words are exchanged, fingers wrap the hilt of a sword, and then the merchant extends his hand over the eggs in a gesture of offering. The warrior yanks a bin, sends it careening from the counter into the street. He continues until the full supply of eggs lies broken—a slop of yolk and white and shell over the orderly mesh of Roman paving stones.

"They have no shame," I whisper.

My father's head wags side to side. "A disgrace."

We keep to the center of the road after that, neither stopping nor slowing until a thin, hollow-chested man steps into our path. "A blacksmith," the man says, directing an open hand toward the loaded cart. He turns to me. "Pretty eyes."

"Let us pass," my father says.

"You've come to trade, and I can be of assistance. I know the ways of Hill Fort. You're all alone here, a newcomer, ripe for the swindlers."

The man looks like a swindler himself, a buzzard with his beak nose and deep-set eyes. My father takes a step toward him. His brawny chest near abuts the man's sharp chin. "I know the worth of my wares."

"I'll walk with you," the buzzard man says, shifting, making a little sweeping gesture that says we should step in line.

My father applies the gentle nudge that tells me I am again to move to his opposite side.

"Chieftain's man won't see you," he says. "There isn't enough work for his own blacksmiths, not with the Romans forbidding even tussles among the tribes. It's turned him sour—Chieftain—idle kin loitering around his household, eating his cherries and drinking his beer; long days without so much as a skirmish to relieve the tedium. Never mind that the Romans take half his wheat."

As we push on, the buzzard man keeps pace. Eventually, he skitters a step or two ahead, turns to me, and says, "You've not had the pleasure of a cherry. I saw it in your face. Small and red like a crab apple but fleshy and sweet. The Romans brought them. And olive oil, another improvement. Delicious, mild, and pleasantly sweet."

Is it a ploy, using such strange words, a way of making my father and me feel like bumpkins? I keep my eyes straight ahead.

"I'm called Luck," the man says, halting. "When you're ready to trade, come find me behind the fishmonger's stall."

We march on. My father has higher sights than to trade with a swindler set up behind a fishmonger's stall. We pass through a wooden gate mounted between the ramparts at the base of Hill Fort and begin to climb the high mound.

The palisade ringing the summit encloses a massive wooden forge with a peaked roof and twenty-three roundhouses, each large, freshly whitewashed, and decorated with bands of ocher, whorls of ruddy red, tendrils of near black. I knew Chieftain was not so impoverished as Luck wanted us to believe. We pause a moment at the opening in the palisade, gaze out over the rolling hills, the never-ending wheat fields, the thousand grazing sheep, the mist obscuring the disarray and frenzy of the commerce far below. My father's shoulders straighten. He grins.

We duck around the heavy oak and iron strapping of the forge's open door. I watch as his eyes light from marvel to marvel—a vast hearth with access from either side; a pair of long cooling tanks; six bellows cleverly suspended from the rafters; a wall hung with hammers, tongs, chisels, rasps, and swages of every size and shape. His eyes land on an iron flagon with an enameled rim, hold steady as he scrutinizes the handiwork. "My work is better," he says, but even as he speaks his voice falls. Is he realizing, as am I, that of the forge's dozen anvils only three are occupied? A blacksmith with the belly of a drinker looks up from an anvil, and I take in the lopsided slant of his mouth. He approaches, waddling, taking his time, but with hammer still gripped in his fist. He introduces himself to my father as Head Smith, not bothering with even a sideways glance toward me. He sneers when my father cannot say who gave us passage, only that the gate was unmanned. "Look at you." Head Smith juts his chin. "Dressed like a hand, hauling a cart. You're a shame to the trade."

My father's smile drops. No doubt my presence doubles his shame. "Should I wait outside?" I say.

My father extends the linen sack toward the man.

"Go!" Head Smith spits in my father's face. "Begone."

My father holds back from wiping spittle from his cheek. He draws himself taller and points to the flagon. "The enameled rim of that flagon," he says. "I can do better. The ridges—"

Head Smith's nostrils flare.

"I'm from the Smith clan at Black Lake."

Head Smith thumps his hammer against his open palm.

"Chieftain once preferred our forge above any other."

Now Head Smith raises the hammer. His eyes say he means to break the skull of so brazen a pauper.

As we descend the mound, my heart aches. We walk in silence, and I ponder. Is he, just now, suffering under the weight of his mother's final words? Or fixating on my mother's worn dress, her hesitation as she decides whether to wrap her arms around his neck? His thoughts do not come into my mind.

"Mother doesn't care that we sometimes go without meat," I say.

His eyes stay put, a step ahead of his feet.

"Hunter should keep his mouth shut," I say.

Only a sideways glance.

"My cape will do another year."

Nothing.

My father sometimes says that by persistence even iron can be shaped. Not today. Today iron does not yield.

We trudge along the road, again hauling the handcart through the cacophony of commerce. He looks neither right nor left, assessing the ironwork on display, the opportunity that awaits. He keeps his gaze on his feet, and I do the same until I catch the stink of the fishmonger's stall. Beyond the stall, overlapping wooden planks form Luck's shed—a narrow rectangle, no more than six paces in breadth. Still, the planks are weathered in a pattern that shows the shed has been increased in size at two points in time. It comes to me that I know that shed. I have seen its crammed interior, the maze of slight pathways cutting through the goods. An old vision—one that had not, until now, made a lick of sense. I knock my elbow against my father's hip. "Look," I say, pointing.

He hardly glances up.

"You can tell his trade is growing."

He does not deviate from our straight path.

I picture our return to Black Lake: my father's crumpled face as Hunter launches into a tale of the wealth that rains from the sky at Hill Fort, caught by anyone with upturned palms; my father's bowed head as Fox sneers disrespect at a blacksmith unable to trade his wares.

With even that imagined moment of Fox again nearby, my throat constricts. My voice quivers slightly as I say, "He's called Luck for a reason."

"All right," my father says. "All right."

And I wonder what would have happened if I had not badgered. Would he have decided on his own to call on Luck? With that old vision, was it cast in stone that I would one day find myself inside that shack? Or had that vision come as a sort of prod so that I would know to alter my father's course, to steer a dispirited man hauling a laden handcart?

The shed's interior is, in truth, threaded with narrow pathways lined with stacks of unadorned pottery bowls, bins of oil lamps, heaps of plainly woven wool and more of skins. Just beyond the skins, the floor is piled with iron bars, more than I have ever seen. The pretty brooches and glass beads and garlanded bowls—all readily available to catch a woman's eye in the marketplace's stalls—are absent from the shed. Luck approaches and my father says, "You earn your wealth supplying the Romans at Viriconium."

Luck looks down his beak nose. "Trade has never been better," he says. "You saw the marketplace."

"Busier than an ox's tail when the flies are thick."

"The warriors on leave are only too happy to part with their wages."

"We saw them," my father says. "Brutish as Fallow."

Luck shrugs. "They've grown bored at Viriconium."

"Now that they've conquered the rebel tribes?"

Luck nods, purses his lips, appearing so much like Old Man when he gives an opinion that he considers a truth. "That defeat has made the druids restless as wind," Luck says. "I can guarantee that."

My father's face is still, and I cannot decipher whether he is thinking he was right to speculate that Fox's arrival at Black Lake is connected to mounting druid anxiety. And what, I wonder, would Luck make of Fox ordering me to divine the outcome of a rebellion? Are Fox's druid brethren, at this very moment, wringing hands and contemplating the tenuous security of their enclave on Sacred Isle? Does talk of rebellion fill their days? And this: Do they discuss how best to appease War Master? Has Julius Caesar's retreat been cited as proof of the usefulness of substituting man for beast?

"I came to trade," my father says.

As sweat dampens my nape, I remind myself that Feeble is the true runt, that I can run like the wind and walk the great distance to Hill Fort. No one would suggest he better earns his keep than I; no one would claim him more deserving of milled flour and hard cheese. Or perhaps they would—if they peered inside my head and saw my low thoughts, the shabby assurances I make for myself. I seek the comfort of my father's hand.

Luck reaches into a bin, holds out to my father something like an oversize nail, except that the blunt end circles back on itself to form a loop. "A Roman tent peg," Luck says. "Better design than we're used to. I can't keep up with the demand."

My father runs his fingers through his hair, makes his opening offer. He would trade his ladles and cauldrons for three times their weight in iron bars. Luck laughs and counteroffers. My father tugs my hand, makes as if we are going to leave the shed, but Luck says, "Stay. Stay."

Luck pours mugs of mead, and after more discussion and my father pointing out the symmetry of his cauldrons, the braid trimming the base, the precision of his ladles, the gentle arc of their handles, the great distance he has traveled from remote Black Lake, Luck ushers us to a small table and goes into the street. He returns with more mead, a small sack of cherries, a plate of sliced bread, and a fist-sized vessel of olive oil. "So that you might see I am a generous man," he says.

"So that you might see I am a skilled blacksmith," my father replies and slides the bronze serving platter from the linen sack.

I watch Luck restrain himself from stroking the handiwork. As my tongue glides over the smooth contours of a cherry, he forces his attention from the platter to my father. My teeth pierce the skin. The flesh is like a plum's, except smoother, sweeter, like honey stirred into thick cream.

He topples the sack and a dozen cherries spill from the opening. "Go ahead," he says to me and then to my father, "Magnificent work, but as you can see my trade does not involve magnificence."

I twist the stem from another cherry, put it in my mouth.

"I'll tell you one thing," he says. "The Romans know about food. You doubt me?"

Though I shake my head, he says, "Just wait until you've tried greens flavored with garlic. Or, better still, meat flavored with rosemary."

He continues, insisting that the tribesmen's diet has been lifted from tedium with the vegetables and herbs the Romans have introduced. He presses further with a litany of arguments in favor of the Romans—never has commerce been so brisk; never has such opportunity come to the tribesmen; with more land cleared and improved yields, the harvest is plentiful; roads and aqueducts have been built and swamps drained and coins introduced; with warring outlawed between the tribes, there is a new order about the land. In Britannia's east, the Roman towns of Londinium, Verulamium, and Camulodunum boast stone temples and marketplaces, halls where the Romans bathe together. No tribesman had seen the likes of such engineering, such ingenuity. He says to me, would not any barbarian, gazing upon those structures or savoring a cherry, embrace the glory of Rome?

I want to say that I do not know a barbarian to ask, also that Roman warriors smashed the Hunters' pottery and tore our woolen partitions, that they leer at women and pilfer pheasants and eggs as though it were their right. But I press my lips shut and wonder if all he asserts is even true and also why any Roman would prefer a stone temple to a sacred grove, why any Roman would want to wash in another man's filth. He tousles my hair, in the same way my father does, and I realize I like this Luck, with his easy smile and breezy way.

I am sucking clean the last cherry pit when he gets back to the trade, to what he really wants. He will take the cauldrons, the ladles, and load the handcart with iron bars equal to twice the weight. My father will come back with half the iron forged into Roman tent pegs. In return for those pegs, Luck will again load the handcart with twice the weight of the forged iron.

"It is best," Luck finally says, "that the pegs come to me in nailed-shut crates. The druids are in the settlements again. They watch carefully now."

My father keeps his face blank, without hint of alarm that his conjecture to me about the druids is confirmed, without hint of surprise that Luck's trade proposal is improper enough to necessitate secrecy, without hint of concern that Fox would surely condemn any industry undertaken on the Romans' behalf. But as my father slides the bronze serving platter into the open mouth of the linen sack, I know he means to abandon the trade.

Oblivious to my father's second thoughts, Luck continues, "They're agitating, those druids," he says, "fanning embers of discontent. I don't think much of them. Fanatics, incapable of reason, incapable of adopting any view other than their own. I wouldn't blame the Romans if they outlawed druidry here like they have in Gaul."

My father stills.

"They call the druids savage," Luck says. "They point to our old ways as certain proof."

He glances to me, then back to my father, and I know Luck is not at all oblivious to the implications of my lame leg.

"I'll take your iron," my father says, "and I'll take a large skin, too. Hobble needs a new cape."

"As you please." Luck sweeps his arm grandly toward his skins. He hands me the vessel of olive oil. "For your mother," he says.

I wonder if my father has the upper hand, and then decide, yes, that Luck needs him. His interest was piqued the moment my father mentioned the remoteness of Black Lake.

My father points to a pile of woven wool. "I'll take a length, enough for a dress." The wool is plain, but my mother will dye it with elderberry or woad, replace the field dress that droops from her shoulders, as worn as a moth's wing.

Luck nods, again sweeps his arm.

It does seem a poor trade on his part, and yet the man with his buzzard face and well-stocked shed is shrewd. Is the undertaking— forging tent pegs for the Roman army—riskier than my father has judged? Luck must think so, and he does not know that a druid lives in the household of the blacksmith he has engaged.

"And also, an oil lamp," my father says. "One of the bronze ones. I saw a few."

"You intend to melt it down?"

"My mate deserves a fine bracelet."

How it would please him to put a pretty bracelet around my mother's wrist. How satisfying to watch her cross the clearing, to see the bronze's warm luster catch Hunter's eye.

Luck nods. "I'll give you the oil lamp, and you'll ask for nothing more."

I can see my father's balled hand beneath the table, the way it drums against his thigh, a quick steady beat, as he works to keep his elation hidden from so shrewd a trader as Luck.

My spirits rise with my father's. He has work, the promise of more to come. My gift proved useful in tipping him toward Luck's shed, and the idea that the trade was fated feels as soothing as Hope's warm breath.

Luck joins us outside as we reload the handcart. "You'll pass through Timber Bridge?"

I remember the large settlement near where we had spent the night. My father nods.

"They say a pair of druids is staying there," Luck says. "Be careful."

My father feigns interest in a lashing holding the iron bars in place.

"Self-interested is what they are," Luck says. "They can't bear their stranglehold loosened. Can't bear the Romans prying their druid fingers from our necks. Can't bear the way Roman rule constrains their power."

I glance toward my silent father—a man content to listen, to discover what he does not know.

"Druids are only men," Luck continues, "imperfect in their judgment."

I stand wide-eyed, troubled, and yet curious that Luck does not seem to believe that the druids execute the gods' will. I think of my father's kin, cajoled into battle and then forever absent from Black Lake.

Luck cocks an eyebrow. "They'll keep conjuring, keep telling us what the gods put in their heads, until they've got us rising up in rebellion."

My father pulls me tight with one arm, and I wonder if his mind, too, has tumbled to War Master and the old ways that are, in fact, not so old.

With his free hand, he tugs the handcart. Wheels lurch from still.

15.

DEVOUT

〜〜〜

EARLY MORNING, as Devout lay awake, a starling flew into
the roundhouse, navigating the narrow gap between wattle
door and frame, and perched on the foot of her pallet. In the
face of so ominous a sign, she scurried to her feet and pushed open
the door with enough force that it slammed into the abutting wall,
waking all the household: her mother, who draped an arm over her
eyes; Second Hand Widow, who bolted upright, her gaze flitting to
her children, stirring amid a hodgepodge of tattered wool; Sullen,
who rolled onto her back; Old Man, who said, "The cock hasn't
even crowed." Once the starling became apparent, all, except a wailing infant, rose quickly from their pallets and began flapping their
arms, clapping their hands, doing their utmost to shoo the bird
outside.

It perched on a rafter and sang the song of a house sparrow, the
incessant chirps and cheeps, and then dove toward the open door
but veered away at the last moment to perch on the high end of a
supporting timber and let out the high-pitched call of the jackdaw.

Though starlings were known mimics, it seemed this particular one taunted the household. Devout's mother dropped to her knees, put the heel of her palm to her forehead, and called out to Protector. The din grew—the wailing, the squawking and chirping, the pleading. A pair of toddlers began to howl, joining the infant, and Old Man threatened them with a stick.

"It's the Romans," Sullen said.

The bog dwellers had had no word, knew not whether the Romans had set out from Gaul, whether they had been turned back by a tempest, a hail of spears. The hands and the tradesmen alike held their breaths as they awaited the Smith clansmen's return, news that the united tribes had prevailed. Sleepless on their pallets, they pulled woolen blankets to their chins, pricked their ears. Were the Romans, at this very moment, moving over the whole of the island, its plains and low hills, its highlands and bogs?

"They'll bash in our doors, bash in our heads," said the eldest of Second Hand Widow's brood.

"Hush," said Second Hand Widow.

Old Man pulled a dagger from beneath his pallet.

"Maybe it's the Smith men," said Devout's mother.

Old Man glared at her. "No bird ever flew inside to foretell a homecoming."

Her face held still, and it came to Old Man that she had not meant the starling heralded the Smiths' safe return but rather dark news of their fate. "Ah." He lowered his gaze. "How long since Hunter's been gone?"

Three moons had passed since Young Smith's yelping kin left the clearing and six days since Old Hunter set out for Hill Fort in search of news. Young Smith had said he would make the trek as First Man, but Old Hunter had been insistent. He knew the route, had traded there since he was a boy. He was acquainted with the locals and the traders and was best positioned to find out what he could about the invasion and the resistance and, more specifically, about Young Smith's kin.

"Six days," Devout, her mother, and Second Hand Widow said in unison. Six long days of hand-wringing as they awaited Old Hunter and the news he would bring.

"He'll be back by nightfall." Old Man jutted his dagger in the direction of the starling. "If not, we'll know the meaning of that bird."

The household grew dejected. Arms hung limply at sides. The starling circled the roundhouse's interior, again called like a jackdaw, and fluttered out the door. The bird had not flown sunwise. Devout and the others touched their lips, the earth.

They stayed fretful as they prepared for the fields—trading their night tunics for field clothes stiff and pungent with sweat and grime, securing worn scraps of leather around their feet, dividing the loaves they would eat midday. Devout remained careful not to comment on the bird, as did all the household, as if admitting it might somehow add to the portent.

OLD HUNTER RETURNED to Black Lake in late afternoon. He was spotted first by Devout, who kept careful watch from amid the stalks of golden wheat. She called out, "Old Hunter comes," and the hands squinted into the distance and then looked to the clearing. Young Smith waved, beckoning them as he left his forge, and because he was First Man now, they knew to abandon the fields.

The bog dwellers gathered around Old Hunter, saying not a word as he set down his spear, his bundled belongings. "It isn't good news." He took a long slug of water from his drinking skin. "I heard nothing of the Smiths, other than that they went southeast with Chieftain's warriors." He looked toward Young Smith. "Some of those men have returned. Most never will. A few are said to have taken up with tribes still holding out against Roman rule."

"There was a battle?" Young Smith said.

"A short one. Two days."

"But we are not defeated? You said tribes still hold out."

"Any of Chieftain's men who joined rebel tribes in the western highlands have sent word to Hill Fort, and your kin have not."

Young Smith lowered his eyes. Devout felt an urge to go to him, to pull his head tight against her breast, to rock and whisper that he would be okay, that he had strength. His mother stood alongside him, her face blank. She offered no soothing touch to her son, no reassuring arms. She held her back erect. "Word will come," she said.

A few of the Smith women began to weep, stirring the smallest of the children to cling to their mothers' legs.

Old Hunter drank again from his skin, wiped his mouth with the back of his hand. "They say eleven chieftains, including our own, have sworn allegiance to a Roman called Claudius. They say he is chieftain to all the chieftains, this Claudius. They say he has pledged to let all compliant chieftains go on leading their tribes as they always have. Chieftain, it appears, will continue to take the same two-thirds share of our harvested wheat and rye and oats that he always has. From this he will pay a tithe owed to Rome."

Devout looked from one bog dweller's knit eyebrows to the next's bit lip. Young Smith's eyes were glassy. He blinked. He had been delivered far too big a blow to speak comforting words, to show himself as First Man.

Old Hunter laid a hand on Young Smith's shoulder. "You're still a boy."

From where she stood, Devout could see that Young Smith swallowed hard.

"I provided the boar for the Harvest Feast," Old Hunter said. "I went to Hill Fort for the news."

How Devout disliked him in that moment, the way he took advantage, the way he grasped.

Young Smith opened his mouth, but Devout saw that he could not manage to speak, would not risk a flood of tears.

Old Hunter wagged his head. "Such a waste, your kin heading southeast." He tightened his grip on Young Smith's shoulder, leaned closer. "I'll step in, take over as First Man."

Young Smith's mother's voice was like ice when she spoke. "His father will return."

"Until then." Old Hunter bowed. "I'll step in until then."

16.

DEVOUT

〜

THREE DAYS LATER it began to rain. As always, the water was collected in buckets and vessels. It was onerous to walk to the ribbon of water that emerged from a mossy crevice and tumbled to the gritstone basin below, and to return to the clearing hauling a pair of buckets sloshing water from their rims. At daybreak Devout opened the door and saw rain falling in sheets. The buckets and bowls left out overnight were full to the height of a man's hand. She and the rest of the hands would not be expected in the fields on such a day.

She thought how she would go to Crone, her small shack. Arc would step through the doorway midmorning, and Crone would place a mortar, a spoon, a sieve into his hands. His touch was light, attentive, she said, like a woman's, and meant it as a compliment. As Devout took up pestle alongside this boy, who knew the industry of bees and the magnificence of the nighttime sky, encroaching Romans and an emperor—both as difficult to fathom as a sea without end—slipped from her mind. Young Smith's agony and the absence of Old Smith's steadying hand fell away. Her happiness was pure. She and Arc had heard the child who was theirs as they walked the length of the causeway, who had come to them from another time.

She woke the following morning even before the rosy tints of daybreak appeared in the eastern sky. She heard Crone whispering from just outside the section of wattle wall closest to her pallet. Devout pulled the door open and stood beneath the thatched eave, yawning and shaking sleep from her head and scowling to be woken before the cock had crowed. The rain had not fully relented overnight, but it had thinned.

"The black henbane has bloomed," Crone said. She shifted her weight from one sodden foot to the other, like a child awaiting honeycomb.

It was an honor, Devout knew, that Crone had collected her to gather the black henbane, the most magic of plants. Crone jutted her chin heavenward to the pale disk. "Only to be picked by moonlight."

As they traversed the fields, heading to the low hill where the black henbane grew, Crone reiterated old instructions, explaining where to look should the known patches fail. Near hare nests; the hares gobbled up the vegetation that tended to choke the henbane but knew enough to steer clear of the plant. In sandy soil; its taproot was deep.

"I know these things." Devout wiped accumulated drizzle from her face.

A few steps farther on, Crone said, "There is the stash of seeds, just in case."

"Yes."

"Soak the seeds twelve days before sowing. Change the water each nightfall."

"I know." Rain trickled from the nape of her neck to between her shoulder blades.

"Never forget."

THE RAIN PICKED UP at daybreak, and the morning was productive with Devout grinding dried meadowsweet, Arc preparing a sweet violet infusion, and Crone stringing the black henbane from her shack's rafters. As the threesome worked, Crone tut-tutted and shook the black henbane, loosening sprays of water, and hung a single plant at a time. Devout did not have to wait long to be reminded that when the air was thick, black henbane tended to rot.

Once it was too late for the fields, Devout began to hope the rain would break, not because she was concerned about rot. Arc made sure to keep the fire too hot for that. But Crone would be feeling the pull of the woodland and bog after so long a time indoors, and Devout wanted Arc's lips on her neck, his hands sliding over her ribs, straying higher to her breasts, with only a layer of wool in between. She glanced up from sewing closed one of the small linen pouches of meadowsweet she had long counted on Old Smith to trade at Hill Fort. Arc was watching her, his gaze steady.

"A breath of fresh air," Crone said, though the rain had not let up. She lifted her cape from a nail hammered into a post. "Keep the fire hot."

The whoosh of cool air that accompanied the leave-taking was barely come and gone when Arc lay back, the rushes covering the earthen floor beneath him and Devout perched on top, her splayed knees alongside his hips. Fingers circling his wrists, she held his arms over his head. She kissed him lingeringly, then a second, third, and fourth time, and felt his hardness beneath her. She straightened her arms, pushing herself away from him. He pulled up from the rushes and caught the neckline of her dress in his teeth. He gave the little yank that snapped open one of the clasps that bound the front of the dress to the back, and it fell from her shoulder to hang diagonally across her ribs. He took in the milky whiteness of the exposed breast, and she leaned forward, felt the warm wet of his mouth. She shimmied the still-clad shoulder free and let her dress fall to her waist. The kissing, the caressing. She thought she could spend the rest of her days so languidly, so dreamily, so urgently, so close to the edge of she knew not what. They were both breathing heavily and sweating, mostly clothed, in the overheated shack, when he took her hips in his hands and rocked her back and forth over his loins. His ecstasy came quickly, accompanied by ragged breath and then a stillness, almost unbearable to Devout, who wanted him closer, inside her skin, who wanted the rocking returned, who needed the unbearableness to come to an end. He pulled her onto his chest and kissed her hair and wrapped her tightly in his arms and said he wished he could give her more than a hand had to give.

She listened to his heart, felt her own slow. She said, "You have all I want," and then a moment later, "I want to lie with you." She had not meant at that exact moment. She meant as his mate, but there was no need to say it. Arc would sling her over his shoulder and carry her across the threshold into her roundhouse. Her fists would pummel his back. Her legs would kick, wildly, in a fine show, an admirable show of fearing the skewering that awaited an intact maiden inside. She thought how only the untouched maidens in the gathered crowd would be fooled.

"You'll be my mate," he said.

"I know," she said, thinking how Hope—the season for unions at Black Lake—felt far away. They had the long moons of Fallow to endure before Arc would move his skin cape and spare breeches, his traps and hooks, his bowl and drinking cup to her roundhouse, and they could live together as mates. Her household had a history of taking in those with few kin and would welcome Arc, a youthful, able-bodied male. Well, all except her mother, who would balk but only a little before giving in. There was that girlhood day she had put her hands on Devout's narrow shoulders and said, "You've a good chance of attracting a young man with a trade."

Devout had thought of Young Smith, Young Hunter, the not-yet-mated Carpenters and Shepherds. Their mothers were not prettier than hers, though they stood straighter and did not share her mother's way of carefully unfolding herself to standing after exulting Mother Earth. It was a tendency common among the hand women, the widows in particular, thin women who touched their lips, the earth with a regularity that suggested the impulse arose as much from want as from gratitude. She had not understood her mother's aspirations that day, only some vague notion that a man with a trade passed to him by his father and in possession of an anvil and bellows, or chisel and saw, could bring comfort to a mate's life.

Her mother had tried again more recently. "You're often with Arc," she said.

Devout felt the urge to smile and wanted to tell her mother about the bed of sweet violets, but she only said, "I admire him."

"He is without a trade, without kin."

It was undesirable, Devout knew, to be without kin. She and her mother were without kin, and her mother sometimes wept when the embers grew dim and the woodpile was exhausted and she was forced into the black of night.

"We'd be his kin," Devout said. "He'd be ours."

"They say Young Smith made his intentions clear."

Young Smith had hardly parted from his forge since Old Hunter had returned with the calamitous news. She had stood at the low wall the other day. "Young Smith," she said, and he lifted red-rimmed eyes from his workbench. "I'm sorry about your kin. Such bravery, all of them."

He nodded, and the lump at the front of his neck bobbed up, then down.

"We all miss your father—always so wise, so evenhanded—more than ever, now that the Romans have come."

He touched a pair of clay molds on his workbench. "Chieftain's territory is far northwest of where they invaded," he said. "Black Lake is at the territory's northern extreme."

"Our remoteness might keep us safe?" she said. "That's what you're saying?"

"It's what we should ask Protector for."

"Your father would give the same advice."

He shrugged, but she could see he was touched.

"Let's hope I can figure this out." He waved a hand over the workbench—the molds, a crucible of iron ingots. "For a sword my father began for Chieftain." He went on, his old assuredness budding as he spoke: The blade was already forged, balanced. Only the easy tasks of polishing and sharpening remained. The hilt was another story though. The shape was roughly there, but the grip was meant to be decorated with two panels of cast openwork inlaid with red and white enamel. "Ambitious for me, even if my father were here."

He lifted the pair of molds. "For making the panels. They'll be smashed to release the panels. I'll get no second chance."

"I've no doubt," she said and stopped herself from adding that she had seen the wonder of his craftsmanship.

―――――――

HER MOTHER WAITED, face expectant, for Devout to comment on Young Smith. If she showed any amount of indecision, her mother would find hope. "I pity him, all alone in the forge now."

"He's got his mother, his brothers' mates, his nieces and nephews," her mother said.

"Women and children."

"Old Man says he'll be First Man again one day."

"Not with the way Old Hunter schemes."

Her mother's chin bobbed. "Still, he'd make a good mate."

Soft lines radiated from the corners of her mother's eyes. She had chosen a hand with a single brother as her mate. Had her mother's mother given her daughter the same advice? Had the words gone unheeded? Had she chosen love and wanted to persuade Devout to do other than she had done herself? Devout lingered on the possibility that her mother breathed in regret each time she hauled water or fetched wood or thought the first sorrel might never come.

Devout sighed a long-drawn-out sigh.

Her mother eased herself to standing; massaged her lower back; and, weary as rot, took up the sling she used to haul wood.

DEVOUT WAS SLEEPLESS, thinking about the time she sat astride Arc in Crone's shack, the kissing and touching that had come afterward: on the stump of an old beech; in the tall grass of the meadow beyond the field; most recently, at a spot where the ferns grew exceptionally thick. Her own ecstasy had come in the tall grass, after she pushed his fingers to the warm wetness between her legs. He had touched her tentatively, then with more certainty, when her back arched up from the ground. He settled into a rhythm as she murmured pleasure. It had come as a shock—the shudder skimming her body like a ripple rolling over the surface of Black Lake, the way her flesh brimmed, wave after wave, the way she fell into the swells, into her body and out of her head, pleasure so deep that her limbs lost strength, that contentment flooded her flesh.

She rattled her head, chastised herself yet again for how fully Arc occupied her mind. This, when Young Smith worked alone unremittingly, as though he might accomplish the work of a dozen lost kin. This, when Romans wielded swords, although at the far extreme of the island, or so she hoped. This, when the fields were pooled with the rain that had barely relented in eight days. It was not right, her lightness, her happiness, the pains she took to arrange her hair, to wash the stink from beneath her arms, to crush a bit of sweet violet against her neck. Her household tossed and turned on their sleeping pallets. Her mother had taken to stillness. The bog dwellers walked with their chins lowered, their faces grim. Devout's mind went to Arc's mouth on her breast, his tongue lapping at a nipple, his hands at her ribs. Almost always, throughout the kissing and stroking, they endured endless rain. Soaked through to the bone, they would return to Crone's shack and hold out dripping willow or purple loosestrife, hastily collected beeswax, each time, a meager haul.

FIFTEEN DAYS OF RAIN, and still the bog dwellers opened their doors in the morning, looked to the southwest and saw that it would not let up. Old Hunter kicked over a bucket swollen with rainwater and stomped across the clearing to confer with Old Carpenter and Old Shepherd. Yet Devout remained heedless, almost jubilant to see rain in the morning and know she would again trade the fields for the bliss of Arc. As they ran from clearing to woodland, from woodland to the dry ground he had found beneath an overhang at the base of Edge, she did not think of the starling that preceded the rain. Thoughts of Arc's wet tongue nudged aside the omen, the lost Smiths, the Romans, the endless rain.

The rain had continued for eighteen days when Old Hunter went door to door advising that every drop of milk be made into the hard cheese that lasted through Fallow rather than used for porridge or the soft cheese the bog dwellers liked to eat with their bread. Three days later he was back. The remaining stores of wheat and barley would be rationed, he said. And then just days before the hands would usually take up their scythes, the first of the small oval spots of rot blistered on the wheat. The men put on brave faces. All was not yet lost. They pointed to the highlands in the west, barely discernible against the churning gray sky, and said it was possible blue skies lay beyond. They had five days, maybe more, before there would be little to salvage in the fields. The women fell to their knees, beseeching Mother Earth.

Still the rain fell, and Devout's mind no longer brimmed with kisses and caresses. With the promise of no wheat for Chieftain, nothing for the stores, she waited for a druid to come, to hold the bog dwellers with a gaze so fierce that some poor soul would drop to kneeling and admit offending Mother Earth.

He came on horseback—a glistening chestnut mare—a sight to behold with his flowing white robe, his beard of curled locks. "Mother Earth must be placated," he said, "but no sacrifice will be sufficient until he who transgressed repents."

His hard gaze moved from face to face. The children whimpered. But no one stepped forward. "Your neighbor will see the troughs between his children's ribs, and he will point a finger. The offender would be wise to step forward now."

A hand finally fell to the ground, fingers clutching the belly that carried her fifth child. She sobbed and muttered, repeatedly touching her lips, the earth. Eventually it was understood that she had not always buried the portion of the nightfall meal due Mother Earth. Devout's fingernails dug into her palms, for that desperate mother's effort to feed her brood seemed a lesser offense than kissing and caressing, oblivious to the mounting woes of the bog dwellers at Black Lake.

THEY GATHERED IN THE RAIN at Sacred Grove. They huddled shoulder to shoulder beneath the six youthful oaks and the ancient one of wondrous girth. Devout had come often. Mother Earth was close amid the gnarled branches hung with mistletoe and the jagged bark silken with moss on its northern face. Today was different, though. Today the grove was dark and foreboding, the ground more mire and muck than lush moss.

A ewe came into the grove, bleating, hauled by Old Tanner and Old Shepherd. Her three good hooves dug into the mud, as though she knew the aged stone altar for what it was, as though the rain had not washed deep into the earth the blood spilled onto the slab. Old Tanner spat onto the mud, said, "Cursed ewe," and Old Shepherd gave the rope a foul-tempered yank.

Young Smith lifted his face to the druid, whose nod showed forbearance rather than true concern.

"That ewe's not a true runt but a breeder," Young Smith said. "Old Shepherd says a week or two out of the mud and the lesion on her hoof will heal. The last three years running, she birthed sets of twins. To offer such a ewe will weaken the flock. I don't see that Mother Earth would find fault with a fox or a hare, not with the wheat rotting."

For a moment, Devout glimpsed his father, his bold manner, the steady voice that showed certainty. The druid's lips pursed for a breath, as though he were considering, but then he dismissed Young Smith's counsel with a wave and hoisted himself into the fork of the old oak. At his side, he wore the golden sickle he would use to cut free the globe of mistletoe to be made into a crown, as was usual when a beast was offered to a god. He chose two maidens to hold the square of white linen meant to catch the severed globe. They took up the corners of the linen and spread it wide. Faces turned upward to the rain and the oak where the druid balanced, his sharp blade cleanly severing the mistletoe. The crowd slouched morosely in their soggy shoes. Devout closed her eyes and imagined the vast wing of Mother Earth shielding the grove from the rain and then beating over the fields, the wet vanishing from the wheat and barley and oats. When Devout opened them, the bleakness of the surroundings glared.

The mistletoe caught and the druid's feet back on muddy earth, he made his crown and set it on his head. The ewe's legs were bound, and she was lifted onto the stone altar, bleating and writhing and thrashing her head. Oftentimes there was debate about the means of slaughter, debate about which of the four gods the offering was intended to appease: Protector, who kept them from harm; War Master, who guided the tribesmen warriors; Begetter, who made man; Mother Earth, who provided. This time, though, the means was set without so much as a hitch of dissent. Everyone knew only Mother Earth could stop the rain, and while an assault to the head appeased Protector; and garroting, War Master; and drowning,

Begetter; Mother Earth sought blood, drained onto the altar, spilled onto the moss, her awaiting mouth.

Those preferences of the gods were reinforced with such regularity that even the youngest at Black Lake understood. A bog dweller striking the heel of his palm against his forehead and calling out to Protector thought quite naturally of the blow the god sought. As that bog dweller drew a finger across his neck and cried, "Heed War Master. Heed him well," garroting came to mind. When he shifted a palm from tracing Begetter's wheel to his chest, it was easy for his mind to flit to drowning, to the breath that would necessarily cease. And when he stooped and murmured, "Blessings of Mother Earth," how ordinary that he should recall blood spilling from the stone altar onto thirsty ground.

Old Hunter and Young Hunter held the ewe, and once the druid raised his arms, Young Smith positioned his knife at the beast's throat. Devout, along with the others, called out, "Blessings of Mother Earth," though the clamor of it was muted as the rain caught their voices and drummed into the earth. She repeated the appeal again and again, as did the others gathered in the grove, yet the rain persisted as the chief source of the din.

What happened next was unclear. Perhaps Old Hunter and Young Hunter prematurely loosened their grips. Perhaps Young Smith applied excessive pressure to the knife even as it met the bones of the ewe's neck. Perhaps the mess was not man's doing, but rather that of a displeased Mother Earth, as the druid would contend in the moments to come. Whatever the case, rather than blood fully drained onto the altar and then cleanly swept onto the moss beneath, as was proper, when the sharp blade of the knife cut into the throat of the ewe, she squirmed. Her bulk twisted in such a way that blood spurted onto the men, streaking their faces, darkening their tunics. Some shot into the air, landed, caught in the deep grooves of the ancient oak's bark. Some mixed with the rivulets of rain crisscrossing the men's faces, the stone altar, the ancient oak's foliage and perhaps found its way to the moss. As the bog dwellers took in the undignified scene, most were certain Mother Earth went unsated, thirsty as salt.

"Now, all for naught, we'll forgo her milk in Fallow," said Old Shepherd's mate, looking as woeful as a shriveled plum. "And the hard cheese we could have made in advance."

A hand called Willow stood with her skin cape spread in such a way that it sheltered her son Lark from the rain. Quick as fear, the druid was upon them, yanking the child away from his mother and toppling him backward onto the stone altar. Lark's hands cast about, for it was through touch that a blind boy discovered his world. His fingers landed on wet gritstone, and, disbelieving, he settled, still as night. Willow screamed, piercing the rain like a cock's crow in the early morning. The druid hooked the point of the golden sickle into the boy's throat and with ease sliced through pale skin, warm flesh, pulsing vein.

"Mother Earth has commanded," he said. "She has shown us her displeasure with the ewe. By her command, we offer a runt boy. With his blood, we atone."

Blood surged from the gaping wound, pooled on gritstone, spilled onto moss—this time, an offering properly made.

17.

DEVOUT

~~~~~~

THE WHEAT ROTTED in the fields. Devout parted under-brush and sat in the woodland with her shoulders hunched forward as her fingers raked decaying leaves and cold, clotted earth. Sometimes she would come upon a clump of mushrooms or a pocket of overlooked hazelnuts and extricate the lot from the debris. With no wheat to harvest and Fallow looming, the mush-rooms were good news, but she was troubled by all that had come to pass, by the way she had smiled as she opened the door to yet an-other wet day. It had not occurred to her, until it was too late, to entreat Mother Earth to stop the rain. In fact, never had she spent so little time on her knees as in recent moons. Never had she been so undeserving of her name. In hopeful moments, she decided her guilt was ordinary, imagined even, rather than born of true offense. Almost certainly a good number of the bog dwellers were counting the ways they had failed, the ways they might have triggered the deluge that had not ceased, the druid who had cut Lark's throat.

Even Arc—good, decent Arc, who stood no chance of drawing the gods' wrath—took up the burden. "Every one of us should've accompanied the Smiths. We just let the Romans invade, and now—" His gaze drifted toward the ruined wheat and then Sacred Grove.

"He knew what was happening," Devout said. "He didn't fight. None of us did."

"Hush," Arc said and laid a finger across his lips.

The bog dwellers had made a solemn pledge. They would not speak of the horror in Sacred Grove, would not bring it to mind by recalling Lark. He was gone from their present and their past, too, a blind boy who sang sweetly, who knew to flavor barley with sorrel and hard cheese with ramsons.

Sometimes as she scavenged, Devout's mind strayed from remorse to the Romans. Though there had been no further word, no sightings as far afield as Hill Fort, those gleaming contrivances from another world could, she supposed, at any moment, arrive in Black Lake. She thought of the druid who had incited the Smith men, of his promise of plunder and killing and torched settlements and tribesmen put into bondage. She felt the cold earth against her shins, raised her face to the heavens. "Blessings of Mother Earth," she said, but her voice pitched higher toward the end of the age-old tribute, turning it into a question for debate. She touched her lips, the decay of the woodland floor.

At nightfall she put her palms on the hollow of her belly, parted her hands to the sharp ridges her hips had become. She could not claim the sharpness arose from necessity, not yet. Still there were the leaves and stems of the chickweed she had picked. The earth remained unfrozen and surely not every edible root—bulbous knots of bulrush, slender tapers of burdock—had been unearthed. She took comfort in the sharpness, those ridges beneath her fingers that provided testament to her piety, her generosity in the portions she set aside for Mother Earth.

Without the usual stores of wheat, the bog dwellers knew the short days and bitter winds of the Fallow soon upon them would not be something to endure but rather to survive. They ate their fills while crab apples still clung to branches, while the elders were more berry than leaf. As far as Edge, they picked the woodland floor clean of nuts and dug up the palatable tubers.

Devout and Crone were in high demand, knowing as they did that the pale mushrooms clinging in layers to a fallen trunk were edible while the darker ones that smelled faintly of rose petals were not. They pointed to plants, the identifying leaves—heart shaped and colossal for burdock, bunched and deeply veined for sorrel, sharply toothed and low to the ground for dandelion. They explained whether it was root or leaf or both that would fill a belly, hush a whining child.

Devout's mother touched the protruding ridge of her daughter's collarbone and suggested she keep a few choice locations to herself. Yes, Devout could make provisions. She had thought of it herself, but surely surrender was the more pious route? She wrapped her arms tighter against her ribs.

The bog dwellers set aside the hard cheese for bleaker days; and in this they were sincere, a claim that could be made for neither the hawthorn berries nor the rose hips. They had agreed to leave those fruits until first frost when they became more appetizing. Still, it was easy to chance upon a cluster of shiny, red berries and notice the sepals already emptied of their fruit and decide that some among the bog dwellers lacked restraint, that one's fair share was better harvested now. They skulked about the clearing with rose hips clutched in fists, tubers hidden beneath skin capes. Better to appear lacking than possessing. Even Young Hunter slunk into the clearing now, the sack at his side swollen with a pheasant or a duck, and went directly to his roundhouse. Crone grew sullen and in a low moment said the bog dwellers deserved what they got—reaping berries before their sweetness had come, digging up tubers in the most haphazard way.

DEVOUT WAS CALLED to Crone's shack and opened the door to find Old Shepherd's two youngest sons gripping their bellies. Loose bowels had plagued them through the night. Their mother wrung her hands. Now more than ever, the boys needed their reserves.

"Willow herb tea, do you think?" Crone said.

It was strange, Crone deferring to Devout, and it came to her that it was a test, that willow herb tea was not the remedy Crone knew to be right. Devout looked from one boy to the other and saw the hint of red about their mouths. She took the older one's hands and turned them over in her own. She rubbed a thumb over reddened skin, skin close to raw. "You've been scratching?"

"Yes."

"And you, too?" The younger brother nodded, holding out his hands so that Devout might see his own damaged skin. Crone smiled, and Devout said, "You've eaten the wrong kind of bulbs." The harmful bulbs had irritated their fingers, their mouths, and then their stomachs cramped.

Old Shepherd's mate shook her head, but then she nodded. "I sent them to find ramson bulbs. I put something that looked like it in their broth."

"Probably daffodil," Devout said. "It will pass."

The mother looked to Crone, who nodded.

"They need water," Devout said.

The mother again looked to Crone, and she repeated Devout's advice, that the boys should take water, and added, "Let them shit. The bulbs will have passed through them by nightfall."

When it was just the two of them, Crone sunk heavily onto the mass of furs heaped by the fire that she called her nest. Devout settled beside her.

"Be on the watch for it: bog dwellers eating what they shouldn't." Crone shifted her hand to cover the top of Devout's. "You've learned well."

Devout was struck by the stillness come to the old woman. Always she dug or chopped or pressed herbs in a colander. Even her eyes seldom rested.

"It's my time," she said. "No point lingering, less with food so scarce."

Devout stiffened. Crone had shown herself watchful and decisive the day the pair first met on the woodland path, and through three years of friendship and shared labor, she had not deviated from what was begun with yellow bloodroot blooms pinched from their stalks. Had Crone foreseen this moment? Had Devout, by her diligence, by recognizing that the Shepherd boys had swallowed bulbs, hastened the arrival of this day? Her eyes flooded with tears.

She put her arms around Crone, and the old woman did not squirm, though it was not their custom to embrace. Devout wept, and Crone said, "Hush," and drew her fingers through the maiden's hair.

"All that is mine is yours," she said, easing Devout away so that her face became visible. "I have said so in front of witnesses to Old Hunter. There will be no mistake."

"But you know better than anyone how to survive Fallow."

"No better than you." She patted Devout's hand, examined her wrist. "You've grown thin."

Devout put her hand in her lap, hid the wrist beneath the fingers of her opposite hand.

"Mother Earth does not find fault with a smaller portion, not when there is no wheat."

She seldom doubted Crone, but just then Devout wondered what the rotted wheat and consequent brutality in Sacred Grove implied about the benevolence of Mother Earth. Her heart quickened that she should have such a thought. A thousand times she had witnessed Mother Earth's generosity. Devout reaped her fields, drew her magic from root and leaf and bloom. She had been the beneficiary, had only to ask—or once, had only to ask.

Still Crone waited, eyebrows lifted, but Devout did not admit the extra fistfuls of chickweed poked deep into the tribute vessel, that vessel where her household set aside the portions owed Mother Earth. Instead she took Crone's hand, and the old woman spoke first of black henbane, repeating instructions Devout already knew. Crone moved on to myriad syrups and drafts and then to her mother's warm hands and how she had a way with bees and then to her father's skill in catching hares, on and on, as the shack grew warmer and dimmer, as flaming wood turned to glowing ember in the firepit. Devout yawned, felt the weight of her eyelids, the weight of her body sinking against Crone's, who slowly, haltingly told a long story about a time when she and her father had become lost in the woods and spent a night huddled in a cave.

Next Devout knew, she startled awake, but there was quiet all around. She listened, but the old woman had ceased speaking. Even the slight wheeze of her breath had disappeared. The girl bolted upright, admonished herself for falling asleep. At one point, as she rocked and wept and cradled Crone, she realized Crone held a small hide pouch tight in her fist. Devout rolled the pouch between her fingers. The contents were loose, granular. She drew open the string, shifted so that her hands fell closer to the weak light coming from the firepit. She tipped the pouch, and seeds spilt onto her palm—small, like wheat in color, like bloated tears in shape. The stink of black henbane filled her nose.

YOUNG SMITH CALLED Devout to the Smith household. One of his brothers' mates had not left her pallet for three days. Without Crone at her side, Devout stood in the doorway, uncertain as a shambling fawn, waiting for her eyes to adjust to the dim light. Young Smith, his mother, his brothers' mates and children—a clan dwindled to seventeen from a once mighty thirty-four—sat at a cluster of low tables. Cook, who had served the clan since before Devout could recall, ladled porridge strewn with wild boar into bowls and poured dandelion root tea into mugs.

Young Smith led her to the sick woman's pallet. As Devout stepped behind the woolen partition, the mate drew skins over her head, retreating, even as the youngest of her brood reached to touch her mother's hair. Devout knew the ailment, the magic to assist, even before she put her hand on the mate's forehead. Goatweed lifted melancholy—a tincture made of crushed blooms and the grain alcohol that preserved the magic.

From beyond the partition, Young Smith's mother spoke. "Make yourselves useful this morning," she said. "They say the gooseberries are ripe. We need water and wood brought inside."

The Smith women—women accustomed to working a loom or

embroidering the edge of a cape—did not respond. Devout shifted to the opening in the partition, just as Young Smith's mother picked up her basket of partially spun wool and stepped from the roundhouse.

Then the mates began:

"We're to haul water while she sits in the sun spinning wool?"

"Someone's got to. They're not coming home."

"The old woman says they're with the rebels in the highlands."

"We all know they're not."

"Can't bear the truth. She loved Old Smith. I'll give her that."

"I'm setting out for Hill Fort next chance I get."

"Better that than hauling water and starving here."

"The old woman's got plenty to trade."

Young Smith slammed down his spoon, though his bowl still held porridge. He got up. "I'll be in the forge," he said.

Cook was prone to a scaly, itchy rash, and a day or two later, she called at Devout's door. As Devout applied a chickweed balm to flared-up wrists, Cook said, "The old woman badgers day and night. She pats the spot beside her and when Young Smith sits, she says, 'You need to take Reddish as your mate.' She holds up a hand, blocking his refusal, insists they need the clan united with a clan on the rise. 'At Black Lake, that's the Hunters,' she says."

"She knows Old Smith isn't coming back," Devout said. That flickering sliver of light had sputtered to black.

"Her eyes glisten, but tears don't come."

Devout thought of the golden brooch daily pinned to the woman's dress now and the belt, decorated with bronze plaques, strung around her waist—ornaments usually reserved for feast days. It made Devout's head wag, that show of wealth and dominance from a woman whose son now labored alone in the forge.

"She's got the persistence of a bull," Cook said. "'No one's fairer than Reddish,' she says, and Young Smith replies that she is spoiled to the core. 'Quite right,' his mother says. 'We all know the way Old Hunter bends to her every whim. You'll use it to your advantage one day.'"

"He's had enough misery," Devout said to Cook and thought of her own part in delivering it.

Young Smith was too gentle for Reddish, and his mother should see it. Devout considered the crop of girls coming up. Beyond the hands and Reddish, the choices were slim, but if he held off a few years, Reddish's younger sister—Second Reddish—was kind and humble and had the same glorious hair as her sister, though one of her eyeteeth bore the shadow that said it would rot.

"And then, he's got Old Hunter to contend with," Cook said.

"He grasps, Old Hunter does."

"He's bent on keeping the Smiths low." Cook shook her head. "You know the sword Young Smith just finished?"

Devout nodded. "The one with the enameled hilt."

"He wanted to take it to Hill Fort himself, along with a pair of flagons and a bronze shield. But Old Hunter said no."

"He forbade it?" Under Old Smith, the tradesmen were free to trade their wares at Hill Fort. For the most part, though, they knew Old Smith's shrewdness, his fairness and were content to let him arrange trades on their behalf.

Cook nodded. "Old Hunter says he'll make the trek himself." She leaned close, whispered, "He can't bear the idea of Young Smith returning with more than his clan needs to get through Fallow. Can't bear him sparing a little dried fish for the hands."

———

THE HAND WHO CONFESSED was next to follow Lark and Crone to Otherworld that Fallow. She swallowed the berries from the bough of mistletoe the druid had brought from Sacred Grove and laid at her feet as a sign of purification. After that, an infant born too small succumbed. The mother, a hand, was thin at the onset of Fallow, thinner still when her labor began, and no amount of stinging nettle would lure milk to her breasts. Old Tanner's mate, nursing a toddler of her own, refused to act as wet nurse to another child. Why waste milk on so small, so sickly an infant? she said. No different from leaving milk to spoil in the sun.

Then it was the mother of Old Tanner's unsparing mate, though she had been taken into the Tanner household, where she lived without want. She had once made a habit of gathering with the other elders, but the woman had not shown her face. It was rumored she had lain on her pallet, declining all but water for the moon since her daughter denied the newly labored hand.

Two more elders refused nourishment, and the bog dwellers laid the bodies with the remains of Old Tanner's mate's mother, the infant, the hand, Crone, and Lark in Bone Meadow. Talk about the nobleness of the elders' sacrifice swelled. Old Man put his chin in the air and, to Devout and his gathered household, said that he had as much right to food as anyone at Black Lake, that those who thought he should not eat forgot the tilling, the sowing, the reaping he had accomplished while they were at their mothers' breasts. Second Hand Widow, who had already accused him of pilfering berries gathered by her brood, sneered and said, "You think you've got more right than children." She went to his pallet and produced, from beneath a tattered skin, a handful of broken hazelnut shells. "You weren't collecting. Too pained in the knees, you said." She hurled the shells, which bounced from his chest and landed at his feet. She went to the pallet where her children slept, yanked down the woolen blanket covering her second youngest boy, exposing the troughs between his ribs.

Devout began giving the boy something each day and to his siblings, too—a bit of burdock root, a few acorns, her allotment of hard cheese. Soon she withered on her pallet, drifting in and out of sleep, vaguely listening to the activity around her—the thud and crackle of a log newly added to the fire, a complaint that its maintenance now fell to so few, a cough, a whimper, the pleas beseeching Mother Earth.

She knew real hunger now, the sort when there was not the strength for pangs. And the boy weak on his pallet, he knew it, too. That he once worked the fields with the diligence of a child twice his age and took the sack from his mother's shoulder and bore its weight himself only added to the household's misery.

Arc did not call at Devout's roundhouse, she supposed, because surviving Fallow left no time. She thought once or twice of the bliss in the woodland, but what she conjured was vapor rather than sustenance. Desire was mere bait, enticement only those initiated in true hardship could see as a trick. It provided nothing more than the feeling of warmth, the feeling of a sated belly, the feeling of a draft of water held to parched lips. It was not hard cheese—mashed to a pulp, pushed to the back of the throat, delivered to the hollow of a belly, where it was not a mere feeling of warmth but warmth itself.

She thought of Young Smith. She had heard about the smoked meat, dried fish, and hard cheese Old Hunter had collected for the tradesmen clans at Hill Fort. Surely some ample portion had gone to Young Smith in return for the sword, the flagons, the shield. He had once set her heart aflutter, and yet she had turned from him—so gentle, so generous, so able a provider. She had been a fool, not yet familiar with the realities of a Fallow without wheat.

Might she rise from her pallet and go to him? Might he spare some hard cheese for the boy with the pronounced ribs? Might he spare some for her? Would he still take her as mate, make true the etching in the old mine? His mother would be an obstacle, but he had gone against her wishes before. The amulet was proof of that. For a glimmer, Devout tasted the richness of fat on her tongue.

She sometimes felt a spoon held to her lips and then tepid water dribbled into her mouth. Occasionally she was fed a thin mash, some blend of roots, though it seemed that her lips were nudged open ever less frequently, that the roundhouse grew ever quieter. But then, one day, the mash was different. There was the taste of meat. "Good fortune," her mother whispered. "Two packets of meat left at the door."

Devout thought to say "Young Smith" who had meat from Hill Fort, but what left her mouth was more breath than words.

It was the same meaty mash at the next feeding and the one after that, and she could not say how many more times the mash met her tongue. The feeling of hunger that had slipped away thundered back into her belly, also the wherewithal to agonize that two packets of meat would soon come to an end.

She had a pleasant dream. The boy with the protruding ribs was on his feet, his mother steadying him, but nevertheless on his feet. She heard Old Man weeping, or so she thought, and she heard quite clearly her mother tell him, "Hush." Devout wondered if she was awake when he said he was undeserving of such generosity.

She took more of the mash and knew the portions she swallowed grew. "Another moon," her mother said, "and the earth will thaw. There will be sorrel and after that chickweed and nettle."

Devout nodded weakly. She attempted a smile.

"The meat continues," her mother said, "enough for the household."

"Blessings for our benefactor," Devout whispered too quietly. Her mother put her ear close to Devout's mouth, and she repeated the words.

Her mother's face glowed, lit by Devout's budding strength, their improved lot now that her daughter fully grasped a tradesman's ability to provide. Young Smith fed the boy, Old Man, her mother, and herself.

Then one day, with enough strength to sit on her pallet and lift the spoon to her mouth, Devout saw that the mash was paler in color. On her tongue, she tasted fish. She felt a strange grittiness.

"Crayfish," her mother said. "I milled the shell."

"Left at the door?" Devout said, thinking it strange if even Young Smith's family was reduced to crayfish.

"Yes. A few dozen. Ugly creatures. More troublesome than the squirrel."

"Squirrel?"

"Old Man was certain."

Squirrel and crayfish, then.

Arc knew the patterns of the squirrels, where to find them docile in their nests. He had told her about catching crayfish with only a length of gut and a bit of bone. It was just like him to feed the weak, just like him to leave a packet and retreat unannounced. He would not want to stand before them, hearing their gratitude and saying the squirrel, the crayfish that saved them were what any one of them would have done in his shoes—his shabby, undersized shoes. She swallowed gritty crayfish and felt warmth in her belly, his tenderness toward her. That tenderness had led him deep into the woodland, then north to the river, to some not yet scavenged place. He had knelt on the cold earth, his breeches soaked through at the knees. She thought of his patience, his watchfulness and his hands plunging into frigid water. He had suffered the harshness of Fallow alone and without shelter, had trapped and fished and told himself he could not return to Black Lake until he had the provisions to feed Devout and the household that would become his.

Her mother ran her fingers through Devout's matted, greasy hair and made as if to get up from the pallet, as if to collect the bone comb, but she hesitated. "He works so hard in the fields, always trying to spare you what he can."

Her mother meant Arc, and yet, with Devout's view so newly altered, she could not grasp that her mother already knew what Devout had only just figured out.

"It's Arc, then, our benefactor," Devout said.

Her mother smiled with all the softness of new grass.

18.

HOBBLE

~~~

I HOLD BACK FROM GALLOPING as my father and I approach Black Lake with our loaded handcart. But then, as we take the last bend in the trackway before the woodland opens onto Chieftain's fields, I see my mother and cannot resist. She catches sight of us and breaks into a smile. She touches her lips, swoops, her fingertips just grazing the earth as she hurtles along the trackway. I meet her arms, feel my slight mother's strength, her lips burrowing, kissing, nuzzling deep into my curls. And then she is off, looping her arms around my father's neck, and hugging and kissing, and then cupping his face in her palms and kissing him again.

With her unfiltered glee, her looping arms, and cupping palms, my usually reticent mother is a conundrum.

"Oh, Smith," she says. "The longest six days of my life."

He grins, radiant as the bloom of day. "Just look," he says, sweeping a hand toward the cart.

She touches the stacked iron bars.

"I have work," he says. "I have a promise of more work to come."

"Chieftain remembered, then."

"I have an arrangement with a trader called Luck."

"Luck!" she says.

"Tedious work. Tent pegs, for now, at any rate. But never mind that."

"Come. I've collected enough eggs for a feast." She slips an arm around his waist, takes my hand.

"Fox?" he says as we begin walking.

"He comes and goes."

"Is he here now?" I say and hold my breath.

She swings my held hand forward and back, as if to make light of the answer she will give. "He just got back."

"Back from where?"

"He never says." She opens a palm empty of an answer. "His horse is worn out."

"They're in the settlements again," my father says. "Luck told us there were druids at Timber Bridge. He claims they mean to stir up the tribesmen."

"Like you said." The merriment cleanly washes from her face, and she drops my hand.

"Anything more—" My father does not need to finish. We all know he is asking about further violence from Fox.

My mother shakes her head.

I look toward the wheat fields, which radiate a first blush of green. "The wheat's coming up," I say, summoning all the vigor of a bird chirping its morning song, but my voice is pitiable. Fox remains at Black Lake and none of us believe we have seen the end of his brutality.

HUNTER IS AT OUR DOOR, even before I have unpacked the bronze lamp, vessel of olive oil, fresh hide, and length of undyed wool bundled inside my cape. He calls out my name, and then with my father standing guard, says, "My mother asks for you."

My father nods that I should go.

I have spent long evenings comforting his ailing mother, combing her hair, rubbing her limbs, feeding her the sweet violet draft that eases sleep. With one foot already in Otherworld and her mind addled, she regularly sets loose the thoughts rattling in her head. I have coaxed, interrogated even, shaking free what I can. Just now, though plucked from my homecoming, I am glad to draw a comb through thin hair and delay the moment when I must face Fox.

"You attended when my mother took Arc as her mate?" I say to Hunter's mother.

She twists around, looks at me doubtfully. Of course, she was there, as was every bog dweller then taking breath at Black Lake. "Not much of a feast as I remember it," she says, "but the bonfire! Such a party we had that night."

She pats my hand, I suppose in consolation that she speaks warmly of the celebration that marked my mother's first union. "Your father loved your mother even then," she says. "Drunk as blazes that night and telling anyone who would listen she'd be his mate one day."

I like the idea—a refuge of drunken certainty—amid what must have been a miserable Hope.

"Your mother and Arc"—an almost girlish smile crosses the old woman's lips—"the sex between those two. Talk of the settlement. In the tall grass, a few strides from the wheat, their scythes barely put down. Atop Edge. In the woodland, with nightfall only just arrived."

I pull the comb, taking care not to disrupt the rhythm, her words, but then Hunter is upon us, hovering, arms knotted at his chest.

"Your father had success?" he says, though he plainly saw a handcart empty of cauldrons and loaded with iron bars.

"Yes."

"Which trader?"

I shrug, because I cannot say to my father's rival that a trader who supplies the Roman army provided the iron. "I went to look at the wool."

"You roamed Hill Fort on your own?" He huffs disbelief.

I draw the comb from hairline to crown to the far reach of the old woman's hair.

"I could send you home with a partridge," he says.

"We'd all appreciate your generosity."

He slides his hands along his thighs as he squats to eye level with me. "You should know I have friends at Hill Fort," he says.

With great effort, his mother lifts herself to unsteady feet. "I'll sleep now." Then, as unsparing as vengeance, she adds, "You'll give the girl a partridge."

I ARRIVE HOME to find the low table set with four mugs, four plates, a platter piled high with fried eggs, and another with hard cheese and bread. My father stops pouring mead and extends his chin toward the partridge. "A cartload of iron and Hunter is inspired to make peace?"

"A partridge? He's feeling generous," my mother says. "You're back just in time."

She calls to Fox, who emerges from his sleeping alcove, eclipsing the moment when I might have corrected my parents. We usually serve ourselves, but my mother knows the hunger of a man and a maiden walking six days and the tendency of Fox to take more than his share. As she divvies up the meal, I look to my father, who nods, and I scamper off to my sleeping alcove to fetch the olive oil that brings sweetness to dipped bread.

My father, my mother, and Fox seat themselves while I pour a small amount of the oil into a shallow bowl. "Try it," I say, handing my mother a piece of bread.

She looks puzzled.

"Like this," I say and dab bread into oil. Sweetness spreads over my tongue.

"Olive oil," my father says and smiles.

"Roman oil," Fox says and swipes a hand across the table, sending the shallow bowl skittering into the rushes.

My father bolts to his feet. "We got it from a tribesman, a trader at Hill Fort"—his voice is almost calm—"a gift for Devout." His fingers clench, unclench.

"Even so," Fox says, "a Roman profited by the transaction." A shadow of exhaustion passes over his face that he should have to explain. "We bring them the lumber for their palisades, the leather for their tents, the cheese for their bellies, these Romans who call us barbarians, who take our gold and silver and salt."

As he speaks the ridges on his brow deepen, the grooves on his cheeks grow hard, and my heart skitters to see the aversion that trade with the Romans puts on his face, to recall Hunter's claim of friends at Hill Fort. My father breathes slowly. He knows better than to repeat Luck's arguments about brisk commerce and opportunity and improved yields, about roads and aqueducts, and order and towns made of stone to a druid who knows with absolute certainty the correctness of his convictions.

My mother gently tugs the leg of my father's breeches. "Sit," she says. "Nothing worse than cold eggs."

He picks up the toppled bowl, returns it to the table, and sits down. Fox mops drippings from the platter that held the eggs with his bread—every smidgen. "He's an ill-considered fool, any tribesman who trades with the Romans."

I see my mother eye my father and want so much to tell her that Luck is not a Roman. The relief would be temporary, though, when Luck is an intermediary, when Fox's view is as unmalleable as a gritstone slab.

My father lowers his chin, a slow, acquiescent nod. "We know little of the Romans here. They set foot here only that one time—chasing prisoners escaped from Viriconium."

"To those brave souls," Fox says and lifts his mug, "men with heart enough to resist."

We return the gesture, directing our raised mugs toward the highlands—an old habit, with those highlands now scoured of the rebel tribes.

"Was there a time when you thought you'd join the rebels?" Fox asks. "From what I've heard, you'd reason enough."

But my father does not rage against the Romans, does not desire retribution for his slain kin, not now, not back when there still existed rebels to join. He had said, "It was a druid who cajoled my kin," and holds our high priests as accountable as the Romans for his loss. He takes the long swallow of mead that lets him avoid the answer Fox does not want. Passion makes the druid deaf to my father's silence, and he continues. "The Romans murdered my father—we have that in common—and the rest of my clan, too." His gaze falls to the mug cupped in his hands. "I was seven, half-starved when a druid found me and delivered me to Sacred Isle. He dripped water into my mouth and chewed the meat I couldn't chew for myself. He lashed my body to his when I could not manage to stay upright on a horse." He lifts glassy eyes.

"He saw your strength," my father says.

As Fox takes a long gulp from his mug, I think of myself at age seven, carefree and loved. It catches me by surprise that I feel pity for so cruel a man. He clears his throat, returns his attention to my father, and says, "Your father would have presented himself to the rebels given half a chance."

A hundred times, I have heard accounts of my father's father's pragmatism—the usefulness of his judgments, his heedfulness of the end result. I look to my father. In the thin line of his lips, I see how it bothers him to let Fox's assumption stand. I gather my nerve and quietly say, "My father's father witnessed the tribesmen defeated in two days."

Fox turns to me, glares that I should speak. I think of the hound pup. I think of a blade held to my own throat. His mouth twists, but he decides me unworthy of straying from the topic at hand and says, "The Romans will come to know the might of our gods."

We eat in silence after that. The vessel of olive oil stands firm atop the table, and I turn to thinking of its presence there as a defiance of sorts. Once Fox at long last excuses himself, my mother and I simultaneously reach for the vessel. I defer, and we share a glance as she whisks it from the table to the folds of her skirt.

A DOZEN EVENINGS LATER, Fox instructs the bog dweller men to assemble around our firepit. I pour mead, refill flagons, collect

DAUGHTER OF BLACK LAKE

wood from the stack beneath the eave. I think my mother will soon make an excuse of magic to deliver and instruct me to accompany her, but Fox says what he would really like is a mug of chamomile tea. As I set the water to boil, my mother stays put, crushing silverweed, though we have an ample supply of liniment.

My father sits drumming his thigh, and I think how that new agitation arrived with Fox. With him on the prowl, my father keeps his completed tent pegs out of sight and leaves ax-heads and ladles in plain view. Yesterday he complained to me about Fox hovering and having to fritter away the better part of an afternoon tinkering with an already finished ladle. A few days before that, Fox left without explanation early morning and stayed away two nights. My father watched for the dust kicked up by Fox's returning horse. I know because the moment a cloud arose, my father's arms plunged into still water and he snatched a dozen as-yet-blunt pegs from the cooling trough, then shoved them into a shadowy gap between his hearth and the wall.

Fox clears his throat at the firepit and, once the low din of the men ceases, pushes himself to his feet. Hands clasped together inside the wide sleeves of his robe, he walks sunwise around the firepit, his pace as measured as his voice when he finally speaks.

"Friends and kinsmen—for I consider you all kinsmen—tonight I speak to you of grave matters." He looks from one man to the next. "You have learned by experience how different freedom is from slavery and though some among you may previously have been deceived by the promises of the Romans, now you have tried both. You have learned how great an error was made in allowing Roman despotism to replace our ancestral ways, and you have come to realize how much better poverty with no master is than wealth with slavery."

Have any among the bog dwellers learned the difference, realized a great error? Always we have handed over the bulk of our harvested grains to Chieftain. At Black Lake we would not know that Chieftain now pays a tithe to the Romans if we had not been told. Is Fox disturbed by his misleading words? It occurs to me that his eyes and ears are closed to any fact that does not support his opinion, that he does not fully see or hear. In his mind, he has recorded only that the Romans deprive us of our wheat.

His hands emerge from his sleeves, and he thrusts his fist into his palm as he says, "We have been robbed of our possessions. We have been despised and trampled underfoot. We till and pasture for the Romans and spend our days toiling first and living afterward. With my druid brethren exiled from your midst to Sacred Isle, our traditions flounder. Roman lust has gone too far."

Fox needs to open his eyes if he has not seen the bog dwellers touching their lips, and burying bread and meat, and palming Begetter's wheel on the causeway. I look from my father to Hunter to Carpenter, wondering if they hear the druid's words as I do. Their faces are blank as they hide from Fox their belief that his words seem intended for different ears.

"But to speak the plain truth," he says, "it is we who are responsible for these evils, in that we allowed the Romans to set foot on our island instead of expelling them at once as we did their famed Julius Caesar. And now, all these years later, we grasp the consequence and we seethe like animals just learning the restrictions of a cage."

Fox strokes his beard, which is insubstantial and reddish brown and does not suggest the aged wisdom of druidry. He looks down his long nose at the faces turned to his, the kinsmen he has claimed. Does he look down his long nose at his druid brethren? My father rearranges his mouth from giving away his distaste.

Fox's hands are back inside his sleeves. "We must do our duty while we still remember what freedom is," he says. "We must leave to our children not only the word *freedom* but also its reality. All this I say, not with the purpose of inspiring you with a hatred of present conditions—that hatred you already have—but of rousing you to choose of your own accord the necessary course of action."

Do tribesmen near and far gather around firepits, no different from my father's, as druids proselytize and thrust fists into palms, breeding discontent? Those days Fox is absent, he surely infiltrates some distant settlement. Never mind his lack of years, like those druids at Timber Bridge, it appears Fox—driven as a ram in rut—has been charged with provoking the tribesmen in some prescribed area as part of a larger crusade.

In flickering firelight, my father sets his mug among the rushes, stills his restless hands in his lap. I want my pallet, the stupor of sleep, my mind shut to druids wringing their hands and scheming how best to rid Britannia of the Romans. A great shudder ripples through me as I remember Fox's final words that evening my father and I returned from Hill Fort: "The Romans will come to know the might of our gods."

The men around the firepit grow quiet, awkward, intent on the mugs in their hands, the frayed hems of their breeches, the rushes at their feet, anything other than Fox. A dozen of them had seen a hound pup pay the price for Hunter's belligerence. Fox looks from man to man, seeking solidarity, but finding not a single met glance. My father's eyes are on me. He flicks his downturned palm through the air in a gesture that says I am to pour no more mead.

The men make excuses—an early morning, a ewe with a swollen teat—and file from the roundhouse. Fox follows a few steps behind, but the burden of him—the evening's lecture—hangs in the air. My mother looks exhausted by the effort of crushing silverweed. My father paces, gaze narrowed to the rushes at his feet.

"Your pegs?" my mother says, and I know Fox's lecture has forced the question that has unsettled her since the uproar over the olive oil.

My father looks up, nods. "Yes, Roman."

"Oh, Smith," she says. "How could you?"

He opens his palms to take in our meager surroundings.

"I hate them, the Romans." She looks on the edge of weeping. "You know I hate them."

"Mother," I say quietly, hesitantly. "The Romans put an end to druidry in Gaul."

She sets down her pestle. She cannot manage "Be careful" or "He can't find out," words of acquiescence, but she swallows, breathes, eventually returns to her silverweed.

"Fox's sermonizing, it changes nothing," my father says, his voice barely above a whisper. "We work at earning his regard. We keep any opposition to ourselves."

Both my parents look at me. I know the words they do not speak: For my sake—my security—we will pander and stoop, and dispute only privately any notion of the tribesmen rising up against the Romans.

A fox lurks close, nose twitching as he sniffs the air.

19.

HOBBLE

~~~

I LIE AWAKE, ears pricked, heart palpitating. A cock has crowed in the black of night. As I strain to hear my father's and my mother's shallow breaths, I am able to make out breathing I know to be my father's. With my habit of listening, I can differentiate between the two. For every eight he takes, she takes ten. "A cock," I hear my mother say, and with both my parents accounted for, my body softens.

To make matters worse, I had heard the flutter of wings in the afternoon. My attention shifted from my scythe to a pair of round eyes, the feathers fanned out in perfect circles from the black pools. A tawny owl perched on a low branch of an ash at the edge of the field, its mottled wings melding with the bark. My gaze went to my mother, scooping felled wheat into a bundle, and then to my father, working the bellows in the forge. I spotted Sliver at the far side of the field and glimpsed Seconds in the clearing, repairing Hunter's handcart. Still, uneasiness persisted. A tawny owl in the light of day.

And now, the cock.

I touch my lips, thread my fingers through the rushes to the earthen floor—uneasy gratitude when the cock crows for someone else's kin. It flickers through my mind that the cock crows for Fox— a wink of relief, gone in a flash, like water hitting iron just lifted from the hearth. He had ridden off four days ago, and for the time being remains away from Black Lake—a small reprieve for all of us who endure his unsettling presence and his continued haranguing at the firepit.

"Smith? Hobble?" my mother says. "You heard the cock?"

"Yes," I say.

Bedcoverings stir as my parents push themselves to sitting and my father says, "I heard."

From outside the wall, footsteps sound and then one of Tanner's boys calls out, "Devout. Hobble."

As I shuffle a woolen blanket from my legs, the wattle door bursts open to show Tanner's eldest son awash in the moon's blue light. "It's Feeble," he says.

I try to remember seeing Feeble earlier, whether he gripped his head in a way that was different from the days before, whether his moans bared some new agony.

The cock crows again, and the boy's face falls. He shakes his head with all the sorrow of dusk.

"Go," my mother says to the boy. "We'll come."

My eyes have grown accustomed to the dark now, and in the dim light of the moon and the few embers still aglow in the firepit, my mother and I exchange the worn linen of our night tunics for the wool of our field dresses. I slip undyed cloth up over my narrow hips and budding breasts, and double clasp it over my shoulders.

As my mother stoops to pluck a small vessel from the bins where we store our prepared remedies, bafflement shows on my father's face. Why select a remedy when her concoctions will prove useless, when the cock has already crowed?

"A draft of sweet violet," she says, lifting the vessel, "to soothe the boy."

Same as he, she is resigned to Feeble's fate.

At the door she fumbles with the ties at the neck of her cape, grows agitated. Her hand falls from the yet unfastened ties. She looks to my father, squatting at the firepit. To watch him is to stir calm, to know his love, and she needs to gather her strength to attend to Feeble, to show me a brave face. She lets her gaze rest a moment on his broad back, the undulating muscle, protruding and receding as he touches a rushlight to the embers. He will protect. She knows it, and yet, with her perplexing coolness toward him, she stays put by the door, forgoing the full comfort of him. She allows herself only a glance, just enough so that she can manage to secure the ties of her cape.

He joins us at the door and hands me the rushlight. How I want to linger, the three of us within our fortress of wattle and daub and thatch, but she and I will set out, as we always do when there is a cough to soothe, a wound to mend.

"I'll go with you," he says.

My mother breathes deeply, taking in his words like sustenance but only offers a meager nod in return, the smallest lowering of her chin.

I put an arm around him, tilt my brow against his chest. His fingers slide through my hair, lower to the nape of my neck. And there it is—familiar as cradle song—his heartache that I understand the implications of a lame leg. How unfair that those pangs come so often now, blunting the pleasure of a man finally reaping success.

He has made a fifth delivery of Roman tent pegs to Hill Fort.

The deal he struck with Luck means that I wear a new skin cape and my mother a bronze bracelet and dusky blue dress, that he brings her enough meat that there is excess to give to the hands, that never has my mother's childhood household eaten so well, that he is greeted with humbly bowed faces. He owns his own handcart now and likes nothing better than to wave away an offer of payment when he lends it out.

Once on his return from Hill Fort, he tipped a fistful of dark seeds onto Shepherd's palm. "Soapwort," he said. "The crushed roots and leaves make a green lather that lifts the grease from sheared wool. The Romans brought the plant over from Gaul." Another time he came home with a trick for Tanner. "Try soaking your hides in urine," he said. "It's how the Romans loosen the hairs." Most recently, he brought me two wooden panels laced together at a central spine. "They call it a tablet," he said. Those panels could be laid open, exposing the inner surfaces, or folded shut, protecting them. The inner surface of each panel was edged with a ridge of wood and, inside that wooden frame, spread with a thin layer of beeswax. It was into that beeswax that the Romans etched their symbols, their words. A Roman, he explained, could record a message in the wax, fold the tablet shut, and then have it delivered to the farthest reach of the empire where the message could be deciphered. I hugged the tablet to my chest and knew I held magic—a tool that made it possible to send words across vast expanses and through long spans of time.

My father had outdone Hunter in providing for the feast that marked the onset of Harvest. With his lavish contribution the bog dwellers' minds had awoken. Sliver had patted her sated belly, yawned. "Your father should be First Man," and Old Man had whispered, "I've been saying that a long time," and Seconds had nudged my elbow. "Look at Hunter," he said. "He can't stand it, your father on the rise."

MY MOTHER, father, and I find Feeble curled into a knot on a sleeping pallet. Tanner pokes at a smoldering log as his other children huddle beneath a woolen blanket on the far side of the firepit. His mate lies wrapped around Feeble. She strokes her son's hair, says, "Daybreak is near," and then repeats the phrase. She speaks to trick the dark fairies, who lurk only under the cover of night.

"The dark fairies have come?" my mother says.

A long silence looms. "He went rigid as wood. His lips turned blue."

My mother nods, encouraging the woman to continue, to say whether the dark fairies danced.

"He bucked and writhed," Tanner says.

"But he vomited. Three times." Tanner's mate smiles a meek smile, as though the dark fairies have been cast out with the vomiting, as though she has not heard the cock.

I step closer, feel my father hold himself back from pulling me away from a haunted child. "He should take the draft while he is still," I say.

With my mother propping Feeble from one side and his mother from the other, he sips the draft I hold to his lips. No hint of morning yet appears in the east, but still the cock crows and crows. Tears roll down Tanner's mate's cheeks without restraint now. Tanner takes a tentative step and puts a hand on her disheveled hair, but she bats it aside. Feeble's back and neck arch away from the sleeping pallet. His arms shoot up from his sides. Tanner's mate places herself over the boy, her back like a shell rounded above his chest. A wrist clubs her ear, an elbow her ribs, a knee her hip, and yet she persists.

My mother's fingers curl around a thick rope of my hair. She clutches, holds fast to her beloved child as Feeble slips from his mother's grip. He lets out a great moan and gulps at the air. Once. Twice. He turns limp, and the color seeps from his face. Then he stills. Slowly his skin grows waxen and takes on a blue cast, not unlike the watery foremilk of a ewe. My hair still gripped in one hand, my mother touches two fingers of the other to his wrist, says, "He's whole in Otherworld." She lets go of me, though what I really want is for her to wrap me in her arms, for my father to hold the pair of us tight in his embrace. She lifts her hands, as if to put them on Tanner's mate's cheeks, but the woman draws away, her grief too consuming, too raw for her to consider that anguish is not hers alone.

Tanner opens the door so that Feeble's spirit might find its way to Begetter in the bog. His mate says, "Not yet," her voice guttural, inhuman, but he leaves the door ajar.

Daybreak, when it finally comes, arises meekly and darkness lingers at Black Lake. The sky hangs pregnant with rain, and the clatter and boom of the thunder is such that children cry and the earth trembles underfoot. My mother and I are not expected in the fields—a blessing, given the few hours we have slept—not when clouds erupt, not when bolts of lightning shoot from the sky.

My father persuades me to lie down in the furs he has arranged close to the fire, but my mother insists she is not tired and settles onto her knees beneath Mother Earth's cross. She kneels there, her fingers stroking the earth through the covering of rushes as the words *Blessings of Mother Earth* form over and over on her lips. But she follows my father with her eyes as he adds kindling to the embers, tents a few sticks over the flame. She thuds her fist against her thigh, takes a long breath. When she finally shuts her eyes, her face pinches with effort.

My father's stomach rumbles, and she glances again in his direction, eyes open just long enough to see him watching, surely wondering why she is taking so long beneath the cross. He lifts the iron cooking cauldron—the graceful lines, his handiwork—hangs it from the hook that holds it above the firepit, spoons barley into its belly, adds two ladlesful of water. Not enough. As he looks toward me, I snap shut my eyes, and finding me asleep, he forgoes asking about a third ladleful. I should rise and make the barley porridge, as I do each daybreak, but I am entranced by the scene before me, most particularly by my mother, on her knees, beseeching and yet failing to properly exalt Mother Earth. I mouth her name—Devout—that promise of piety, goodness, sincerity in all things. As a rule, she appears serene, elated even, as she kneels. Not now, though. This morning, an infirm boy departed and her daughter has reemerged as least deserving of a teat.

Lightning flashes vigorously enough to brighten the roundhouse for a beat. The thunder that follows rustles the herbs hanging from the rafters and rattles the collection of small clay vessels, but still she stays put on her knees. My father opens the door, no doubt fearful that the bolt has struck near the clearing, and then returns to the fire. Nothing smolders, then. Nothing has burst into flames.

I lie still and know by the rasp of metal against metal that he is scraping a portion of the barley porridge into a bowl for himself. Shepherd's mate, who brings the sheep's milk each morning, will be consoling Tanner's mate, her old friend, and we will go without. He will not enjoy the porridge. Too little water. No milk.

The rain falls heavier, and the thick, still air adds to the morning's burdens. Eventually my mother gives up. I watch through a veil of lashes as she rises to her feet, straightening knees bent too long, like a woman who has worked Black Lake's fields more than her thirty-one years.

"I made porridge," my father says and adds, "There's no milk."

"Hobble can tend to the ewes when she wakes."

I suppose she hopes a quiet morning with Pet nuzzling close as I milk her kin will help mend what ails. That favorite ewe's upper and lower jaws were misaligned at birth, so much so that as a lamb she was nudged from her mother's teat. With Old Shepherd's blessing and the small bucket of milk he provided each day, Sliver, Pocks, and I had, as children, taken on the lamb—cradling her head, coaxing open her crooked jaw, squeezing milk from a scrap of linen held over her mouth. By the end of Hope, Pet went to pasture alongside the other lambs, and, despite her jaw, managed clover, grass, and forbs. She grew into a ewe prized for her frequent twins, beloved for the affection she still shows the three of us who had nursed her.

My mother spoons porridge into a bowl. My father watches as she lifts a spoonful.

"Devout," he says. So forlorn a voice.

She goes to him, drops to the spot beside him on the bench. Keeping her voice low, she says, "I'm so afraid."

"I know," he softly says. "Me, too."

It comes as a relief, even if I am not meant to hear. A burden shared. No different from a load of wood split between many hands.

"Luck said he's heard rumblings that druidry will be outlawed here, like it is in Gaul," my father says.

This idea—that druidry could be extracted from our lives—feels as unfathomable as the heavens. My mother wants me safe, I know, and so she nods in response to such a notion—a faint, uncertain nod, because how are we to live if not with our ancestral ways?

It seems to me that my family—that all tribesmen—navigate an ever-narrowing ridge, one with steep slopes on either side and a thick layer of cloud that prevents us from seeing which slope is preferred, which promises a lesser fall. Am I to lean toward the familiar slope—our customs and traditions, our gods, the authority of the druids, the only way I know of being in the world? The alternative is to lean toward Roman rule and the wealth available to my father and roads paved with stone and symbols strung together to record words. But some claim our conquerors abduct and enslave at their leisure. I witnessed a merchant's livelihood whisked from a counter, smashed atop paving stones. I heard the Hunters' pottery shatter, saw our woolen partitions ripped. I know about the snatched amulet, the dagger wielded when my father said to give it back. The abuse fills me with fear, though I cannot deny a long history of feuding tribes behaving toward one another in vicious ways, of heads skewered on stakes, of women violated and men ransomed, of property pilfered and destroyed.

By leaning toward Roman rule, do I embrace existence as a second-rate inhabitant of my own island? The druids recoil at such an existence, at all they have to lose, but I am a hand and already sinew wraps my ankle, tethering me to the fields. And now this possibility to ponder—that the Romans deliberate a decree that would see Fox vanished from our lives. That would mean a lame leg threatens nothing more than a gait marked by a limp.

My father's palm slides the length of his thigh. "Luck also said the Romans point to the old ways as justification, but that in reality they want the druids gone because only they have the influence to unite Britannia's tribes in rebellion."

I want to blurt that it sounds like the Romans have cupped their ears to our wall as Fox agitates, but more than that I want to hear more.

"So much uncertainty, and now Feeble gone." In her lap, my mother's fingers lace, unlace, tuck into her palms. "I'm dreading Fox hearing. I can see it now, his chin poking toward Hobble, his smirk as he says, 'Black Lake's true runt now.'"

My father reaches to pull her closer, and she does not draw away. No, she allows it, even nestles her head against his shoulder. "Fox's favor can only help," he says.

Without raising her head, she nods her agreement.

"And my trade at Hill Fort," he says. "The better off a man, the more sway he holds."

Now she lifts her head from the warmth of him.

"It's not ideal, I know," he says. "But my first concern is Hobble, our family. I can better protect the both of you from a position of strength."

When my father first said he would go to Hill Fort, I thought a desire for returned status drove him to undertake the trek. But now, as my mother returns her head to his shoulder, I understand that his ambition is inseparable from a need to keep me safe, that she knows it, too. How different from Fox, I think, who plots and pushes forward for his own gain—so that he might rid himself and his brethren of Roman interference, so that he might ensure the druids' authority.

They sit in silence awhile until my mother says, almost too quietly for me to make out, "The gods can be merciless."

"And benevolent, too."

Any other day it would be my mother pointing out the hundred ways the gods provide. She wraps her arms around her waist, squeezes.

"There's something you don't know," she says. She begins to rock in a peculiar way, and I am reminded of my own childhood habit of shifting my weight to and fro before confessing a hide cap lost in the woods, a mutton stew left to burn black.

I hold my breath, somehow certain I await the riddle of my mother's coolness toward my father solved.

"A long time ago I—" She licks her lips, as though to ease the passage of words. But the interior of our roundhouse flashes a paler shade of gray. A clap of thunder rises, deafening and close. I jolt, as do they, my father's shoulder slightly jostling my mother's nestled head.

He is on his feet and then whipping open the door to reveal the clearing coming alive with bog dwellers hauling buckets and flagons and cauldrons slopping water from their rims. I am quick to my feet, quick to grab hold of a water bucket.

Like everyone else, I tip my bucket and stamp lit underbrush and slam the heel of my palm to my forehead and call out, "Hear me, Protector," only ceasing once the bay willow at the fringe of the clearing is little more than a heap of smoldering ash.

20.

'HOBBLE

~~~~~~

B Y THE TIME I come in from the barley field, the low walls
of the forge have been extended to the roof. My father holds
a final rough plank in place while Carpenter nails it to a
supporting timber. I put my weight onto one hip and wait for my
father to explain.

"I have no use for rain blown sideways or for wind cooling my
hearth," he says. "I've got too much work for that."

But I know the truth. No longer will he risk forging Roman tent
pegs in open air, not with Fox agitating and War Master waiting
and Feeble gone and his daughter confirmed as the most imperfect
at Black Lake.

"I told him he's going to cook in there," Carpenter says.

I swing the forge's new door to and fro, finger the newly fastened bolt.

"You forget the bitterness of Fallow," my father says.

Once the final plank is nailed into place, Carpenter takes his
leave with the three dozen nails bartered for the work. As my father

kneads his shoulder, I see exhaustion that he has spent a full day assisting Carpenter—a full day, when he is behind on his pegs, when Fox remains away, offering my father a chance to work without hindrance. In return for his toil, he has gained the walls that will prevent the hearth's heat from drifting away and isolate him from our neighbors' conversation and block him from glimpsing my mother and me in the fields.

He steps inside the forge, and I am left wondering a moment, until he emerges with his prized bronze platter and offers it to me. He grins as I take it, then lifts me by the waist. He holds me aloft, directly in line with a pair of mounting brackets fastened to a timber brace over the forge's new door. I take in the platter's perfect oval as I mount it, the flawless swirls of polished bronze.

My feet back on solid earth, I remember my mother saying that to see the amulet was to wonder whether the gods had a hand in crafting it. Might they, on occasion, awaken his heart and eyes and hands, guiding him in some way? How very similar to my own moments of white light and knowledge beyond what I should know.

Most often I turn to my parents in contemplating the source of my gift. Why not, when Young Reddish's tresses glint the same rusty red as her mother's, when Hunter's face flushes the same crimson as his father's, when Sliver's front teeth hold the same pretty gap as Sullen's? My mother has seemed the more likely candidate. I share her straight nose and bright blue eyes, her regard for the tender green of a new leaf, the dew clinging to a blade of grass. I share her reverence for Mother Earth's abundance, the magic held inside. And there was her easy acceptance of my visions, that long-ago day when I confirmed what it seemed she had known all along.

We had been foraging when the woodland flashed white, and I saw in my mind's eye how the next moment would unfold. I held the bottom edge of my dress up in front and fixed my eyes on the thick canopy overhead. As my mother peered upward, squinting to see what I could, a hawfinch fledgling tumbled into the woolen sling of my dress. I went to my knees and began patting dried leaves and twigs into the rough shape of a bowl. She continued to scrutinize the canopy, eyes sliding along the high horizontal branches of the beech, but she could not spot the makings of a nest. "I don't see a nest," she said.

"No." I gently slid the fledgling from my dress to the makeshift nest, where it righted itself, looked up at her, and chirped a dozen times.

"But you saw a nest?"

"No."

Her gaze went to the fledgling. "You saw no nest but expected the bird to fall?"

I nodded.

She crouched beside me and the chirping fledgling and put a hand on my knee.

"I see things." My shoulders crept skyward. "I don't know why."

She drew me to her. As my cheek pressed to her breast, she stroked my hair.

"It's beautiful," she said.

In that moment it seemed to me that it felt as natural and promising as light to her that I sometimes saw beyond the here and now.

"Imagine a world without magic," she had said and threw open her arms, baffled by the impossibility.

Now, though, I consider my father anew. Perhaps he experiences firsthand those disconcerting flashes when a mind is overtaken, powerless to halt a moment, to regain one's self. Perhaps it is meaningful that his thoughts alone come to me, a mistake to decide it is only a result of our closeness, those many nightfalls we have trekked to the bog.

I tilt my face to the platter and could weep at the sight of it above the doorway—that evidence of my father's returned pride.

"Fox should see it," he says. "He should know what I'm capable of."

Inside the renovated forge, I turn in a slow circle, taking in a space grown smaller, dimmer, stiller by the extension of the walls. He slides the bolt shut behind us, pulls on the door's handle, and then pulls again. The door does not budge. He brushes one hand against the other—a satisfied man. But then, the next moment, when he opens the door to exit, we find Fox there, still mounted on his horse. His eyes wander over the transformed forge. Dust dulls his face and robe, and the saliva of a hard ride clings in a thick layer to the horse's bit. Salt crusts its hooves.

"You've improved your forge," Fox says.

My father gives a gentle nudge, urging me out the door. As he pulls it closed behind us, poof, I know his mind. He sifts through how to best respond. Should he say that he needs protection from the rain, when he has always labored without walls, or that he prefers seclusion, when Carpenter and Shepherd have so often stood chatting with my father over a low wall?

I say, "You brought your message of freedom to the salt marsh?"

From atop his horse, Fox's face shines benevolence. "The tribesmen are broken with overwork there."

"I hear Roman demand means the salt makers are forced to tend their fires through the night," my father says. He had once told me how the salt makers fill clay urns with brine from the marsh and then boil the brine until only the salt remains.

Fox nods, pleased. My father and I, we have grown adept at this game, where we speak the words the druid most wants to hear.

"I've heard children take their last breaths carrying loads of wood to fuel the flames," my father says. It was something a trader come to call on Tanner had said; also that there was trade in rounded-up orphans to put into bondage in the salt marsh.

"They turn orphans into slaves there," I say. "That's what the hide trader said."

Fox climbs down from his horse, pats my shoulder like Hunter pats his hound when it trundles into the clearing with a bloody hare gripped in its jaw. He claps my father's back and leaves an arm wrapping his shoulder. "Now, show me the improvements you've made."

As we step aside, allowing Fox to pass into the forge, I see my father's apprehension—never mind that his finished pegs are housed in nailed-shut crates.

"You will work in privacy here," Fox says.

His head is nodding in what appears to be good opinion, and I suppose it makes sense that a druid would have an affinity for seclusion.

"You're an intelligent man," Fox says, looking approvingly around the darkened forge. "I knew that first day your support would come early."

The hairs at the back of my neck stiffen.

"I have access to iron," Fox says. "You needn't command a supply."

My father ducks from beneath Fox's arm, moves away until the hearth blocks further retreat. It is one thing to hide opposition or even feign support, but quite another to be enlisted as an ally.

"Our stockpiled armaments grow even as we speak," Fox says. "Still, there is much to accomplish."

Fox, it seems, has correctly read the walls as a shield against prying eyes but has not considered that those eyes are his own. No, it appears he assumes his words have opened my father's mind to ironwork that requires a wooden shroud, ironwork for which Fox will provide the iron.

"I have my regular trade," my father says. "I'm already overworked."

What other resistance might he offer?

"I have Devout and Hobble to feed and clothe."

"Of course." Fox waves away the concern.

He lifts a pair of tongs, a rasp. He runs his fingers along the cooling trough's rim, looks evenly at my father, and smiles, seemingly pleased with how his scheme is unfolding. He chose Black Lake, where no Roman would come upon him while he campaigned for rebellion and now has enlisted the settlement's blacksmith to assist him in forging arms.

"You are not alone," Fox says. "You join many of your brethren already making spearheads, daggers, and swords." He clasps his hands. "The desolation here—there is no better place."

I assume he means no better place for forging weapons, but he continues, saying, "You know the land here. Is there some spot where we could stockpile the armaments being forged in less secluded settlements?"

I think immediately of the old mine at the base of Edge. How many times my father and I had wandered its tunnels and caverns, always stopping a moment at the etching there—a family of three cut into gritstone. He liked to tell me about the long-ago day when he and my mother knelt before that gritstone wall, each clutching a sharp stone.

If Fox were shown the old mine, his palms would meet, slide one over the other, his delight apparent. The entryway is as innocent as a shallow cave; the walls, as impenetrable as the sky; the tunnels, as chaotic as the branches of an oak; the space, as vast as time. He waits, brow lifted, expectant. As silence hangs, I do not need to glimpse my father's mind to know he is thinking of me, my lame leg, and druids agitating and Romans edging closer to Sacred Isle. He makes his face ponderous, as though he is mentally combing bog and woodland, though he well knows the perfect hiding place.

By speaking of the old mine, he will enter into an agreement with Fox that cannot be revoked. He knows this, and so he hesitates a long moment. Then he clears his throat and says, "There is the abandoned mine at Edge."

21

DEVOUT

~~~

HAIR LATHERED and rinsed with a brew of chamomile, body scrubbed with dried moss and scented with sweet violet, Devout stood on the causeway with Arc, just beyond the bog dwellers gathered on the shore. Her dress was new, a fine rust and brown check, woolen but of lighter weight than that traditionally woven at Black Lake. When Devout had found the cloth alongside Crone's tools—a trowel, a funnel, a mortar and pestle, two colanders, two scythes, four knives—she slumped onto the same nest of furs where she had held the old woman's hand as she slipped from this world. Devout had wept into the wool—wool woven in secret, a gift so that she might wear a fine dress the day she took Arc as her mate.

He wore shoes of thick hide not yet softened by wear, a gift from Devout to mark the day. Old Tanner had agreed to the shoes after she delivered enough dandelion purgative to see him through to Fallow and promised to milk Shepherd's ewes through to Growth, for which Old Tanner would be owed, on her behalf, two coats of sheared wool. Arc reciprocated with a large collection of eggs and a pledge to provide three each day for the remainder of Hope, though three would become two each nightfall as an egg was returned to Mother Earth. "To pad your bones," he had said. The ribs exposed in Fallow protruded still, like wattle barely skimmed with daub.

On the causeway he lifted a pouch from her neck, undid the ties, and shook a half-dozen stinging nettle leaves into her cupped hands. She put three leaves on his tongue, and he did the same for her. They closed their mouths, worked their teeth. She felt the nettle's magic, a sensation less painful than invigorating. Each year as Fallow softened to Hope, as Mother Earth unleashed the earth's riches, new clumps of nettle sprouted around old wizened stalks foretelling the abundance to come. Devout touched her lips, the timbers of the causeway. "Today I receive Arc as my mate," she said, keeping her voice solemn, though she felt as blissful as a romping lamb. "I take Mother Earth's nettle and ask that she bless our union with fertility."

At Black Lake, tradition held that a declaration made in front of four witnesses hardened to unyielding fact. It meant that they were careful, that men turned their backs in heated conversation, that women clamped their mouths shut against hasty words. Best to let stirred dust settle, to give reason a chance. In this instance, though, the declaration was made without hesitation. Nothing felt more right, more urgent, than that she should receive Arc as her mate.

The union was the third at Black Lake that Hope. First Sullen took Singer, and then Reddish took Second Carpenter. At that second union, Young Smith's mother held her head high, wore her golden brooch, her belt decorated with bronze plaques. Even so, a pall hung over the festivities. At the onset of Hope, three of her sons' mates and their broods had set out to find more promising lives at Hill Fort. With that parting, the once mighty Smith clan dwindled to nine, and almost certainly Young Smith was decided unworthy of the Hunters' prize. Reddish's union with Second Carpenter confirmed the speculation. Reign had passed, evermore, from the benevolent, evenhanded Smiths.

At nightfall Old Man worked his flint and lit the bonfire—a mountain of heaped beech and ash and oak, all of it collected by the hands to honor Arc and Devout. Bog dwellers pushed capes from their shoulders. They took into their mouths the smoky gaminess of the roasted venison provided by the Hunters, the sweetness of the mead provided by the Carpenters, and dared allow the optimism that had been creeping back into their lives.

Nearly a year had passed since the Roman invasion, and as one day settled quietly into the next, the bog dwellers less often turned to scan the horizon, less often imagined the sound of pounding hooves. Days came and went without mention of the Romans— where they might be, whether they might thunder into the clearing. Old Hunter had gone to Hill Fort, returned with the news that not a single Roman was stationed there, watching over or otherwise molesting the market town. He reported that only the occasional small band of Romans called at Hill Fort and made their way to Chieftain at the palisaded summit where he lived. It was said he drank a strong brew of fermented grapes with the Romans, and laughed and nodded and promised his fields would be thick with wheat come Harvest. He would pay the tithe owed the emperor. Without protest. Without deceit.

Hunter had described, too, a means he had learned for detecting the presence of Roman warriors nearby. The footprints, he said, would be pitted by the short, large-headed nails studding the soles of their shoes. For a while the bog dwellers had taken to examining the earth, fingers palpating the contours that never once made known a Roman in their midst.

JUST BEYOND THE BONFIRE'S LIGHT, Devout and Arc tilted a large tribute vessel over the communal pit, dumping Mother Earth's portion of the venison and mead. He placed a hand on the back of her neck and pulled her toward him. She heard his heart, felt his lips on her hair, his arms around her. When she raised her eyes to his somber face, he said, "I thought you would choose Young Smith."

Throughout the evening, Young Smith had occupied himself with pitching pine cones into the bonfire, his aim deteriorating as his drunkenness increased.

"I won't forget it," Arc said, "that you chose me over all he could provide."

"You brought the squirrel and the crayfish," she said. "I won't forget that."

He kissed her, and her lips fell open to the warmth of his mouth. After some time, the drumming began and then came the low voice of Singer crooning old words.

Partake as two
A final time.
Unite as one,
Flesh entwined.

Arc did not shift, nudging her toward the clearing, toward Singer's beckoning drum. "Are you afraid?"

She knew what to expect. Within the roundhouses, the partitions were of woven wool or nothing at all. "No," she said, touching his hand, a hand that sometimes skimmed the tall grass alongside the path, the inner sides of her forearms, her ribs. She laughed. "But I'll be kicking and pounding with a man's strength."

They returned to the firelight, and as was their tradition, she walked innocently among the bog dwellers swallowing mead and pulsing to the beat of Singer's drumming hands. Eventually Arc swept her into his arms, heaved her onto his shoulder, darted sunwise around the bonfire three times, and then made for the roundhouse that was now his home. The bog dwellers taunted and cheered, and she hollered and lashed her fists and kicked her feet.

He set her on her pallet—their pallet. A jumble of tatty skins and stitched-together scraps of cloth newly partitioned the alcove from the one she had long shared with her mother. He undid the clasps at her shoulders, the braid of gut at her waist. She was still as he removed her dress, edging it past her shoulder blades, her waist. She did not lift her hips, and it was awkward as he tugged her dress past her backside.

She would not tell that the moment before Arc swept her into his arms, she had knocked elbows with Young Smith. He had turned, unsteady on his feet. "The etching," he said, "it foretells what will come."

She smiled at Arc fully—an effort—and his mouth went to her neck.

Young Smith had sounded so sure.

She felt Arc's hot breath, dampness at her ear. A hand went from shoulder to breast.

The etching, just as she had seen it with Young Smith, flared in her mind's eyes. Stone blazing orange, golden, and red. The chalky, ginger lines.

Arc's hand went lower still. She parted her legs and tried to muster the yearning that came so easily in the woodland. He eased himself into her, and her teeth gritted with the pain.

ONLY THAT FIRST time was dire, and soon she and Arc were so adept, so familiar that it was nothing to lie naked in some sun-dappled spot, their laughter unrestrained as they remembered the clumsiness. "You were terrified that first time," he said.

"Wasn't."

"Oh, yes. Paralyzed with fear."

She lifted her cheek from the warmth of his chest. "You saw me naked and, in a wink, you were finished, on your back, staring up at the rafters, looking lost."

He rolled onto his side, nuzzled her neck, slid a hand to her breast. Her lips parted, met his. Her back arched as his hand slid from breast to belly to between her thighs.

She closed her eyes, inhaled slowly, thought how pleasant that low ache between her legs was, and then how unbearable, unbearable that it should continue. She pushed him onto his back, lowered herself onto him. It was bliss, the knowledge that he would push more deeply into her, the way she undid, opening to him. She leaned forward, put weight onto her arms, and began a slow rocking.

And so it went—groping, writhing, yearning, wet mouths, damp flesh, sopping squelching groins, and then two spent bodies and laughter and agreement that no one had ever been so much in love. They continued as the seed was sowed, as the rain came—a light sprinkling that evenly dampened the earth, that did not chance washing away the unmoored seed. Pale shoots poked from the soil, pushed upward, sprouted a deeper shade of green, and Devout and

Arc slipped into pleasure. They fell into bliss as the wheat turned golden and tall. Once it lay cut in the fields, they set down their scythes and thought of long, empty Fallow and drawn-out evenings and the boundless lovemaking to come. She touched her lips, the earth.

Such a blessing—this yearning carnality that built and built, that toppled, that left her happy and full of hope and light and charity.

22

HOBBLE

~~~

I KNEEL AT THE QUERN, circling the handle that causes the upper stone to rotate on the lower one, milling wheat to flour. My father sits by the fire, drawing a rasp over the blade of one of Fox's daggers and then the next, imprecise work he could complete in his sleep. My mother is out. Late afternoon she had gone to the forge to tell my father that Sullen labored yet again. Though it is her sixth, her pelvis is not made for childbearing, and my mother expected she would be required well into the night. He had come in, carrying the rasp and a dozen daggers. As a maiden, I am not yet permitted to attend childbirth, and, though neither has said so, I know they have agreed not to leave me alone with Fox.

He sits on a bench, sipping steaming broth from a mug and staring into the fire. I want to speak to my father, some light conversation about the woundwort I have gathered or Sullen's tendency to birth girls, but I do not want to pull Fox away from his contemplation and have him start in on the abuses of the Romans, the tragedy of all our lives.

How I long for my family of three alone at the firepit, my father's softening face as my mother rubs silverweed liniment into his shoulder. How I resent those evenings when Fox works himself into a fist-thumping fervor. How I miss my overworked father as I trek to the causeway, on my own now, except for those few evenings when Seconds is able to accompany me. I duck into the forge afterward and report some minute improvement, reassuring my father, reassuring myself, when once I sprinted the causeway's length mainly because I liked to run.

With work to accomplish for both Luck and Fox, my father is at his anvil daybreak until nightfall. His existence consists of little more than pegs and daggers—pegs when Fox is absent, daggers when he is not. Daggers exactly as Fox ordained—plain ugly things, with one straight edge and one curved, and a narrow handle curled back on itself in a way that keeps the leather strapping in place. How many times has my father's hammer fallen onto the iron bar gripped in his tongs, molding it into a cylinder and then flattening the blade section and shaping the curl at the opposite end? After that comes the curve of the sharp edge, then the diagonal score that marks the blade's point and then more hammering on the anvil's edge so that the iron snaps at that score. And the blows are not the end of it. When he puts down his hammer, it is only to pick up a rasp, then a series of sandstones, and finally a strop.

As sometimes happens, I sense someone coming to call before they arrive at our door. In this instance, it is Sliver and Pocks, no doubt dismissed from the blood and gore of childbirth. Rather than quickly getting to my feet and making a beeline for the door, I wait for them to call out, announcing their arrival. Fox is at the firepit, and I cannot bear him wondering how he missed their approach when I had not.

The sisters nod to my father and then kneel before Fox a moment, touching their lips, the rushes. I beckon, and the three of us sit near the fire in a small enough circle that our knees touch. Each of us holds a bone needle in one hand and, in the other, a strip of roe deer hide in some state of transformation into a decorated belt. Sliver's is closest to completion, almost covered end to end in embroidered blue spirals. At the center of each swirl, she plans to attach a bead. Most often, at Black Lake, the beads trimming the belts and drinking skins are formed from hollowed, severed lengths of bird bone. Sliver, though, has ideas of her own and tells us she intends to use a snake's backbone as the source of her beads. "Think of it," she says. "Each bone is already pierced, already a bead."

"No severing required," I say.

"And all those spurs. Nothing so dull as a smooth cylinder of bone."

"It should be easy enough to find a snake skeleton already picked clean," I say.

Fox's gaze stays on us as we push our needles into the hide strips and pull through loops of colored wool. I hate the way he watches, without even bothering to look away when my glance snags his.

Eventually Pocks tires of needlework, puts down her belt, and cajoles Sliver and me into joining her in a game where we clap our hands against each other's and our knees in an ever-evolving sequence. She giggles and points a finger and tips onto her back each time one of us makes a mistake. Her laughter infects Sliver and me, and I give little notice to Fox as he trades scrutiny at the firepit for time on his knees beneath Mother Earth's cross or to my father as he lifts yet another dagger.

At the Harvest Feast, Sliver had said my father should be First Man, and the idea has proved true in the moons since. Those evenings the men gather around our firepit, swallowing the grilled boar he no longer lacks the means to provide, my father sits on Fox's left. That prized position means I serve only Fox before him as I move sunwise, pouring mead, and confirms his status as First Man at Black Lake.

Fox stops mid-sermon on occasion and says to Hunter, seated on his right, "Our provisions of salted meat continue to grow, do they not?" and Hunter nods.

Fox turns next to my father. "Our stockpiled armaments expand each day, do they not?"

He nods.

Now laden handcarts arrive in the clearing and my father directs the traders hauling those carts to the old mine. Once I crept behind a cart loaded with swords and, at the old mine's entrance, announced myself and offered to hold a rushlight as the trader continued to the cavern housing the stockpiled weapons. I learned that the swords had come from a valley dweller settlement, that there is brisk trade in transporting armaments, that Fox orchestrates their production and collection across the northwestern tribes. Even so, when we reached the cavern, I stood agape, taking in the upended spears lining the wall three deep, the shields stacked on the floor to the height of a man's thigh, the swords piled to toppling, the daggers spilling from dozens of large crates. And that unnerving hoard was, according to the trader, dwarfed by those of the tribes in the east.

Early on, the bog dweller men had mostly rolled their eyes amid the privacy of the woodland and agreed that Fox liked to talk, to provoke courage that none among them would be called on to demonstrate. That easy dismissal of Fox's ranting had come to an abrupt close one evening late in Fallow. As he eyed the men sternly, he said, "Glory will be awarded to those who seek freedom, to those who defend our ancestral ways, and woe to those who do not." Then he went from one man to the next, questioning, "Glory or woe, which do you choose?" Like sticks of tented kindling falling to ash, one man toppled, choosing glory, and then inevitably the next.

With my father's contribution to the rebellion so apparent, I had wondered if the bog dwellers might turn away from him, at least drop conversations midsentence as he approached, but I have watched and the opposite is true. They appear at our door, seeking the opinion of Black Lake's First Man. Which ram should be set on the ewes? Was Carpenter required to replace the wooden hide stretchers Tanner claimed were warped long before he left them out in the rain? Old Man meant to make an offering, and was the one-legged hen the best choice? My father's opinion is sought on everything but Fox's proselytizing, his scheme. On this they assume they know my father's mind.

AFTER A DOZEN ROUNDS, Sliver, Pocks, and I end our game and get to our feet. We drink ladlefuls of water as we pick stray lengths of rush from one another's dresses. At the door, the sisters grow solemn and call out "Blessings of Mother Earth" to Fox, still on his knees beneath Mother Earth's cross, and shrug their shoulders when he does not so much as open his eyes. Then they turn to the night outside and holler into blackness, "Daybreak is near," so the dark fairies will know to scatter from their path.

As they cross the threshold, Pocks stops and looks over her shoulder. "Tomorrow, then, we'll find the bones? You're sure?"

"Yes, tomorrow." I nod.

"Let's go," Sliver says and yanks Pocks's arm.

"Where will we look?" Pocks waits, feet rooted, as though at any moment, I will reveal a secret sweet as honey.

How best to make them leave? I arrange my face to show doubt. "The causeway?"

"Come on." Sliver yanks again.

But Pocks holds her ground. "Not until she does it right. Hobble, shut your eyes."

Panic rises that she intends to reenact our childhood game. I close my eyes, meaning only to satisfy Pocks, and though I keep them shut hardly more than a blink, I see a knobby, white spine and curved ribs, also the chiseled slab of gritstone that marks the location of the bones as Sacred Grove.

"Now!" Sliver snaps.

"Not until she tells us where."

Fox is still on his knees, his face blank, his eyes lightly closed. "The stone altar," I whisper.

Pocks eyes me skeptically, blurts, "I've never seen a snake in Sacred Grove."

Sliver does not yank this time. This time she loops her arm around her sister's neck and hauls her into the black night.

I close the door, go back to the quern. My father's attention has left the blade, the rasp, and settled on me. Fox's eyes are on me, too.

"You said you can't choose what you divine?" He watches so intently.

"I can't."

"And yet you close your eyes and tell a pair of maidens where to find a snake skeleton?"

"A nonsense game," my father says with enough certainty that I know he is unaware of the stones I prophesied as a child.

My hands grow damp. As I let go of the quern's handle and wipe them on my dress, Fox says, "You girls are almost like lambs in your innocence."

Lambs? Like those bound on the stone altar?

His white robe glows yellow in the firelight, and his cheeks shine orange beneath the black hollows of his eyes.

23.

HOBBLE

≈

Fox makes haste in the early morning, his cape rippling and flapping as he lodges himself from the roundhouse into pelting rain and gusting wind. As I step from behind the woolen partition of my sleeping alcove, my father emerges from his. He, too, then, had been waiting for Fox to leave.

"A tempest out there," he says. "You won't be tilling today."

"Mother's still with Sullen?"

He nods. "A day to catch up on my pegs."

It seems, then, that he assumes Fox is off to rally in some far-flung settlement rather than to search for a snake skeleton in Sacred Grove, and maybe he is right. Maybe my late night of tossing and turning was the senseless product of an overcharged mind.

"I'll bring out your barley porridge."

He juts his chin toward the tumult beyond the door. "Not in this," he says though he takes his morning meal in the forge these days.

I take my time wrapping the alternate—a wedge of hard cheese and a thick slice of bread. "You'll have some dandelion tea?" I say.

"Water will do."

He drains his mug, tucks the wrapped meal under his cape, ducks his head as he tramps into the deluge.

I picture him alone in his forge—working the bellows, building up the fire. I think of him clasping a peg in his tongs and, worn down by the monotony of a thousand pegs, lobbing it into the cooling trough though the point remains crude. When will Fox leave for good? When might my household return to the simplicity we all so badly miss? I need a break from my mind, the never-ending loop of the worry he has brought to my household, to all of us at Black Lake. I hate the man—Fox—his watchfulness, his shameless staring. I close my eyes to the thought, but it is true. I hate him—a druid, an emissary of the gods. My recklessness frightens me, and I touch my lips, the rushes at my feet.

I have only just decided we are free of Fox for the day when I hear the commotion of feet slapping puddles and water kicked up in the clearing. I stand stock-still, listening, then let go my breath as I recognize the laughter of sisters making chase. With Fox truly away, and Sliver and Pocks again dismissed by their laboring mother, the three of us will spend a rainy morning being as we should, easy and carefree, without the anxiety of a druid watching and judging and likening us to lambs.

As I usher the sisters inside, I see my father peering around the forge's door. Same as me, he listens. He waves. I wave, and he turns back to his unmade pegs.

The sisters have barely finished exclaiming about the tempest and shaking the rain from their capes, when the door pulls open behind them. Fox brushes inside, looking as stirred up as the day outside. "Over to the firepit, the three of you," he says.

Fox crowds close on our heels, rainwater spilling from the sopping, mud-splattered cape he has not taken the time to remove. "Sit there," he says, pointing to a bench.

He squats to his haunches, directly facing me. "You'll do as you're told," he says. "You'll do as I've already asked."

I lace my fingers, put my hands between my knees.

"Go on. Tell us of the awaiting glory."

I pinch my thighs, my hands together. How to explain that I cannot conjure his rebellion, cannot conjure the result he awaits. "I can't."

Fox reaches into the pocket of his cape. His hand emerges to reveal what I knew it would. "From the altar at Sacred Grove," he says. He holds out his hand, quivering with excitement. The dangling snake skeleton exactly matches the one I had divined—white, a knobby spine, endless pairs of curved ribs.

He turns to the sisters, trembling, gripping each other's hands. "You've heard her divine," he says. "You've seen her accomplish it all your lives."

Pocks nods a single slow nod.

"Explain yourself," he says to me, and then, when I say nothing, he turns back to the sisters. "Perhaps one of you can tell me what your friend won't."

His eyes burrow, and Pocks whimpers, buries her face in Sliver's chest.

"I picture a place," I say, "a place I know well, and sometimes—"

"Picture this." He straightens, begins to pace. "Picture a horde of seething tribesmen. Picture them spilling over a ridge. They jeer and leap and rattle their steel. They howl promises of ruin, defeat." As he continues—the unending horde, the boundless weaponry—I know it is a scene that has played over and over in his mind, that has become his truth.

Had my father heard Fox return? Was he at this very moment

snatching the peg from atop his anvil, replacing it with the dagger he keeps in his jerkin? I want my father, want to know he is coming, and so, as my heart pounds, I press my eyes shut. Same as I focus on the spring's shallow pool before divining a smooth, milky stone, I focus on my father's anvil—black, pocked, tinged with orange, sloped on one side. I focus on the dagger that I want placed on its surface—plain, inelegant, curved along one side.

Then I taste metal. The backs of my eyelids flash white light. A hand clutches that inelegant dagger's narrow handle. A hand belonging not to my father but to a boy. He jabs the dagger, jeers amid old men heaving stones and frenzied women waving sickles, among enraged tribesmen thrusting swords. The boy shrinks to reveal a plain teeming with an unfathomable mass of tribesmen facing a wall of shields. Swords protrude from between those shields, and behind those shields, the armor, helmets, and weaponry of an immense army gleam. The lines of that army rotate with practiced efficiency—the second line, stepping forward in unison to take up the position of the first and that spent line retreating to the rear to recoup its strength. The front boundary of that Roman army is shaped like the teeth of a saw, and the trough of each tooth serves as a pit in which the tribesmen are compressed. Those gleaming men press forward, trampling the tribesmen still taking breath, treading on the fallen. The hobnails of their sandals tear the flesh underfoot. The earth grows thick with mounded corpses, slick with blood.

THEN I AM BACK in the roundhouse, quaking, realizing I have lured a vision, forced it to appear. It might seem momentous, an achievement of sorts—a prophetess honing her craft—if I had conjured something other than the tribesmen's slaughter. Fox bellows, "Tell me. Tell me what you see."

"Romans wearing helmets and armor march with their shields in front like a wall. They step on bodies—tribesmen's bodies—countless bodies spread over a plain."

Fox's face hardens, intensifying the deep grooves of his cheeks.

I know his conviction that the tribesmen should fight, that the gods demand the Romans be expelled. With my prophecy, I have made myself an obstacle in pursuing that end.

"Any one of us could describe what she did." My father stands in the roundhouse doorway now. He keeps his gaze steady, his voice easy, light. "You forget that Roman warriors sat at our firepit."

"You forget that she foretold the arrival of those Romans," Fox snaps.

"We've all known for years that one day Romans would arrive in Black Lake."

Fox's gaze falls to the snake skeleton still in his hand.

"Admit you put the skeleton on the altar, Hobble," my father says and locks his eyes on mine. Lie, admit trickery, no matter the truth.

Fox made me prophesy. He had only considered some positive revelation, and now I have divined defeat. But my father understands Fox's ability to erase any fact that contradicts his view, and he hands Fox a way out: discredit me and my naysaying prophecy is undone.

I shudder as Fox hollers, "Admit it!"

I hold my gaze firm. "I put the bones on the altar," I say in a strong, clear voice.

Fox turns from me to the sisters. "Your friend divines nothing." He spits the words. "She deceives you. She pretends."

The sisters cower. Pocks begins to sob, low mournful cries.

"This game where she"—he sneers—"leaves bones one day and tells you where you might find them the next, who else joins in?"

Sliver clears her throat. "Usually it's stones," she says. "Only bones, this once. We don't play anymore. We haven't played for years."

"I asked, who else?"

"Harelip and Moon," she says. "Sometimes Young Reddish."

Pocks shifts so that her face peeks away from sister's chest. "Mole. The young Shepherds."

"Who else?"

"Seconds," Sliver says.

Fox waits, his gaze darting back and forth between Sliver and Pocks. He pitches the bones into the firepit and says, "Tell your friends Hobble deceives them. She foretells nothing. You have heard her confess."

His fist clenches. "A false prophetess lives among us," he bellows. His narrowed, raging eyes look first to my father, then to me. "We'll gather in Sacred Grove at nightfall," he says.

The taste of metal swamps my mouth. The white flash, when it comes, is such that pain flares behind my brow. My hands fly to my eye sockets, and I feel myself collapsing forward from the bench.

I see my mother turning a placenta—round, flat, deeply veined, blue red as meat, and most important, fully intact. She places her hands on Sullen's belly, feeling for a womb gone hard from boggy, shrunk to the size of a man's fist. She lifts the newborn—a girl—from Sullen's breast, provoking a spirited howl. "Won't be browbeat by the older ones," my mother says.

She wipes waxy vernix from the newborn, small clots of blood. She has only the child's nether regions left to clean when Sliver and Pocks burst into the roundhouse, capes dripping, wet hair snaking their flushed cheeks. Pocks runs straight to Sullen and hides her face in the crook of her mother's arm, never mind the blood, the glistening umbilicus, the blue-red meat. Sliver stands in the doorway quaking, eyes roving over a scene she is not yet meant to witness.

"The druid," she cries, and then she, too, begins to wail, fitful panting sobs. "He'll turn us into stone."

My mother grasps Sliver's shoulder. "Hobble?" she says. "What has happened to Hobble?" but Sliver only blubbers, and my mother jerks her in a way that draws a futile attempt from Sullen to push herself up from her pallet.

"Devout!"

The girls bawl and sniffle, catch and lose their breaths, snort snot and smear it on the backs of their wrists. In between, they gasp that I lie, that I put a stone in a pool and snake bones on the altar, that I described bodies ripped and torn under the Romans' hobnailed boots, that Fox hates their game, that they do not want to be turned into stone or beasts, that they said the others' names, that he will banish all of them.

My mother's eyes dart, as though she means to flee the round-house, the incoherent blather, but first she must free herself of the infant held in her hands.

Sliver says, "He's making an offering tonight in the grove."

My mother plunks the howling bundle at Sullen's breast, spins around to leave. Pocks says, "Pet, she's my favorite ewe," and bursts into renewed sobbing.

Sliver says, "I told him how we nursed her. He didn't even care."

My mother flattens a hand against the wall. "It's Pet he means to slay?" she says. "You're certain?"

Pocks nods and puts her grim, wet face in her hands. Sliver wipes her eyes with the folds of her dress and whimpers, "He told us to find Shepherd, to tell him to prepare a beast—the ewe with the deformed jaw, he said."

"Hush," coos Sullen, stroking the girl's hair. "Hush."

But they do not hush. Without even bothering with her cape, my mother flees into the torrent outside.

I am lying in the rushes when I awake. The mishmash of roots and leaves hanging overhead sharpens into focus and then, my father's hand as he passes a cool cloth over my brow. "Sliver and Pocks?" I say.

"They've gone." He puts a finger to his lips. "Quiet now. Rest. You fainted. You've been out a good while."

I shift to prop myself onto my elbows, but my father puts a hand on my shoulder, gently easing me back. "Fox?" I whisper.

"Making the rounds," he says. "We're offing a ewe at nightfall. Fox said so after you fainted."

The relief is like thunder, a cloud burst open, a deluge dropped to earth.

"I need to get your mother," my father says. "I'll be quick."

But she has already left Sliver and Pocks and exhausted Sullen and her newborn. At any moment my drenched mother will come hurtling through the doorway. "She's on her way."

And Pet? My fingers curl into fists for Pet. First the Hunters' hound pup. And now Pet. It is as callous a choice as Fox could make. He meant it as a warning: He would not put up with another episode of treachery—for that is what he considers my description of the trampled tribesmen—not from my family, not from me, a maiden briefly lifted to the status of prophetess and then quickly relegated to the status of lying runt.

24.

DEVOUT

≈

DEVOUT SET DOWN the round frame used to winnow the
wheat. As she headed to the cesspit, she made a fervent
wish that she was mistaken. But then, squatting over the
reeking hole, she took her hand away from between her legs. A
smear of blood clung to her fingertips—vestige of a child Mother
Earth had not blessed.

She and Arc had been joined in union six moons now, and still,
with the arrival of each new moon, she felt a fullness come to her
breasts, a heaviness come to her belly. She had woken the night before and recognized that familiar feeling. Rather than woozily rolling onto her side, she snapped her eyes open. What sliced through
her grogginess, like a blade through a ripe plum, was instant knowledge that she would bleed the next day.

She and the other hands had taken up their scythes as the wheat
turned golden, had bound felled stalks into sheaves, and hauled
loads from the fields. For twelve days now they had selected harvested sheaves, beat the laden heads with a thick stick, and then

trampled the battered remains until the grain came loose. Just that morning, finally, they had begun the lighter work of loading the wheat onto skin-stretched frames and tossing the grain into the air. It was satisfying work—watching as the chaff drifted away in the breeze, as the grain that fell back onto the skins grew ever more pure. Usually they sang as they worked. But this Harvest, on Devout's return from the cesspit, though she took up her frame, satisfaction did not come and she did not join in the song.

Three moons had passed since Sullen came to her in the fields and took Devout's hands in her own. The gesture was not uncommon among the bog dwellers. The warmth of it was strange for a girl as meek as Sullen, though, even if she had grown surer of herself since taking Singer as her mate. Devout saw her friend's dewy skin, her gleaming hair, the fullness of her face, her breasts. Sullen let go of Devout, smoothed her hands over her skirt, a belly rounded by the blessed child in her womb.

That first day of winnowing, Devout anticipated more sly comments about her exhaustion if she yawned, a knowing look if she did not rise from the pallet immediately at daybreak, a lifted eyebrow if she took a second slice of bread. The flesh she had lost the Fallow before was mostly returned, and she had grown accustomed to the pause that came after she was told she looked well, a pause that was really a question about the status of her womb. Had she been blessed? Though her mother kept any comment to herself, Devout noticed the thin set of her lips when bloodied rags were among the items they scrubbed. And then there was Arc, who did not need to ask, who knew she would tell him the moment she was sure, who kissed the back of her neck with such tenderness those nights she bled.

She would start with a tea of nettle and red clover, move on to an infusion if stronger magic was required. She would put a stalk of nettle under their pallet, tie a pouch of its seeds to her waist, so that it might hang close to her womb. She would find occasion to share Sullen's mug, to drink from it, siphoning some of the girl's fruitfulness. Acquiring the first egg laid by a hen would bring humiliation, but Young Carpenter's mate, who kept the brood, was kind. She would hand over an egg without making Devout stammer through saying she needed the yolk to swallow, the white to spread over her belly, a hen's new fertility to rouse her own.

But then, even before she had gathered the resolve, Young Carpenter's mate came to Devout when she was alone in the meadow adjacent the fields. She looked up from pinching red clover leaves from their stems.

"It was almost two years before I was blessed," Young Carpenter's mate said. With the hand that did not hold an egg, she fiddled with a fold of her dress. "Crone gave me red clover, and I put nettle under our pallet, but still I bled. I was honest in setting aside a third of the chicks—but I chose cockerels over laying hens and, in doing so, built up the brood but cheated Mother Earth. I wasn't blessed until I'd made an offering of my three best laying hens. Make careful accounting, Devout."

Young Carpenter's mate placed the egg on Devout's palm and closed her fingers around the shell. The kindness put a lump in Devout's throat. She bowed her head and thought how she possessed no laying hens.

WITH THE WHEAT, barley, and oats finally winnowed, Devout and Arc found a moment to lie back on a flat rock and look up at the sky. The bitter winds of Fallow skimmed their hands and cheeks, infiltrated their capes, and she huddled close. It was an effort to lie still, after moons of gathering hazelnuts, moons of preparing the magic of comfrey and burdock, all the while, little thought given over to the tasks, her mind a low drone of praising and beseeching and bartering: Mother Earth is bountiful and generous. A child, just one. I will do better, put more in the tribute vessel, surpass even Crone in unleashing your magic, in serving the bog dwellers.

And yet she must stay still on the flat rock. She must feel the rise and fall of Arc's chest, hear the passage of air through his nostrils, take in the smell of him, a mixture of smoke and sweat and the earthy fragrance of the dried moss he used to clean himself. "You're lost," he had said, more than once. "You've drifted away." Other times she would glance up to catch his eyes on her, his eyebrows knit for the flicker before he returned his attention to the fox he was skinning, the wood he was stacking beneath the eaves.

His breath and then his lips were on her hair. She wrapped an arm more tightly around him so that he would know she was not lost. "Devout?" he said so softly it was like a drop of rain. "What troubles you, Devout?"

Might she pretend not to know the strangeness that had afflicted her recent moons, gaining foothold as Sullen shared her news, thickening as the nettle and red clover failed, burgeoning as Young Carpenter's mate instructed her to make a careful accounting. She thought, as she often did, of the day she had clung to Arc on the causeway after hearing their child in the mist. "That child we heard, I thought we'd seen our future," she said. "And now I think, was that it? That flicker? Was that the only child we'll ever know?"

"It was a good omen."

After a long pause, she said, "Sullen is soon to birth, and we joined in union just after she and Singer."

"It's been eight moons, not even a year. You told me yourself Young Carpenter's mate went unblessed for two."

"She had laying hens to offer Mother Earth."

He was silent, and in his silence, she heard insecurity that he had nothing—neither laying hens, nor other prize, certainly nothing so worthy as a silver amulet.

"I'll see what I can catch at Black Lake," he said. "We'll make an offering."

She had felt a flicker of hope as she placed a nettle sprig beneath their pallet, as she swallowed the first egg's yolk, as she scraped too large portions of wild carrot and fox into the tribute vessel, but always the flicker dimmed, went out as she bled. She resisted latching on to Arc's fish, a flicker of promise blinking like sunshine through a leafy canopy, but she could not.

"Yes, maybe fish," she said.

25.

DEVOUT

≈

ARC SAT IN THE FIRELIGHT, whittling a straight stick and securing a length of sinew knotted with an iron hook to one end. Old Man paraded about the roundhouse, saying how sensible Arc was to hunt the fish now, early in Fallow. They had matured from fingerlings to adults and become sluggish in the cold water. "You'll come back," he said, "stooped under the weight of your haul." As Devout crumbled dried sweet violet for the draft that kept Walker from pacing through the night, she thought of a bucket chock-full of perch. "He's right," she said.

Arc turned his attention from his whittling.

"A large haul." She smiled.

Old Man clapped Arc on the back and his usually labored gait took on a little skip as he continued around the firepit.

Once the completed fishing rod was propped against the wall and her sweet violet draft put aside to steep, she and Arc snuggled close under furs and woolen coverings. She touched her nose to his. "You'll catch a dozen fish."

He put his lips against hers. "I will," he said, his breath hot. "Their bellies will be so fat."

She drew his hand to her breast, a nipple grown achingly taut. He stroked, kissed, pulled her to him. She took him into her loosened body, rode the swells, until they were spent and quiet amid a tangle of furs and wool.

As HE TENDED the fire at daybreak, she made barley porridge and dandelion root tea. She separated the third due Mother Earth without generosity and did not mind that Arc kept up his habit of looking often in her direction as she accomplished the task. She packed a midday meal of hard cheese and bread. As she wrapped the cheese, Arc's hands slipped around her waist from behind. She closed her eyes, tilted her head back against his shoulder. She turned away from the cheese and bread, put her arms around his neck, and gave a sly smile. "We'll enjoy Fallow's quiet this year."

A burst of bitter air slipped past the open door as he crossed the threshold. He shut it quickly, preserving the warmth around Devout and missed seeing her arm raised in farewell.

She drained her tea, set another log on the fire. The day stretched before her, long and strangely, luxuriously blank. Full of vigor, she lifted her cape from the nail beside the door. Today she would sort through the last of the vessels, roots, and leaves remaining in Crone's shack.

As THE SUN fell low in the sky and the light coming through the doorway lessened, Devout hauled a final vessel-crammed bin close to the fire. She sat down with heaviness, feeling the weight of arms held too long overhead. Arc would at any moment come into the clearing and Old Man would tell him where to find her, and they would eat a quick meal of bread and honey and hazelnuts and go by moonlight to Sacred Grove.

She identified the aroma of white bryony and then lesser celandine wafting from the vessels held beneath her nose. She had already decided the place where they would bury the fish—on the eastern edge of Sacred Grove, beneath a particularly fruitful rowan. It could only help. She tapped a small amount of reddish-brown powder onto her palm and considered what she knew about improving the sway of an offering. Through a sort of overkilling more than one god could be placated. She drew a finger through the powder on her palm and saw by its color it was common bistort root and brushed it back into the vessel. Should Protector get his blow to the head, War Master his garroting, and Begetter his drowning? Each fish could first be struck with a rock and then wrapped behind the gills with a piece of twine twisted ever tighter, but a fish returned to the lake where it had swum hardly made sense. But enough, it was not Protector, War Master, and Begetter who would bless her womb but rather Mother Earth, and she wanted only the blood drained from the fish. Devout shook her head, brushed stray bits of plant from her skirt. She had spent too long in the smoke, the close air. She stood and doused the fire, eager to be rid of the shack.

A thin layer of white newly blanketed the clearing. The snow was as yet unmarred, and before lifting her skirt, she hesitated a moment, eyes sweeping a world made pure, without rot, without darkness. Arc was not in the clearing, only Young Smith, who glanced up from his anvil and then quickly back down again before changing his mind and nodding to Devout. He turned back to his work and, with a show of effort that caused tenderness to well in her throat, pounded his hammer against a narrow strip of glowing iron. She wanted to ask if he had seen Arc. There was no one else, and it was unnatural not to ask, as she would any other bog dweller. Even so, she only said, "Fallow is fully arrived."

"Don't mind the coolness, working alongside a bed of scorching coals." He wiped his brow with the back of the hand holding a pair of tongs, and it left a sooty streak. She drew her finger across her own forehead, showing him the place, but he only looked at her. She pointed to his forehead. Still he did not understand. She reached across the half wall of his roofed shelter and with her thumb erased the streak.

"Oh," he said, heat coming to his cheeks.

"A line of soot."

"Gone now, then?"

"Yes, gone."

She went off to find Arc, but he was not chopping wood. No pair of legs showed beneath the wattle screen surrounding the cesspit. He was not in the roundhouse, and the buckets where they kept the water were full to the brim. "The fish are hurtling themselves onto his hook," Old Man said. "Won't be seeing him until the sun is fully set." And so she busied herself with milling the flour for the next day's loaves and heading out to the larder dug into the earth to collect a round of cheese. She went down clay stairs and pulled back the door's thick leather. Though she shivered in the damp, the cold, she took her time letting her eyes adjust to the dim light and then selecting a round poked with the three holes that marked it as belonging to her household.

Arc was not in the clearing when she emerged, and she thought perhaps she had stayed too long in the larder, that he had already stepped inside. She went back to the warmth and clamor of the roundhouse—the children squawking, their mother scolding and instructing, Old Man blowing his nose, her mother saying, "Oh, good, you've been to the larder." For a count of ten, Devout held her eyes from drifting to the place by the door where Arc's bucket would be if he had come in from the bog. The roundhouse smelled of woodsmoke and hides and wool and bodies too long unwashed. She could detect no hint of fish. She inhaled long and low, but the stink did not change. Of course not, when no laden bucket rested by the door.

She turned and went back into the clearing, night now fully arrived. She thought about a rushlight, but she knew the path well and the snow glistened beneath a cloudless sky, a moon on the cusp of full, and she did not want to explain the need of a rushlight to her household. Adding their anxiety to her own seemed like giving weight to something that was nothing at all.

The fish were there, on the shore of Black Lake, a bucketful of perch with broad dark stripes reaching around their bellies and red fins and glassy, unblinking eyes. Beyond, the lake was rung in white—a band of ice extending a few paces from the shore and bleeding into a narrower band where the white lost its brightness before transitioning to gray. Near the lake's middle, the ice ended with a feathery edge, and beyond that, open water, blackness. Her gaze swept the carpet of fresh snow, landed on a place where the soft white contours abruptly gave way to stirred leaf litter and trampled earth. She moved closer, knelt, touched a footprint that she knew to be Arc's. The size was right, and the impression was smooth, cast by a foot snugly wrapped in leather. Her fingers went to a second footprint, one of myriad others. For a moment she could not decipher the pitted basin of that print. Then her hands flew to her mouth. She pressed her eyes shut, opened them, but still, Arc's smooth footprint was there, amid a tangle of others, each pitted by the short, large-headed nails that Old Hunter had described as studding the soles of Roman warriors' shoes. She staggered to upright, lurched away from the spot where it appeared Arc had tussled with the Romans before being—what? Shackled? Carted off to live out his days building the road said to extend from southeastern Britannia? Forced onto the ship that would transport him to the faraway slave market from which he would never return? She shoved the bucket. Even before it tipped, she knew she would count eleven gulping, flapping perch. For she had said, "You'll catch a dozen fish," and he had stayed too long seeking the final one.

She stepped farther out onto the ice ringing Black Lake's pool, at first gingerly and then not, for the gods would not open up the ice for her. They would not permit the relief of Otherworld. Never mind: she would outwit them, would step into the blackness beyond the ice. Her skin cape, wool dress, and leather shoes would be sodden weights. She would not kick or splash or pull herself up onto the ice but allow Black Lake to close its yawning mouth, to swallow, delivering her to its watery depths.

But then the night air shook with a bang—blunt and hollow and far away. It was only that the ice had buckled and cracked at the opposite shore, but she stood rigid, unable to propel herself forward. She dropped onto the ice, defeated, and lay there weeping and blubbering, "Arc," "my beloved," "my peace."

She did not care that she grew chilled, that her cheek adhered to the ice with frozen tears, frozen spittle, frozen snot.

26.

ᴴOBBLE

~~~

As I leave my mother's childhood roundhouse, I see Hunter, of all men, standing outside my door. I take a quiet backward step. He has not called in moons, not since that first evening of my return from Hill Fort. I take in his stance, his chest flared like a hot bull's, then scurry along the back of the roundhouses. When I reach my own, I creep along the wall until I have an unobstructed view of Hunter in profile at our door. "I thought we might speak," he says.

My father's voice reaches me from just inside the doorway. "Speak, then."

Now more than ever, I like visiting my mother's childhood roundhouse, the reprieve it provides those evenings when the druid lurks. No one is as entertaining as Old Man. He tells stories—the crucial gifts of crayfish and squirrel provided by Arc during the most harrowing of Fallows, his promise of eggs to fill the troughs arisen between my mother's ribs. Old Man takes an interest in my tablet, watches as I etch *HOBVL* into beeswax, those five symbols that Luck showed my father at Hill Fort. Old Man repeats after me as I say, "Huh-aw-buh-uuh-luh," and point to the symbol corresponding to each of those sounds. Eventually he winces, bends and straightens his legs, waiting for me to ask about his afflicted knees. A moment ago, I had said to Old Man, "Let me fetch some silverweed liniment. I'll be back quick as a beating wing."

HUNTER LIFTS HIS CHIN. "Your tent pegs," he says. "I saw similar ones at Hill Fort."

My father steps fully outside and pulls the door shut behind his back. I flatten myself against the curved wall.

"They're Roman," Hunter says.

"I've heard you boast," my father says. "I remember a boar traded for a flagon, a deal struck with a Roman."

"Not since Fox. Fox says it's treason."

My father folds his arms, and I think how Hunter clings to the Black Lake of old, before the Romans, that time when still he was First Man, when still my family was downtrodden, when still my mother's wrist was bare.

"Fox might find out," Hunter says. "About your pegs."

"From you?"

Hunter shrugs, shifts as though to leave.

My father takes a fold of Hunter's tunic into his fist. "The boar and venison you trade at Hill Fort, you think no morsel finds its way to Viriconium?"

Hunter breathes.

My father presses. "We're not to provide the pegs that secure the Romans' tents? We're not to feed them? You're suggesting I advise Fox to ban all of us from trading at Hill Fort?"

Hunter's eyes flit from my father's. "I only meant you should be careful."

"Of course." My father drops his hand.

Hunter retreats a few steps, then a few more. Once he is beyond my father's reach, Hunter's chest puffs again and he spits, "Don't claim you weren't warned."

As he turns away, my father wipes his hand against his breeches, like he is ridding it of filth.

How much I dislike Hunter; how I would like to deny him the dandelion draft that keeps his flush face from exploding to red. He knows the danger Fox poses to me. He must. He knows the harm that could come from raising Fox's ire against my father, and yet he stands at our door, threatening to do exactly that. Or maybe his hunger for status runs so deep that he is blind to any implication beyond diminishing my father.

My father stands, looking out over the clearing, inhaling and exhaling long steady breaths. He taught me the technique as a child, after a snorting, pawing wild boar had come into the clearing and set me trembling. "I know a trick for stilling terror," he had said.

I BOLT UPRIGHT on my pallet. A vision of a sea—red with blood—retreats. The here and now enters. My heart pounds the wall of my chest like an urgent fist. I know by my limbs' exhaustion that they have just stilled, by my throat's ache that I was hollering.

In the vision, the beach alongside that grisly sea had teemed with white-robed druids—some stooped, crippled with age, others with arms held aloft and faces tilted to the heavens. They bellowed incantations as women clad in black darted among them, howling and waving firebrands and kissing the robes of their masters. At the shoreline, gleaming men streamed from flat-bottomed boats and re-grouped behind a wall of shields. They moved with precision as they marched onto the beach. The rheumy-eyed druids did not hesitate in their bellowing or lower their arms to impede the steel ripping into their chests. Smooth-skinned apprentices looked to their supe-riors for some absent signal that said they might resist. The black-clad women fled, wailed as they were knocked from their feet, pleaded as swift kicks urged them onto their backs so that they might know for a moment the terror of a thrust dagger. Blood spurted, pooled on flat rocks, slithered over hard-packed sand, col-lected in rivulets, streamed to the sea. My mother rocks me now, smoothing my hair and cooing, "Wake, my child. Wake." My father crouches with one hand on the wool over my lame leg, and the other holding a rushlight. My cupped palms hide my mouth, and when I take them away, I say, "The men with the shields were in boats this time. Druids waited on the shore with their arms raised up to the gods. They didn't fight back. They were cut down. All of them."

My parents glance toward the entryway of my sleeping alcove, and I discover we are not alone. Carpenter, Shepherd, and Tanner touch their lips, reach for the rushes beneath their feet. Hunter stands with arms folded over his chest. Fox steps away from the tradesmen into the warm glow of the rushlight. My nighttime raving had drawn the men away from Fox's evening oration at the firepit.

"How many?" Fox says.

And now, fully awake, I hesitate. Am I to confirm any rumors of my soothsaying for those men in the entryway?

As the fields were tilled and sowed, neither Sliver nor anyone else mentioned the foretold snake bones or tribesmen underfoot, and I had come to believe that word of that naysaying prophecy had not spread beyond Sliver's family. The fields had blushed fully green before I learned from Seconds that I was wrong.

I sat shelling peas on the bench just outside the door of my roundhouse as Seconds approached. He dropped down beside me and said, "Your father lost his entire clan to an earlier round of druid goading. Yet same as everyone else, he lifts his mug when Fox calls out some beloved phrase—"Righteous vengeance!," "Freedom!," or "Roman lust has gone too far!" I've watched him, though—your father—and he doesn't show any more enthusiasm than he must. He might sit on Fox's left and forge his daggers, but your father doesn't support his rebellion. I'm sure of it."

I shut my eyes, tilted my head back against wattle and daub.

"Look," he said, his voice so gentle that I knew he had not meant to unnerve me. "Fox has already questioned the cowardice of any man unwilling to join the rebellion. Next, he will promise the persecution of anyone who stays put to farm the wheat we all need to survive. Your father is our best hope."

I opened my eyes, sat up straight. "But what can he do?"

"Try to reason with Fox." He twisted to face me on the bench. "It's true, what I've heard? You foresaw defeat?"

And then words tumbled from me, like a spring spewing from a high crevice—the teeming plain, the wall of shields, the gleaming men pressing forward, Fox's sneering mouth and narrowed, raging eyes. "It's why Pet was sacrificed. Because I told him what he didn't want to hear."

He got up, walked the length of the bench, returned. "The man's a fanatic," he said and slumped beside me. "He's incapable of balanced thinking. He can't fathom any opinion other than his own." He put a hand on my knee. "That prophecy—if anyone asks, say you made it up."

"TELL ME," Fox says now, as he squats beside my pallet.

"The sea turned red."

"The sea?"

"It was the sea around Sacred Isle. I don't know how I know."

"Describe the boats."

Visions come to me, and I have long thought of those visions as delivered by a benevolent hand; they revealed the sites of pretty stones, the hollow where morel would soon sprout. Had I not put to good use that vision of Luck's shed and its crammed interior? But perhaps that argument is flawed, when my father regularly scoops Roman pegs from his cooling trough and hides them between hearth and wall. I wonder now if, rather than benevolence, malice delivers the revelations. I think of Pet on the stone altar, her yellow eyes still, forever dim, because I had spoken a prophecy that Fox could not accept.

"Made of willow," I say, recalling the only boat I know. It holds a single man and is constructed of arced willow boughs covered with hides and made waterproof with pitch. "Like the one tethered to the causeway here."

Fox raises an arm, as though to club a lying maiden, but my father clasps the druid's pale wrist.

My mother takes my chin in her palms. "Speak the truth, Hobble," she says, and my father nods.

I swallow, start again. "They were made of planks. The bottoms were flat."

Fox's arm slackens, and my father lets go his grip.

"The sort of boats the Roman army uses in shallow water," Fox says. Then his voice booms. "We allowed the Romans to set foot on our island. We grow rich feeding and housing those who enslave us, those who seek to cut down our lawmakers, our historians, our astronomers, our philosophers, those high priests who divine the will of the gods."

His hard gaze shifts to my father. Fox raises an eyebrow, as if to question my father's familiarity with such treasonous trade.

I look to Hunter, who had threatened, who had said Fox might find out about the Roman tent pegs. I cling to the idea that even Hunter would not stoop so low, but guilty eyes flit from the small family he has jeopardized. Those eyes stay put on his feet, and my already trotting heart gallops.

"Go," Fox thunders. "All of you."

As the tradesmen skitter from my alcove's entryway, Fox retreats from the halo of light.

He begins treading to and fro at the firepit, halts to add kindling, to blow until it is caught, and then returns to pacing. My family huddles close on my pallet, my mother on one side of my curled body, and my father on the other. She strokes my brow and he, my back. Twice their fingers interlace. The second time they keep them that way, bound together over my deformed hip, and a restless sleep comes.

Fox leaves with first light. I hear the whinnies and blusters of his horse and after that the fading clatter of galloping hooves. I shift, stretch so that I can reach the woolen partition screening my parents from my view. I lift the bottom edge just as my mother gathers her skirt and settles onto her knees, at the spot directly facing my father. I can see only his back, hunched forward as he sits on a bench. He pats the spot beside him, and when she does not so much as lift her red-rimmed, swollen eyes, he touches her arm. But after such a night, she is oblivious to his invitation and continues to kneel. "He'll be back," my father says.

"Yes."

"We don't have a lot of time."

I wait for my parents to tip their heads together, to speculate and concoct what exactly Fox knows about the tent pegs, what revenge he might seek, to question where he has fled, whether he might be galloping home to Sacred Isle, whether we might be rid of him and the great anxiety he has brought to all our lives. But they do not. No, my mother puts her face in her hands, shakes her head. "I've deceived you, Smith," she says. "Hobble's imperfection is my punishment."

I am reminded of the confession she did not make—interrupted by a lightning strike—the morning after Feeble departed.

"Devout?"

"It was a long time ago," she continues. "I was desperate for Arc."

They rarely speak of Arc, and as she says his name, I focus my mind, trying to bring shape to mist.

"I'd started to forget him."

"Devout," he says, shaking his head. "I don't want to hear."

I glimpse something then. A truth. My father's wariness—his mind slipping to Arc when he hears my mother's nighttime sighs— is not unfounded. Even gone from our midst, Arc intrudes.

I let the woolen partition fall, shimmy deep beneath the pallet coverings. "Stop," I whisper. "Leave him alone."

Swallowing sobs, she says, "I was broken with grief. I wanted to be lifted to Otherworld."

The bench creaks as my father stands. Rushes swish. Feet clomp. "I said I don't want to hear." His voice is a whisper hollered through gritted teeth. The door whooshes open, thumps shut behind his back.

27.

DEVOUT

≈≈≈

EACH DAYBREAK DEVOUT BLINKED her eyes open to a moment of oblivion before she remembered what she had forgotten during a dreamless night. How many times would she wake astonished? How was it that the vast emptiness felt wholly new when she had experienced the same emptiness yesterday and the day before that? How was it that the present moment, no different from the moment just passed, seemed the first moment she fully knew the loss of Arc?

He came to her in morning light, an image as disturbing as it had been the day before: Blank eyes. A shackled neck. A Roman spear tipped to his shoulder blade, daring him to stray from the parade of tribesmen trudging southeast, prodding him to board the ship that would carry him to some distant place. Old Hunter had come to her roundhouse, had said he released her from the bond of union. Arc, he said, was departed to Otherworld, or as good as departed to Otherworld. He drowned or the Romans took him. Either way they had seen the last of him. She wrapped her arms over her face, shuddered with cold, despite a woolen blanket, heaped furs. Her breath felt shallow, her gut hollow, her limbs weak—as though her flesh cowered, withered. She knew the sensation. Grief, she thought, felt like fear.

How was it the bog dwellers went on? Her mother, who lost her mate. Old Man, who lost all. The hand, who produced no milk, who had cradled her fading child. Walker, who had witnessed the unfathomable, her own son's throat slit. The easy answer was to decide Devout's grief surpassed theirs, but had not Old Man lain with his mate twenty-six years? Had not her mother described the blackness she had sunk into for a period of time? To think of her suffering as comparable to Walker's was indulgent. Devout's grief was commonplace. The gods were cold, without heart. And the Romans? Fiends. Demons, the lot of them. She could murder now, could plunge a dagger, cut open a heart.

Her mother stroked Devout's brow. "I understand," she said. "I do, but you must get up." She looped her arm around Devout's and urged her to sitting. "I had you to care for. I had no choice. Now, come have some broth by the fire."

"I'm queasy," Devout said, though it was untrue.

Light came to her mother's eyes, and Devout realized her mistake. Even now, she bled, as she always would with each new moon.

HER MOTHER HAD COME to the bog, and Old Hunter and Young Smith, too, carrying rushlights. They saw the toppled bucket, and then out on the ice, midway to open water, the shadow of crumpled Devout. They paused, drawing Begetter's wheel in midair, putting their hands on their chests, all except her mother, who stepped onto the ice and did not hesitate until she was bent over her child, a cheek pressed between her shoulder blades.

Old Hunter held out an arm, barring Young Smith from following. "The ice is thin," he said.

Young Smith maneuvered around him, went onto the ice. He breathed his warm breath into the gap between Devout's cheek and the ice, all the while prodding with his fingers, whisper by whisper freeing her skin.

"Leave me be," she said, between sobs. "Leave me to Otherworld." She knew self-pity formed the words. She had had her chance to step into the black pool.

Once she was on her feet with Young Smith supporting her by the waist, she managed between sobs to say, "The demon Romans took him."

Old Hunter was cold and had no time for a hand's hysteria, particularly not if Romans skulked nearby. Clouds had drifted in and obscured the moon, and when Devout was unable to immediately find the patch of hobnail-pitted snow, he said, "He shouldn't have been fishing with the ice so thin. We're asking for the same fate out here now."

"You need a fire, warm broth," Young Smith said and wrapped his arm more tightly around quaking Devout. "I'll come back in the morning."

But in the morning, the snow was gone along with any trace of the Romans, any trace of Arc swallowed up by the frigid water of Black Lake.

After her mother tried to coax Devout from her pallet, the wretched girl lay there, telling herself to get up, but she neither pushed back the covers nor took a cup of broth by the fire. When she finally rose, it was because Sullen had come into the roundhouse, looking stricken, with Singer holding her by the arm. She stepped forward, ripe with child. "My water spilled at daybreak but—" She waved a hand across the hard mound of her belly.

"She is your friend," Singer said, his voice insistent. "You're a healer, and you're obliged to help."

Once Devout would have counted Sullen's arrival at this particular moment, a moment when she needed to be prodded from her pallet, a blessing orchestrated by the gods, but Devout had turned wise on the ice. The gods did not care whether she rose from her pallet. She kept her face brave as she ground the dried raspberry leaves that would bring on labor, as Sullen swallowed the ground leaves. "Go back to your roundhouse," Devout said. "Rest. You'll need your strength."

She looked longingly to her pallet but turned away and poured water into a large cauldron and hung it over the fire so that she might wash away the sweat and grime and stink collected on her body in the moon since Arc was lost.

As FALLOW DREW to an end, Devout prevailed, making her teas and poultices, teaching the children to forage for sorrel and chickweed, assisting Sullen when one of her breasts grew red and swollen and hot to the touch. Had Devout fully given up on Arc? Undeniably. Earlier on, she had sometimes let her mind wander to a joyous moment when he would inexplicably emerge thin and bedraggled from the woodland's underbrush, but that fantasy ended when a trader described the merciless Romans setting beasts on slaves for sport and hollering enthusiasm as men were torn limb from limb.

Young Smith came to the roundhouse and handed her an iron pestle that fit so beautifully into her fist that she knew he had made close examination of her hands. That evening the bog dweller maidens would eat boar and dance and receive trinkets as they celebrated the Feast of Purification. "No one knows whether you're coming tonight," he said, "and so, well, I thought—"

"Ah," Old Man said, once Young Smith was gone. "He's still besotted and makes his intentions known."

"You make something of nothing," Devout said. "He has little work."

Her mother cajoled. "You should go tonight." She said how her back ached, how her strength waned. "I have you for my old age, but you—" she said and drew her brow into the knot that suggested the uncertain fate of a widow hand with only a mother as kin, particularly a widow hand who had gone unblessed eight moons.

"I can't," Devout said. Her mother did not know the evenings she spent on the causeway, thighs pulled into her chest, forehead dropped to her knees. She did not know the way Devout's shoulders shuddered and heaved. She did not know the bit of nettle Devout swallowed each day, how she said "Today I receive Arc" in a sort of reenactment of the afternoon he had become her mate. She did not know how studiously Devout avoided the shelf holding the bowl he preferred, the cup he had made from a horn, the leather sling he had fashioned for carrying wood. She would not open the rush basket where he kept his hooks and traps and an old shoe so that he could, in happier times, slice free a strip of leather when he needed a new lace. She slept facing outward on the pallet's edge, when once she wanted only to open her eyes to his slumbering face. She would never again trek Edge, could not bear passing a mossy glade or gritstone outcrop where she had lain with him. Certainly she could not bear Arc's sweet violets. The familiar dredged up memories, and memories led to sorrow, vast and flooding.

"Young Smith is a man and won't wait," her mother said.

Devout went to walk in the woodland and to instruct herself to smile easily, to laugh. She barred herself from retracing her steps until she felt firm in her resolve to be light at that evening's festivities. When finally she reached the clearing, she spied the half-dozen maidens collecting for the feast just outside the Smith roundhouse door. Young Smith's mother handed over a single flagon of middling size.

As the girls filed into the roundhouse, Devout—no longer a maiden—stayed put in the clearing. There had been debate about whether she would be permitted to attend the feast. But released from the bond of union, she was eligible to take a mate, and Old Hunter had noted the surplus of young men at Black Lake. Her mind drifted to the bed of sweet violets, presented to her by Arc on that same day two years earlier. She struggled, then, blinking back tears, working to keep them from spilling onto her cheeks. Not today. Not now, not when Young Smith's mother had left the roundhouse and appeared to be approaching Devout. She gathered her strength.

"It was I who argued against you joining in tonight," she said. As she spoke, she had put her hand on Devout's arm, a benevolent gesture as far as anyone watching could tell, but the message delivered was anything but: The sky would collapse before she let her son take Devout as a mate.

As Young Smith's mother wandered off, relief swept through Devout. She would have neither to laugh nor to pretend. She could put away the worry of someday enduring Young Smith's hands on places that belonged to Arc. She would not lie with Young Smith, eyes pressed shut, all the while thinking of another. She would have no part in draining his good heart drop by drop.

———

LATE IN THE EVENING, Young Smith approached her amid the swell of Singer's drum and voices bolstered by mead and wheaten beer. "Enjoying yourself, Devout?"

"I make poor company."

"You're ailing, almost like a bird with a broken wing." He sipped from his mug. "You need someone to provide—sheltering and feeding until you're back to full strength."

The idea was appealing—herself an ailing bird, her every concern attended to until her bent wing grew straight.

"The bird would come to know the goodness of her caretaker," he said.

She dropped her gaze, and he ducked lower so that she could not avoid his eyes.

"She wouldn't want to fly away once she could," he said.

"The mead is making you brave."

"Some things need to be said, Devout."

In that moment, he was self-assured, bold enough to think he might defy a mother known to be fierce. But what might daybreak bring?

"I know what you think." He looked her directly in the face. "I won't bend to her. She forbade the pestle."

IN THE DAYS that followed, Old Man told Devout of the ranting Cook described to him, of a pottery flagon hurled by Young Smith's mother and smashed at his feet. She howled that Devout was barren. Eight moons and no child! She slapped her hand on the table and spoke of Sullen, the child suckling at her breast while Devout's belly remained empty as the fields in Fallow, her breasts dry as chaff. Was Young Smith a fool? she wanted to know. He had been hood-winked by a hand's great beauty, beauty that would fade. Did he not understand his clan's dubious position? And what of the old edict? she said. He knew as well as she that no tribesman could take a barren woman as his mate. Who did he think would till the soil and mine the ore and shape the knives and fish the rivers, if young men put their seed into vessels too brittle to sustain a child?

"He argues that you aren't barren," Old Man said. "He said he's got all the proof he needs in the old mine. Cook tells me that the old woman hollered back that she didn't care about childhood whims."

Devout wrung her hands, remembered the footsteps on the causeway, her certainty she and Arc had heard their child. How easy it was to attach meaning to something that foretold nothing at all.

Old Man said, "Young Smith sent for a druid. He told her the druid would divine your child."

Alarm rose that a druid would come, that she would be called to stand before him. She stiffened at the thought that Young Smith was desperate enough to risk enticing a druid to Black Lake. "A druid won't come. They're in hiding. All the traders say so."

"Young Smith packed up a set of silver goblets as payment," Old Man said. "And now a trader is off to Sacred Isle with a laden sack."

"You think those goblets are bribery enough?"

"Old Smith made them," he said, "the finest in the household, decorated with a band of leaping deer." He leaned close, lowered his voice to a whisper. "Apparently the old woman snatched a goblet from the sack and threatened to club Young Smith if he tried to get it back."

Devout pulled her bottom lip into her mouth, held it clamped between her teeth.

28.

DEVOUT

~~~

THE BOG DWELLERS WOKE IN the nighttime to the sound of hooves against the earth. They edged open doors to find a druid discarding the black hooded cloak that masked his white robe. Fingers flew to anxious lips—never mind that Young Smith had sent for him. The last of his kind to call had toppled Lark onto the stone altar and the one before that had goaded the Smith men into slaughter by Roman steel.

Midmorning, Young Smith's mother came for Devout. Although the clearing was strewn with puddles, she strode a step or two ahead of Devout, never deviating from the straight line leading to the Smith roundhouse. Devout's legs were weak as she sidestepped puddles and dodged the woman's kicked-up spray.

Devout balanced on one foot just inside the Smiths' doorway, scraping wet mud from a sodden shoe with a stick. How was she to stand before a druid and not collapse from fear? How was she to endure his moments of deliberation, let alone the judgment he would make? Divined as evermore forsaken by Mother Earth, evermore unblessed, she would live out her days without the security of a tradesman. That she could bear. But to never know an infant cradled at her breast, to never hold the hand of a tottering child, a child calling out *willow herb* and *cowbane* as they passed each bloom? She soothed herself with the idea that whether she stayed put with her mother or moved her skin cape, the fine checked dress sewn from Crone's gift, and the rough woolen one she wore in the fields to the Smith roundhouse was of no consequence. The Romans had captured her happiness, kept it shackled in some distant place, never to return.

"Come closer, girl," the druid said.

She went to him, seated on a low bench with a thick layer of sheepskin. The small table before him was loaded with a platter of bread, nuts, and cheese; a second, heaped with meat; a bowl of steaming lentils; another of soup; another of greens. As he lifted a silver goblet rimmed with a band of leaping deer, she thought of the browbeating Old Man had described.

The druid ate carefully, and Devout stood still, her hands clutched beneath her cape. When she risked a glimpse, his gaze was on her, and she averted her eyes. Old Man had told her a trick of deciphering temperament: Lines deeper on the forehead than those radiating from the eyes meant a tendency to scowl rather than to laugh. In that snatched glimpse, she saw a thin beard more gray than white, hollow cheeks, eyes shadowed by drooping folds of skin, a smooth brow.

"You shiver," he said.

"Yes." The druid did not suggest she warm herself at the fire.

As the remaining nine members of the Smith clan gathered behind her, she dared not turn. She wrung her hands, heard breath, rushes stirred by moving feet, a blown nose, a whimper, the threat of pallets for a pair of children unable to keep still. She thought of Young Smith, his shoulders so broad now, so able. She thought of gritstone and a halo of light, of him kneeling beside her in the old mine as he traced the arc of the circle enclosing the stick figures etched into the wall.

"Devout, an earnest name." The druid shifted, leaning slightly toward her. "A well-deserved name?"

"I'm not without fault."

He sat back on the bench, folded his arms over his chest, and ordered the table cleared. Once the task was accomplished, he beckoned her still closer. "Your barrenness is in question," he said. His eyes slid over the emptiness between her hips. "They tell me you joined in union eight moons and yet remained unblessed."

"I'd been unwell the Fallow before."

The noise of a throat cleared came from behind, and then Young Smith's mother's voice. "Mother Earth is greater than a girl's weakness."

The druid's gaze left Devout, and those lines that marked him as unkindly appeared on his brow.

"Mother Earth is all-powerful," Devout said, hardly above a whisper. She touched her lips, the rush-strewn ground.

"A name well earned," he said, stroking his beard. "Mine is Truth, for it is what I speak."

In each palm, he cradled a bronze object, like midsize spoons in shape but with shortened handles. A small hole was punched through the bowl of one. The perforated spoon, he said, would hold the question being asked. Devout's query, he called it, that question he would put to the gods. Her knees felt weak, as though the sinew holding the bones in place had gone slack, and she gripped the supporting timber beside her, steadying herself.

From behind her came huffed breath—a mother's disgust. Devout let go the timber.

The second spoon's bowl was engraved with a cross that divided it into four quadrants. "This one gives sight," Truth said, raising the engraved spoon.

He took her hand in his and produced a small blade. Before she had a moment to consider his intent, he cut into the pad of her middle finger. He shifted a tiny bronze cup into position to catch the trickling blood. Her finger was bound with a strip of linen, and then the linen tied in a knot.

He glanced up from beneath the folds of skin draping his eyes. She thought she saw merriment, though it was but a flicker.

He turned the perforated spoon over and placed its concave face over the engraved spoon. The result was like a mussel with its two halves shut tight. He gave her a thin reed. "Suck a small amount of blood into the reed."

In her desire to comply, she was overzealous and tasted iron.

"Now," Truth said, "align the reed with the hole"—he tapped the small perforation in the upper spoon— "and blow."

With a small puff—she would not be overzealous this time—she blew the blood through the perforation and into the hollow between the two spoons.

He opened the spoons and examined the pattern of the splattered blood while she held her breath, one long last moment when she was suspended in the world, ignorant of some great detail of her life.

His finger tapped the engraved spoon's rim. The bowl was the year, he said, and each quadrant a season. The quadrant splattered with blood—the only quadrant marked by so much as a speck—was Growth.

Truth lifted the palm holding the spoon and extended his arm so that the onlookers behind Devout could see what she had. "Her child"—his gaze shifted and she turned to see Young Smith's mother on the receiving end of his words—"will be born in the season of Growth."

He set down his spoons.

29

ᛏHOBBLE

‿‿‿

M Y FATHER STAYS ALL DAY in the forge. When he returns at nightfall, neither of my parents has forgotten
that she spoke of Arc earlier and they remain distant
from each other through the evening, quiet at the firepit. My mother
is overly considerate with offers to fill a mug, to fetch a woolen covering, and gives wide berth as my father fuels and pokes the fire. All
the while, my mind churns. Fox will return, and I will kneel before
him, a runt who promises the futility of rebellion, who promises
druid slaughter. My father—who aids the Romans—will drop to his
knees alongside me, an enemy now, too. And what might all of it
bring about? How might it end?

Eventually my father, mother, and I retreat to our pallets. I listen
to their breaths and wonder if I detect slumber no matter that a
druid schemes: How best to deal with a naysaying runt, a treasonous
blacksmith? I finally drift off to the comforting thought of Fox on
the shore of Sacred Isle, arms raised overhead as his neck is slit.

The second nightfall of Fox's absence, the moment my father lies back on the pallet, I hear my mother whisper words I cannot make out. Woolen blankets begin to stir and breaths to deepen. I hear the tender sound of lips and tongues and wet. Lovemaking is useful, then, in begging forgiveness for pining the lost mate who fed her squirrel, who had not given her a child.

By daybreak I have mellowed and begin to question whether the intimacy of the evening before was not solely an act of contrition. I hover on the edge of believing the mate my father feeds and shelters and wholeheartedly loves has come to know his goodness. Of Arc she had said, "I'd started to forget him," and it seems to me that my mother has not remained impervious to my father's charms, that Arc had in fact slipped away from her—as my father warmed her night tunic before the fire, as he placed tender lips against her skin, as he brought a flagon of cold water to her in the field, as he waited ever patient for her love.

The idea stays with me into the evening, bringing a scrap of light to a day of foreboding, a day of looking southwest, of straining to hear the low drum of hooves against the earth. I keep up the surveillance as I return from the spring with a yoke across my shoulders and a slopping bucket weighting each end. My eyes sweep the clearing, and I stagger backward a step. "Luck?" I say, hardly above a whisper.

At the far reach of the clearing, he has dismounted a horse. He pats the beast's neck, as he surveys his surroundings, surely questioning whether he might find my father inside the walled forge. Why has he come? Even with a horse, we must be a half day from Hill Fort. I slip the yoke from my shoulders, toppling a bucket, and run toward him, deviating from my beeline only to thump the forge's door. My father appears and, quick as lightning, he is on my heels, loping toward Luck.

The men embrace, grin, embrace a second time. Luck ruffles my hair. Then my father throws open his palms. "Why?" he says. "Why are you here?"

With a brief tilt of his head, Luck indicates the bog dwellers emerging from their roundhouses. They peer and point toward the three of us, then walk in the direction of the curiosity just arrived at Black Lake. "We've only got a moment." He exhales through fluttering lips. "I had business with a nearby salt maker and thought I should come. A druid called on me yesterday, a druid called Fox."

My father's face collapses.

Luck forces a smile and then knocks my father's arms. "Know how I answered when he asked who I knew at Black Lake?" Luck continues. "I said, 'Black Lake? I think I know the place, in the east, near Londinium.' That druid hurled an oil lamp, kicked over a stack of pottery. 'Oh, wait,' I said. 'I was thinking of Black Wood.'"

His face turns serious, and he clasps my father's shoulder.

"I was steady in my denial, Smith. I did not expose you. But that druid, he was as unrelenting as fate. He stopped harassing me only when the marketplace erupted. That turmoil—the arrival of grave news—saved the both of us."

"For the time being," my father says, shaking his head. "What news?"

But Luck does not answer, for the bog dwellers are close now, and my mother, too. They look our guest up and down. A tribesman who lacks the handcart of a trader? Who possesses wealth enough to own a horse?

"I'm called Loyal," Luck says, without hesitation. "I come from Timber Bridge with news."

"First, you'll rest." My father takes the horse's reins. "Come."

"There isn't daylight enough." Luck cannot linger in a place he has denied knowing, not with Fox's uncertain whereabouts.

Luck steps closer to the waiting crowd, makes his face solemn. "They say ten thousand Roman warriors marched on Sacred Isle. They say every druid present on that small island was cut down by Roman steel."

It is as I said, then. Though my parents and Seconds and perhaps Sliver and Pocks, too, do not doubt my gift, though I do not doubt it myself, I brim with alarm and edge closer to my father.

Bog dwellers reel, put the heels of their palms against their fore-heads, call out to Protector. Their palms shift to their chests. "Blessed be Begetter," they say. "Blessed be his flock." Like me, my mother knew the massacre would come, and yet her head slowly wags *no*.

The bog dwellers' eyes begin to settle. One pair at a time, eyes land on me and hold fast. Comprehension flickers, catches, burns bright in alert faces. I see it in the way Hunter nods and strokes his chin. Almost certainly he is recalling some instance where I showed myself a true seer, like that time a stag stepped into the clearing after I told him to ready his spear. I see realization come to Shepherd, too. He whispers to his eldest son, reminding him of further evidence—perhaps my mother's claim that I was a seer the day Fox first arrived. Tanner and his mate share the sort of glance that passes between mates thinking the same thought, and I can guess the thought—that the news of the massacre I foretold provides firm proof. Sullen shifts her hand to cover her heart. She knows I saw tribesmen underfoot, that vision reported to her by Sliver and Pocks, that promise of certain end for any tribesman goaded into rebellion. For a moment I wonder who beyond Sullen, her girls, and Seconds knows about that prophecy. Then Carpenter flings the chisel gripped in his fist to his feet. "Hobble's a seer," he says. "You've made it indisputable." He gestures toward Luck, the news he brought. "Fox and his lunatic rebellion. He should heed her every word."

"Fox knows what she saw," Sullen says.

"He chooses what he believes," Seconds says.

"Maybe he isn't coming back," Sliver says. "Maybe he's been cut down." Her eyes are on me, her eyebrows lifted with the question she does not speak: In the vision of the massacre, had I witnessed Fox's demise?

I shake my head. That vision had revealed nothing of Fox. He was not on Sacred Isle but rather in Hill Fort, hounding Luck, when news of the massacre arrived. With that small shake, a newly proven prophetess puts to rest for an entire settlement any notion that we are rid of Fox.

"Chieftain should be told what Hobble saw," Carpenter says. "He should know rebellion will end in catastrophe."

"Not even Chieftain will cross a druid," Hunter says.

"He could rally the other chieftains," Carpenter says. He turns to Luck. "You've got a horse. Hill Fort is just beyond Timber Bridge. You could convince Chieftain to come at once to Black Lake." He sweeps an arm toward the gathered crowd. "All of us could vouch for Hobble. All of us know she foretold the sea turned red at Sacred Isle."

Luck holds up a palm. "Wait," he says. "You're saying—" His fingers reach but stop short of my shoulder. "You're saying Hobble foretold the druid massacre? You're saying she foretells the defeat of their rebellion?"

Carpenter nods amid a flock of bobbing chins.

"You're certain?"

"As certain as wanderers' star," Carpenter says.

Luck looks to my father. Without my father's confirmation, I remain a maiden soothsayer in a remote settlement, with a narrow audience, narrow credibility.

"Smith?" Luck says. "Hobble is a seer? Is it true?"

The tiny hairs at the nape of my neck bristle straight.

My father nods a whisper of a nod.

30.

ᴴHOBBLE

~~~~

FOX RETURNS AT NIGHTFALL. He does not speak—neither as I bring him a cloth and a bowl of warm water so that he might wipe the dust from his face, nor as he swallows the mead my mother puts before him. My father's eyes follow him as he sits—glowering—then stands, then circles the firepit, then sits again. The hand holding the cloth falls to a table, as if cleaning himself is too inconsequential a task for such a night.

"It is as Hobble described," he finally says, "my brethren cut down on the shore of Sacred Isle." His eyes fix on my father, and he continues: "The Romans, after that slaughter, moved like a giant net over the whole of Sacred Isle, its wheat fields and low hills and cliffs plunging to a blue sea without end. They clouted doors from hinges, toppled looms so that blankets mingled with the entrails spilled onto earthen floors. They hauled thatch into the sacred groves, set aflame the ancient oaks, the pyres of piled druids. The druid who found me, who chewed my meat—an invalid, without the strength to lift himself from a pallet—his limbs were severed from his body and his fingers, too. They were shoved into his mouth."

He gets up, makes his way to my father.

"You!" Fox hammers a finger against my father's chest. "You and your Roman tent pegs. You are as responsible as any Roman."

My father slowly lifts his shoulders in imitation of a man ignorant of Fox's accusation, ignorant of Roman pegs.

Luck had not lingered after my father answered him. He said he would go to Chieftain and left at a gallop, without first embracing my father, who knew him only as a news bearer as far as the bog dwellers were concerned. My father stood a long moment afterward. Then he steered my mother and me into the forge and bolted the door shut behind our backs.

He pried open two crates of finished pegs, loaded those pegs into a dozen linen sacks. He lifted his tunic, strung a rope around his waist, affixed four laden sacks to that rope, and then smoothed his tunic back into place, roughly concealing the bulk. Once my mother and I had copied the effort, the three of us set out and, at the far end of the causeway, dumped the sacks' telltale contents into black water. As we turned to leave, my mother touched my arm. Together we put the heels of our palms to our foreheads and murmured, "Hear me, Protector."

Fox TAKES A FOLD of my father's tunic into his fist. He makes as if to thrust, as if to hurl my father, but in his fury, the druid has misjudged the heft of so muscled a man. He leans close, spits, "To your forge! Now!" When my father offers no objection, Fox's eyes narrow. "You've unburdened yourself," he says and flicks his hand free of the clasped wool.

My father makes no comment, only breathes his long, steady breaths.

A slow grin comes to Fox, the pleasure of a man who has not been outdone. "Hunter will make a declaration. I'll get him now." He hesitates a moment in the doorway. "You'll pay, Smith," he hisses. "I promise you that."

As my father turns to pacing, my mother crouches alongside the bins holding our remedies and selects a small, sealed vessel. As she scrapes the beeswax from the vessel's mouth, the stink of black henbane taints the air. She glances up to see me watching, lays a finger across her lips.

I know black henbane—its urn-shaped pods, the tiny wheat-colored seeds. When I was a child, she had shown me the plant cupped in her palm. "A tea made with the leaves is enough to set a man soaring," she had said. "The strongest magic is in the seeds, though. A dozen and a spirit lifts to Otherworld. More than that and the spirit won't return."

She tilts several dozen seeds from the vessel into a mortar and works her pestle. I watch, frozen, as she taps pulverized seed into the silver goblet, as she fills the goblet with mead, as she returns it to the low table where Fox usually sits at the firepit. Her hands, all the while, remain as composed as the gliding moon.

WHEN FOX RETURNS WITH HUNTER, I do not like the tribesman's face. His chin is lifted, and his cheeks are held rigid as though resisting a satisfied grin. Fox orders the men to the firepit. My father lowers himself to the prized spot on Fox's left, and the druid launches a belly laugh as false as water captured in cupped hands. "There," he says, indicating the spot on his right.

Once Fox is seated, he puts a hand over the goblet's base, as though he might at any moment slide his fingers to the stem and deliver the mead to his mouth. I bite my lip, glance toward my mother—wide-eyed, though dropped onto her knees beneath Mother Earth's cross.

Fox clears his throat. "Hunter has made a serious accusation against Smith—an accusation of treason," he says. "Tonight he will speak his accusation openly, and in doing make his declaration in front of four witnesses." He beckons. "Devout, Hobble, come close."

As we shuffle to the firepit and seat ourselves, his thumb and index finger slide over the goblet's stem, up, then down, then up again. Drink the mead, I holler inside my mind.

Fox sweeps a hand toward Hunter. "Speak," he says.

Hunter nods deeply, as though acquiescing, as though the choice to point a finger were not his. "I saw tent pegs exactly matching Smith's—strange pegs with the blunt end curled into a loop—in the marketplace at Hill Fort. I made inquiries and was assured the pegs are Roman."

"The pegs are superior," my father says. "Tribesmen have adopted them."

"He deals with a man called Luck"—Hunter glances from my father to Fox—"a trader widely known to supply the Roman army."

My father wags his head in slow denial.

Hunter raises his chin further. "Why, then, did that very trader call at Black Lake this afternoon?"

As the grooves in the druid's face deepen, my mother blurts, "Loyal," and his attention snaps to her. "The one who came was called Loyal." She continues, voice quivering, "He was from Timber Bridge and came with news of the massacre."

"And left," Hunter says, "with the intent to tell Chieftain about a maiden prophetess who foretold that massacre."

The druid is on his feet now, fingers clenched into fists. "Luck or Loyal?"

"Luck," Hunter says. "A nose like a buzzard. I've seen him at Hill Fort."

"And what would be the point of this Luck speaking to Chieftain?"

"To entice him to Black Lake."

"For what purpose?" Fox's knuckles protrude, as smooth and white as bone.

Haltingly Hunter says, "So that the bog dwellers might convince him Hobble is a true prophetess." His eyes dart to the door.

With that the druid crosses the firepit, squats in front of me. He balances there, fingers tented, his flush face radiating hostility.

I attempt my father's steady breathing, attempt any breathing, but only manage to suck air as though through a wet cloth.

Then Fox grips my shoulders. He shoves, then yanks, causing my head to jerk forward, then backward. "What did you tell Luck?"

"Nothing. I said nothing."

Hunter's palms push the air, as though urging restraint. Too late, I think. Too late to decide better than to turn a druid against the maiden who prepares your dandelion draft, who brings ease to your mother's old age.

Fox leaves me, returns to Hunter. "What else does Luck know?"

He wags his head back and forth.

Fox's lips draw back from gritted teeth. Eyebrows lower toward his rutted nose. He threads a hand though Hunter's hair, pulls as Hunter's backside parts from the bench. "You deny a druid!"

Hunter twists to face my father, and in doing so, his head tilts. Wet overflows the rims of his eyes. "I am not a brave man," he says and then lifts his face to Fox. "He knows she prophesied defeat. The idea is to sway Chieftain."

A further yank. "To what end?"

Hunter winces, sputters, "So that he might rally all the chieftains against rebellion."

Fox sets Hunter loose with a mighty heave that topples him backward from a low bench to a crumpled heap.

Fox kicks his foot hard into the rushes and then into the underside of a bench, toppling it. When will he grow thirsty, take the mead? I want the goblet drained now, before he topples the table holding it.

He overturns a second and third bench, chest heaving, and then suddenly halts, as if transfixed by some moment that is not now. He circles the firepit in silence—once, twice, three times. Then he looks up from contemplation. "We will not delay further," he says. His mouth twists. "Now is the time."

I grip the bench beneath me.

He continues, explaining that four legions of Roman warriors occupy Britannia, that two remain on Sacred Isle, that another is stationed in the south, and the fourth in the northeast. In their arrogance, the Romans have left their largest town unprotected, ripe for attack. Camulodunum, that place they had named their capital and settled in large numbers, brimmed with advancement—paved roads, according to Luck, and stone temples and marketplaces, a hall where the Romans bathe in large groups. Camulodunum, Fox spits, is a debauched colony of veterans—the worst dogs. The closest Roman legion, he says, that one in the northeast, blights the land a full eight days' march from the town.

As Fox harangues, my father sidles nearer to where my mother and I huddle on the bench.

Fox paces more, thuds his fist into his palm. His face quivers rage as he describes how the eastern tribesmen have long despised the veterans who robbed them of their farmsteads and spat on them in the street. And now one of the eastern chieftains—a mighty woman called Boudicca—has been publicly flogged, her two maiden daughters raped, her male kin chained and hauled away to be sold. Her great offense: speaking out that half of her newly departed mate's estate belonged to his daughters. "This, when he had willed the other half to Rome," he bellows. "This, when he had been a loyal chieftain, one of the first to swear allegiance to Rome. Her abasement is the final kick. Obedient hound has turned against master. Tribesmen flock to follow Boudicca into battle."

My father drops beside me on the bench. He reaches around my back to my mother and draws both of us snug.

The eastern tribesmen, Fox says, are hungry for the vengeance they are owed and are already gathering in camps and making ready to descend on Camulodunum. "Tomorrow we march. We will unite with our eastern kin."

The gods turned back Julius Caesar, his flocks of warriors, his hundreds of ships; but first, I remember, in every settlement a runt—a human runt—was bludgeoned, garroted, drowned, and bled. I sit still, negotiating with the gods. I will pitch any further tent pegs my father forges into the bog, join my mother in the liberal portions she allots Mother Earth, drop more frequently to my knees. I wait, fingers clenched, body taut.

"I'll make the rounds, command the others to prepare," he says.

"You're exhausted," my mother says. "You must rest. I'll fetch your mead."

"We will make good with the gods at daybreak, before we set out," he says. "With blood we atone for our failings as a people"—he turns, directing his words to my father—"failings that are without precedent."

I swallow. Blink.

"What are you saying?" my mother asks, her voice thin as a reed.

And then, like leaf quitting bough, his gaze falls to me. "We will look to the old ways."

How long, how diligently I have clung to the idea that I possess a gift, that I am unique, not because I am a runt, but because I see what others do not. I am chosen, I told myself, and waited to see the splendor that would unfold. "You'll outdo me as healer," my mother had said. "You have your gift." And Seconds—his face had radiated wonder, admiration that I could foretell what had not yet taken place. But he had turned to saying, "That prophecy—if anyone asks, say you made it up." Through foretelling, I have made myself the enemy of a druid, a druid who will not risk his rebellion halted, who will not permit Luck time to rally Chieftain, who will at daybreak rid himself of a final threat to achieving his rebellion. This is the last moment of my innocence, the last moment before I swallow the truth. There is no benevolent hand, no triumph on the far horizon. This is the moment when I know the reality of my visions. My curse.

My father leaps up. "The fields will sprout in Fallow before any-one is laid out on cold stone." His voice cuts with the severe edge of a sharpened blade. Nostrils flaring, he thrusts his fist into his palm, and I look away from a man I do not know, a man, in this moment, so much like Fox.

The druid's palms turn heavenward. "Don't you see, Smith? It is the will of the gods. They have spoken, and it is divined."

With that he lifts the goblet.

But then his nose wrinkles, his face shudders, drawing back from the tainted mead. On his way to the door, he pauses at the tribute vessel and turns the goblet, spilling its contents onto the day's collected slop.

I look to my mother, find her dropped from the bench onto her knees, rocking now, hands over her heart. "Forgive me," she says, bowing at my feet.

But what am I to forgive? What grave offense stirs her to say "Hobble's imperfection is my punishment" and puts torment on her face and hardens her from accepting my father's love?

What has my mother done?

31

'HOBBLE

~~~

MY FAMILY ENTERS SACRED GROVE as though wading through the thick murk of the bog. The low branches of the ancient oak reach like gnarled fingers. The globes of mistletoe protrude like diseased joints. The canopy above smothers, dense, unrelenting. Moss clings thick and black to the oak, the rotted fallen trees, the boulders marking the perimeter of the place. Darkness hangs at Sacred Grove.

As we take our places in front of the stone altar, I look from bog dweller to bog dweller—my fierce father on my left; my quaking mother next in line; Carpenter and then Tanner after that; scores of weary faces; and last, Fox's, set as iron. He looms on the altar's far side, his skin wiped clean of yesterday's streaked dirt, his body cloaked in an immaculate white robe.

The Shepherds come into the grove, and I count all six sons. As I endeavor to catch sight of the ewe that I know will not follow the boys, I notice others straining to glimpse a trailing ewe and understand that my family is not alone in its fear. My mother grips my father's arm.

My gut roils as my eyes wander over the chiseled slab of cold gritstone, and then over Fox's pristine robe, his hard face. He lays a golden sickle, a square of folded linen, an ax, and a garrote on the altar, and I wonder whether a sickle made for hacking mistletoe would cleanly slit a man's throat. Would it be as useful as the dagger hidden inside my father's breeches? Yes, it is true. Never mind that blades other than those used in sacrifice are not permitted in Sacred Grove, a dagger rests against his hip, held at the ready by his woven belt.

After Fox announced a return to the old ways and left the roundhouse, my father straddled a bench, and took up a sandstone in one hand and that dagger in the other. He sharpened the blade, tested its mercilessness with his thumb, returned to circling stone over iron. Then, finally through with the dagger, he shifted to instructing my mother. "Appear to make ready." he said. "Let the druid think the men will set out in the morning."

I wrapped hard cheese and three loaves in linen, cut slabs of salted pork from the bone, all the while my mind reeling, deliberating a scheme I could not fathom. My mother collected his second pair of breeches, warmest tunic, and two woolen blankets, bound the lot inside his skin cape. The chill had not yet left the turf, and I wondered whether that cape would provide enough warmth as he slept. In my stupor, I had misplaced the idea that my father plotted, that in his fervent mind Fox would not lead the bog dwellers east to unite with the assembled tribesmen.

I hauled the skin-cape bundle to the door, briefly rested my forehead against the wall's wattle and daub. I squatted at the quern, anticipating the comfort of a familiar task, but I felt my father's eyes and looked up. His thoughts came into my mind at that moment. Like a thunderclap, I knew his frustration that my face appeared as blank as snow, his disgruntlement that I appeared unable to prophesy the futility or necessity or folly of a scheme about which I knew nothing beyond a sharpened blade.

Early this morning, before the sun had fully risen, that scheme became less opaque. "Hobble," my father said, "the tribute vessel needs to be emptied." His concern with chores seemed out of place on such a morning, but after a moment, I understood the task was an excuse to direct me away from the roundhouse and Fox. Then, sure enough, as I tipped the slop into the communal pit, my father appeared. From beneath the waist of his breeches, he slid the dagger. "No harm will come to you," he said. "You have my word."

"You'll kill him?" My head wagged wariness. "But the gods?" Somehow a dagger drawn across a druid's throat seemed a greater offense than a goblet of tainted mead.

"I forged them a thousand daggers."

I stared a moment. Did the gods even know about those daggers? Did they care? And what was the point of wondering when no number of forged daggers could make up for the single one concealed at his hip?

"I can't see that there's any other way," he said.

I threw my arms around him and felt his fingers thread my hair, the palm holding me close.

FOX HOISTS HIMSELF into the crotch of the ancient oak, severs a globe of mistletoe with the sickle, lets it fall to the linen a pair of maidens hold open below. He fashions a wreath from the mistletoe, sets it on his head, and puts both hands on the altar. "We have become diseased, a people that turns away from our ancestral ways, that wrongly collaborates with our enemies. The whole head of our people is sick, and the whole heart faint."

He pauses, scowls his loathing for the lot of us, and we shift, minutely drawing away.

"But the gods are merciful," he says. "They have breathed into the ears of my brethren, instructing us in making amends. We will earn their favor and then, on the battlefield, rid ourselves of the plague that has brought us low."

Fox knows my prophecy and yet he proceeds. For a year now, the tribesmen's small resentments have been fed by the druids, transforming a breeze into a gale. Would any druid put himself in the path of that gale, that seething multitude of incited tribesmen? How much easier to proceed—eyes shut, hands over ears—than to take on the tempest they themselves have made. I suppose early on the words were measured, sincere, that with each retelling the story of our enslavement grew more deeply etched into the speaker's mind, that at some point it became impossible to conceive of that gale as anything other than a righteous opportunity to sweep Britannia clean. To put themselves in its path is an idea as inconceivable as a hatched chick returned to inside its shell.

"With blood spilled onto stone altars," he says, "we wash clean our corrupt souls and earn benevolence."

Not a single chin nods in shared opinion. We stand united, leery of spilled blood when there is no ewe.

"On occasions, such as now, when the situation is dire and we have sunk low, the sacrifice demanded of us is of real consequence. Not a boar with a deformed hoof. Not even a ewe with a record of twins."

I look from Hunter to Tanner to Carpenter, from clenching jaw to pursing lips to narrowing eyes. My father's hand shifts to his hip.

"On this day," Fox says, "our offering will be of the highest worth."

My father grips the dagger at his hip, and I feel a shift among the others—bodies tightening.

"The gods demand the firstborn of your First Man," Fox says.

Heads turn in my family's direction. My father pulls the dagger from his hip, holds it out in front, both hands wrapping the grip, the glinting blade cutting the air without the slightest quiver of uncertainty.

My mother's eyes gleam in terror. Her mouth gapes open, shuts, a fish gulping for air.

The bog dwellers part for their First Man, clearing a path to the stone altar, to Fox on the far side.

"Kill him," I whisper.

My mother pitches forward, cries, "Wait, wait!"

She throws her arms around my father's waist. She clings to him, clings with all her might, holds him rooted to earth slick with black moss.

"He means to slaughter our daughter," my father hollers, though she surely understands.

He wrenches his torso to free himself, but still she clings. "My daughter." Her voice breaks. "Mine and Arc's."

My father halts.

She unwraps herself, slower than a drifting cloud. Then she beckons, quaking fingers calling me.

I shuffle near, and she reaches. As she touches the pair of clasps securing the front of my dress to the back at one shoulder, the crescent on the small of my back pulses its strange beat. She unfastens a single clasp, and then the remaining three. I keep my arms tight against my chest to hold the wool in place as the back of my dress falls, revealing a reddish-purple crescent—that long-held secret between my mother and me.

Necks crane. Bog dwellers look from my back to my mother. She draws a fingertip over her cheek in the shape of a crescent. I swallow dumbfounded and wonder how, with my tendency to wonder, to prod, to surmise, I had never thought to ask the reason my mother's first mate was called Arc. With that reminder of the stain that marked his cheek, the bog dwellers swallow and nod recognition, agreement. Yes, that reddish-purple crescent on the small of my back exactly matches Arc's.

My mother collapses to her knees. My father reels. His arms drop. The dagger hangs inert at his side.

32.

DEVOUT

~~~~

EVOUT TOOK YOUNG SMITH AS her mate three days after Truth divined that she would bear a child in Growth.
She had noticed Smith's gait lighten over the moon since,
noticed, too, that he seldom put down the hammer to massage the
shoulder that seemed now to bother him less. When they walked
together, he called out to Young Hunter or Singer and put his hand
on the small of her back, as though to remind them, and perhaps
himself, that he had succeeded in taking her as his mate. He laughed
often and wholeheartedly, and streaks of white now radiated from
the corners of his eyes, marking the tiny crevices of skin hidden
from the sun.

She put her fingers on the streaks and told him they were there.
It was the sort of thing a mate should do, and he reached for her as
he often did, pulling her close. There was a fleeting moment of regret that she had touched the streaks. She whisked away the
realization—as she did when she caught Arc's name nearly fallen
from her lips, or when she lay in Young Smith's embrace, still warm

with exertion, and knew she had closed her eyes to him and let herself believe he was Arc.

At mealtimes Cook served Young Smith, then his mother, and then the two remaining mates of his brothers, after that their broods. Devout was served last, for she was a hand by birth and a hand she remained. It might have meant she chewed gristle and sucked marrow and pried scant meat from bones, that those meals when Cook was careless doling out the portions, she went without a spoonful of chickweed. But Young Smith passed from his plate to hers drumsticks and thighs, tender slices of loin, the thickest fillets. She told him that it was unnecessary, that even marrow was a treat. "You're my mate," he said. "You're a Smith."

Once she said, "Your mother doesn't scold anymore when you give me the choicest cuts. She gave me a length of cloth—woven from dyed wool. She went to Old Hunter on my behalf."

His mother had petitioned Old Hunter, saying that Devout was Black Lake's healer, a prize the bog dwellers could not do without. It was not right, her in the fields daybreak to nightfall, without a moment to prepare her remedies. How would Old Hunter manage without the dandelion draft that kept his face from bloating red like a ewe's forgotten teats? Eventually, he relented, and Devout was told she could leave the fields midafternoon.

"Has she changed toward me?" Devout said.

Young Smith took Devout's hand, enclosed it in the envelope of his palms. "Only the Hunters are above us and only because my father and brothers had the courage they lack. I owe it to my father and brothers to earn back the title of First Man. You can help by having the bearing of a Smith."

"I'm a hand."

"And so you must stand taller."

The bog dwellers would not be fooled by squared shoulders, a long neck. She would work in fields as was her lot, until she grew weak and Old Hunter decided her time of rest had come. It was a possibility, now that she had kin to feed her. Unlike Old Man, she would not take her last breaths in the fields.

"The Smiths will rise again," Young Smith said. His gaze was steady, his focus beyond her.

She slid her hand from between his palms. She could not explain herself if she were asked, only that an uneasiness had come to her that he should want more, that he should plot. "We have enough."

His gaze persisted, steady on some moment that was not now.

"Our pallet is heaped with furs. I have a length of fine cloth. We eat meat."

"You'll have more." He took her hand back into the envelope of his palms.

SHE WENT OFTEN to the bog, more often than was right, and always at nightfall, when the bog dwellers stayed close to their fires. She went without rushlight, prodding roots and rocks with the toe of a shoe and curled into a ball at the causeway's farthest reach, weeping and shuddering no different from the earliest days after Arc disappeared, no different from the nightfall before. Eventually she collapsed onto her side and stared into the mist's thick murk. The exhaustion that accompanied the blubbering had become a prerequisite to her desired state of being neither awake nor asleep. She navigated the narrow band in between, a liminal place where Arc fully inhabited her mind—his long face and watchful eyes, his pale lashes and eyebrows, the gentle curve of the crescent marking his cheek, the fine hairs that matted against the damp of his neck. She could conjure him and with her mind so weary, she knew the heat of his breath on her cheek, the lightness of his palm on her back.

Nightfall came earlier, an infinitesimal progression, unremarkable for days, and then the cumulative shift, when she realized it, was as astonishing to her as waking to the earth blanketed in white. It was like that on the causeway, too. She looked into the mist, recalling the minutia of his face one nightfall. The next it was his hands. After that she remembered the weight. She felt quite distinctly the mound at the base of his thumb.

By daylight she understood that the weight, the mound were remembered from an earlier time, but on the causeway, the texture of her skin altered to gooseflesh beneath his palms. How vivid. How very nearly real. How she wanted more.

She began to construct her days around a gap at nightfall. She rose before the cock crowed and built up the fire and milled the wheat to flour and made the cheese if Cook had put out milk laced with nettle juice to curdle overnight. With both hands, she plucked chickweed and sorrel from the earth, her eyes always a shade ahead, flitting to the next clump. She gathered alone, unhindered by a child's gait, a sister-in-law's desire for talk. Her privacy was complete as she indulged in her daily habit of taking a nettle leaf into her mouth, of saying "Today I receive Arc." At mealtimes she savored little, so busy was she swallowing her meat, in order that she might scour the cauldron with a handful of sand and then, with a clear conscience, leave the soiled plates and bowls. Late afternoon she collected white bryony, hung lesser celandine, ground dried comfrey root. She had become meticulous in monitoring her supplies. Nightfall was for the causeway, and she planned against the duties that could keep her pinned to the hearth, the heartache of needing to unearth comfrey as night fell.

She said nothing when she left the Smith household, neither that her stash of raspberry leaf was low, nor that Sullen's baby needed a dose of meadowsweet rubbed into her gums. If Young Smith wanted to look, he would not know where to start. Crone's shack? Her mother's roundhouse, where she often prepared her drafts and salves? She thought it good fortune now that Young Smith's mother had barred Devout's stinking vessels and rotting herbs from the Smith roundhouse. If he was determined and called but did not find her at her mother's, there were still seven more roundhouses where she might be patting chickweed balm onto a rash or applying a purple loosestrife poultice to a wound. He would not suffer the humiliation of going door-to-door asking for his mate.

Something shifted. The number of evenings Young Smith's mother wanted company increased. Perhaps her mind was in fact altered toward Devout. She had made a gift of the cloth and recently said Devout's cheese was better than Cook's. Once when it poured rain, housebound Devout sat among the others gathered that nightfall—like most every nightfall—in the fire's flickering light. When she looked up, Young Smith's mother was watching, her hands stilled from trimming a cape with fur. "Living among the Smiths suits you," she said. "Your paleness has grown becoming."

Most likely, it was only that she disliked her son so often without his mate at the fire. He sharpened a blade on sandstone or removed burs using a leather strop without the comfort of a mate's light touch on his shoulder, without a cup of water fetched on his behalf. Whatever the reason, the moment Devout pushed herself up from the low table, Young Smith's mother began to make it difficult to do anything other than stay put in the roundhouse. She complained that the ache in her big toe was like a nail pierced through the bone. Might Devout apply the magic so an old woman could be spared?

She needed assistance rinsing her hair with chamomile or untangling a skein of wool. The nightfall she announced Devout's needlework as lacking and said she would teach the girl the skill, Devout grew dismayed. How many nightfalls on the causeway would she miss? She turned to Young Smith, hoping he might read disgruntlement in her face and remind his mother that his mate was a hand who worked in the fields in a dress unadorned with embroidery, or that with her drafts and balms her days were already full to the brim. What she saw were eyes full of pride that she would be taught something as noble as needlework.

She missed three nightfalls in a row, then four. She held a bone needle, licked the wool, passed it through the eye. She rushed, and it meant her stitches varied in length or were wide of the line scratched into the surface of a scrap of hide. She slowed down, held out her work to Young Smith's mother, and though each stitch was of equal length, Devout missed another nightfall on the causeway. The running stitch was but single stitch, Young Smith's mother said. There was the backstitch to learn. Devout learned the backstitch, and another nightfall passed before Young Smith's mother gave a satisfied nod. But then there was the split stitch after that and the stem stitch, the chain stitch. "How many more?" Devout said, jutting her needle into the hide.

Young Smith put a hand on her shoulder, as though to say he understood her weariness, and then disappeared behind a woolen partition. Devout heard a chest creak open, and then he was back, holding out a tiny hide cap. "For our child," he said. "Decorating it might help the needlework feel useful."

Tears brimmed, rolled onto her cheeks, joyful tears that their promised child should wear an adorned cap, sorrowful tears that she was not a better mate, mournful tears that eleven nightfalls had come and gone, that she would sit in the firelight and make the cap a thing of beauty, that she would rush, that her mind would be on completion, the causeway, ridding herself of the task keeping her away.

Devout took the cap from Young Smith, gave in to a sudden urge to touch his cheek.

She selected yarns—the deep yellow of goldenrod, the rusty red of bloodroot, the blue of woad. The running stitch was quickest, the stem stitch best for curved lines, and the chain stitch most pleasing to the eye. She drew her needle around the cap's edge, scoring the place where her first round of stitches would lie. She tied a knot, poked her needle up though the hide, hesitated a moment before arranging her yarn in the way that committed her to the running stitch and less time in the flickering light. Then she poked her needle down and back up again though the hide.

She realized one day she had neglected to take nettle, to say "Today I receive Arc." The next occasion, she could not remember with certainty whether she had forgotten once or twice. Sometimes as she squinted across the clearing to Young Smith in his forge, she glimpsed deep affection, profound tenderness. She had known love as a fever that took hold independent of will, and she gathered might against the unbridled force of it. She plucked a handful of nettle leaves; let the hot throb spread over her tongue, inner cheeks, and gums; denied herself the relief of the dock growing nearby. How could all that had been between her and Arc slip away? How could she let it? Love was not as fleeting as that—ever present one moment, gone the next. She would not retreat from him, fail him. He would not disappear.

She began to lie. With the new moon almost arrived, she said she had valerian root to prepare for the bog dweller women whose menses brought cramps, when in fact her store was ample. Young Smith's mother cocked her head, drew her lips into a tight ring. The night was bright, Devout said. She knew a patch not far from the clearing. Another time, she said Old Man needed a poultice for his knee but stopped short of saying the poultice was already made, that he knew the routine, that she need not slip away.

In between the lies, she spent evenings in the firelight, needle in hand, glancing up to study Young Smith, to see that his thick-lashed eyes were not hazel but rather gray flecked with gold, to appreciate the way he scrutinized a blade and often returned to perfecting it against a strop, to feel a spreading warmth as he heaved a yelping, laughing nephew over his shoulder and spun him around.

She had spent thirteen consecutive nightfalls away from the causeway before the first lie, eight before the next, after that six. Even so, on the causeway, as she recalled the minutia of Arc's face and hands and held them in her mind, her teeth gritted with effort. She wept, her usual prelude to invoking him, but her grief was fraught as she mourned the passage of yet another fruitless nightfall. She wanted to club her fist against the timbers, but, no, clubbing was not part of the chain that drew him close those other times. She returned to the clearing dejected, probing the exact sequence of those other nightfalls, the duration of her tears, the position of her knees as she rolled onto her side. She would do better, would shorten the gap before the next lie. She would not rush on the causeway, would not grasp. She would let the feeling of Arc come to her. But the next time and the time after that her skin did not alter to goose-flesh. He was slipping away, nudged little by little as Young Smith drew close, took up residence in her heart. She held her face in her palms.

The Night of the Departed approached, that threshold when Harvest gave way to cold, barren Fallow. On that night, the gates between this world and the next stood ajar, and the spirits of fore-fathers and lost children and mates lingered close. The bog dwellers congregated on the shore of Black Lake, reached for their departed loved ones, drew them near. That night, when it came, would be Devout's best chance to hold tight to fading Arc. Her breath caught a moment, snagged by the realization that his presence on the Night of the Departed would imply that he dwelt in Otherworld rather than some corner of the Roman Empire.

She touched her lips, the earth. At least she would know.

33.

DEVOUT

~~~

DEVOUT CLUTCHED the small hide pouch hidden between the folds of her dress, the seeds within. Had Crone foreseen this Night of the Departed? She had instructed the girl in black henbane's collection and preservation, how to hang a lone plant, giving the leaves a chance to escape rot. She had held a pouch of the seeds tight in her fist that last night. It was as though, even after all the instruction, Crone would not chance Devout neglecting to maintain the stock, as though she knew the severity with which Devout would one day yearn. It was a gift—that pouch, a gift given as Crone took her last breath.

Devout, Young Smith, and his kin joined the bog dwellers amassed on a high patch of Black Lake's shore, each clan spreading woolen blankets, unpacking plates and mugs. They feasted on the sheep culled from the flock as unworthy of feed through Fallow, the honey-slathered bread provided by the Carpenters, a roe deer speared by Young Hunter, the wheaten beer acquired by the Smiths in exchange for a partition Devout had unbound from the rafters and beat clean with a stick. "Still plenty of alcoves for what will come," Young Smith's mother had said and gestured toward Devout's belly, still awaiting the foretold child.

The rushlights made a pretty sight, staked into the ground, their flames reflected on the pool's flat water and then, when a fish came to the surface, shimmering on tiny rippling waves. There was a single rushlight different from the rest, as there always was, burning brightly inside the skull Old Hunter had removed from over his door and brought to the bog for the night. The effect was chilling—two bright recesses where once there were eyes, another shaped like a linden leaf where once there was a nose, a bright grinning mouth where once there were teeth, and at the temple a last bright void where Old Hunter's spear had entered the skull. Setting eyes on that ghoulish, glowing face, the dark fairies flitted afar, clearing the way for tranquility as forefathers were named and praise given and blessings sought, as Old Man spilled tears, as Walker remembered Lark's song, as the hand who was refused milk by Old Tanner's mate pitched bits of roe deer into the bog for her starved child. Devout took in the sidelong glances, the whispered words of the gathered bog dwellers. How might a hand, newly joined in union to a tradesman, pay homage on this first Night of the Departed since her beloved disappeared?

Devout stayed late, biding her time until the causeway was hers alone. Young Smith had not denied her. He had not put his hand on her shoulder and said, "It's time," but rather had reached toward her, seen her separateness from him, and taken his hand away. He withdrew a single step and cleared his throat. When she did not stir, he took another step and then another.

She tipped the pouch over her open hand and licked a dozen black henbane seeds from her palm. She had never so much as tasted a single seed, and as she ground her molars—knowing that the grinding would hasten the magic—her face knotted with the bitter pungency. She lay back on the causeway's rough timbers, her tongue drawing the acrid mash from her teeth, her gums, and pushing it to the back of her mouth. As she swallowed, she looked right and left. Six rushlights still burned on the shore.

Her eyes closed, and when she opened them the rushlights were spent and the mist was thick. Her head rolled to one side. Her eyelids fluttered shut. The mist grew heavier, at first like a blanket and then like heaped furs. She felt warmth on her cheek, like breath. Her skin grew damp beneath the exhalations. She waited until the feeling of heaped furs grew uneven, until she felt the heaviness of hips, thighs over her own. Fingers traced the ridge of her collarbone. She turned her face ever so slightly toward them. Then a palm cupped her cheek, and she felt fingertips—familiar, dry, slightly ragged, like they rolled grains of sand over her skin.

She opened her eyes and looked beyond the mist to the stars, to the pinpricks of light swirling, coalescing, drawing close. They became like two eyes, and then like Arc's eyes—watchful, framed by pale lashes, pale eyebrows. She put two fingers just below one of the eyes, felt the resistance of flesh, the bone beneath. She traced the reddish-purple crescent on his cheek.

She felt the sensation of soaring, her spirit leaving her body, watching from above as Arc unclasped her dress and slipped it from her shoulders, past her ribs, her waist, her hips, her knees, her ankles, and yet she could feel rough wool sliding over her skin, his strong hands, his wet mouth, his hard sex, her parted thighs and tilted hips, the moment he entered her, and they became one. He was slow and gentle, and she clung to him, her face buried in the crook of his neck. She pulled him closer, deeper, until it was not possible to be any closer than they were.

SHE WOKE ON the causeway to bottomless night and her dress clasped at her shoulders, her mouth dry, her tongue thick. She rolled onto her side, lay with her cheek resting against her outstretched arm before getting to her feet.

She could detect no warmth, no dampness between her legs, no lingering sensation of friction, no tenderness. Still Arc's watchful eyes, the ragged skin of his fingers had been so tangible, more than a recollection, more than a window briefly opened to an earlier time. She knew in that moment that Arc had succumbed to Roman brutality, that she had called him to her from Otherworld. She had lain with him on the causeway, rapturous, though Young Smith was now her mate.

Young Smith slept alone on their pallet or, more likely, was just now blinking into the blackness of night, wondering how time could slow, how the sun had not risen, how the cock had not crowed. Why had she not returned? Would she forever pine for her lost mate? Had he been a fool to think a warm nest could mend an ailing bird?

She thought of the amulet, her claim to have offered it to Mother Earth. She remembered an uncertain feeling, the idea that with that first lie she had thrown open the door to deceit. She wiped tears from her cheeks. She would push and shove and lean her full weight into that heavy door. By will, she would force it shut and become the mate so worthy a man deserved. Never again would she reach for Arc on the causeway, seek the weight of his hands on her skin. Never again would she spend a Night of the Departed apart from Young

Smith. Rather she would sit with him in the evenings, her thigh against his, and touch his arm when she brushed past him in the doorway, at the firepit. She would mill his wheat and mend his breeches with care and linger at the low wall of his forge, showing an interest in glowing iron and bellows and she knew not what, but she would learn. She understood now that she had felt herself slipping toward love as she gazed across the distance to Young Smith in his forge. She would let herself fall. She would lie back and part her knees, let desire mount, peak, topple to a lingering glow.

She would give him a child as the druid had divined.

34.

HOBBLE

≈

No BOG DWELLER looks at my father alongside the stone altar, alongside Fox. No one dares. Almost certainly, same as me, same as him, they stand in the ancient oak's shadow counting the moons between Arc's disappearance, a dark evening early in Fallow, and my birth, a warm afternoon with the sun crowning high in the sky. The season was Growth, but not the one that followed Arc's disappearance. Rather, the one after that. Close to twenty moons. How very strange. How very difficult to swallow. But still, there is the telltale mark on the small of my back, and I have proven myself uncanny, a prophetess. And everyone knows the rumors about the extended period when my mother disappeared almost nightly, when she keened on the causeway reaching out over the bog's pool, that place where Otherworld breathes close. I think of black henbane's usefulness in releasing a spirit from a body, and how she had said, "I wanted to be lifted to Otherworld." I think of her saying "I've deceived you," and "Hobble's imperfection is my punishment." I bend toward belief.

I count back from my birth. The Night of the Departed, that one night when the gates opening onto Otherworld stand ajar, falls nine moons earlier. I put a hand over my heart and count again. I swallow truth.

Fox claps, a hard clap, and for a moment, faces jerk in his direction. A dozen women touch their lips, then the earth.

My mother gets up from her knees, puts her palms on my father's cheeks, holds his face toward hers—her pale skin and rosy mouth, her straight nose and dainty chin. "Smith," she says, like a plea. "I was wretched. I don't seek him anymore. It was a long time ago."

He averts his gaze, and she firms her grip.

"You're her father in every important way," she says, shifting so that she returns to his view, as if with her lovely, sorrowful eyes she might always hold him under her spell.

He turns his face, looks at Reddish, who now takes up the central frame. She watches him, skepticism apparent in her cocked head, as though she is all too familiar with him and the way he surrenders to the woman he has trailed since boyhood, a tiresome, never-ending chase.

He puts his gaze back on my mother. "I banish you," he says, in a strong clear voice, as is the right of a man with an adulterous mate.

The bog dwellers gasp. It takes me a moment to catch up, to realize that today my mother has pummeled my father's already battered heart a final time.

Fox claps a hand against the stone altar, and when the bog dwellers continue to mutter the names of the gods, familiar words of homage, he strikes it again.

"You can love her still," my mother says, hands fallen from his face. "You will love her still?"

He remains silent, withholding comfort, as she deserves for all she has withheld from him.

He will love me still. I know this. His love will persist undeterred by lineage. He cannot help himself any more than can I.

Arc fathered me, but my true father feeds me and clothes me and shelters me. He repairs the thatch, the wattle and daub. Bitter nights, he rises to stoke the fire and draws the furs tight under my chin. He takes my hand, strokes my hair, kisses my brow with a tenderness foreign to most men. He wields a dagger as he nears a druid, undaunted by the repercussions promised by such an act.

My mother grasps, pulls me close, plasters my face to the crook of her neck. She weeps, shoulders heaving, breaks her sobbing only to kiss my hair, my dry cheeks. Sullen and Old Man put their hands on me, on her, as though she is not banished, as though she remains one of our own. Her embrace, her weeping persist. I keep my arms pressed to my sides.

Suddenly I taste metal, await the flash of white light that comes in an instant. Then I see my mother skirting a wheat field. Her hand moves to her neck, to the amulet resting at her throat: A silver Mother Earth's cross. Finely detailed and magnificent. Handiwork meant to capture an indifferent heart.

Then, I am again prisoner in her embrace. As I breathe in her familiar scent, my rigid arms soften. But that vision—that glimpse of the past rather than of days to come—appeared so that I would be reminded of her first lie, told at a long-ago Feast of Purification, a claim to have offered the amulet to Mother Earth at the bog. Or perhaps, it was not at all the first.

"Be gone, adulteress," Fox bellows. "Be gone from this place where our sacred traditions are upheld. Be gone from Black Lake."

But still, her grip does not loosen, not until I squirm and duck from her arms. She stands dismayed a moment, then extends a hand toward me. I think of my curse. I think of afternoons pondering its source. With our many likenesses and her easy acceptance of mystery, I had wondered if she knew firsthand something of prophecy. I had thought of my father, his ironwork, how certain pieces appeared guided by the divine. How grossly naïve. My curse is born of neither but of darkness, infidelity, my mother clutching tight to what we are not meant to find in this world. I step away from her extended hand.

My mother stumbles in the direction of the path, and stumbles three times more before I can no longer glimpse swatches of her blue dress between the trees. My heart beats steadily, calmly, for I am outside the scene, detached, as though all that might come is as impossible as what has already taken place.

Next I know, Shepherd is snatching up his two youngest children and Second Hand Widow one of hers, as if they are making ready to flee the grove. But then I spy a strange sight, a staggering red fox—its twitching ears and white throat; its trailing, bushy tail—and I understand they are clearing their children from its path. Its yellow eyes shine, the pupils round and full, grossly dilated.

I find myself seeking my mother, her opinion of the diseased creature. But, of course, she is not here, and I glimpse years of looking over my shoulder to catch sight of her attentive face, her absent face. I sway on my feet.

The fox lumbers in loopy circles, falls onto its side. Four paws stretch open; each digit splays wide. The limbs tremble and jerk. A hind leg repeatedly grazes the sharp edge of a rock until the fox grows still, lifeless. In that instant, I know. The creature had feasted at the pit where I emptied the tribute vessel holding the black henbane and mead poured from the silver goblet last night.

Then the bog dwellers appear to remember why we are gathered, and the fear they brought to the grove—fear magnified by the edict of human sacrifice and then briefly interrupted by a reddish-purple crescent and a fox—comes back full force. If not me, then who?

My father stoops, picks up the red fox by the tail. "First we learn that Hobble isn't—" His voice breaks, and he swallows. He flings the creature onto the altar. "Then a fox comes into the grove and takes its last breath."

He looks at the druid, and I understand the portent he is assigning to a fox collapsing in Sacred Grove just now.

His gaze holds steady on Fox as the druid works out for himself the conclusion my father has already reached. And then, like kindling taking up flame, one bog dweller and then the next catches his meaning and stands with chest flared.

Carpenter pulls a dagger—another forbidden dagger—from his breeches. "Divine for us," he says, pointing the blade toward the druid. "Tell us the meaning of the departed fox."

"Tell us how you were prepared to slay Hobble," says Hunter, who also brandishes a dagger, "when it's you the gods demand."

"None of us would let you slay Hobble," Seconds says, his gentle face as fearsome now as his raised dagger.

"Or any one of us," Reddish says.

"Fox or no fox," Sullen says, holding a dagger at the ready.

"Never again," Walker cries out.

A chorus of "Yes, never again" echoes through Sacred Grove.

More daggers are slid from beneath breeches, from between folds of wool. I feel the warmth of sunshine raining down, though there is no chance of rays penetrating the grove's murk. My father feels it, too. I can tell by the slight lift of his chest. I again seek my mother, confirmation that she, too, perceives the bog dwellers' embrace. But she is not here and does not know the bog dwellers are moving toward Fox. This, when even Chieftain would drop to bended knee in a druid's presence. This, when a poisoned fox lurked at the grove's fringes, awaiting the precise moment to show itself.

Fox holds his hands out in front, palms up, gently pumping the air.

There had been no collective sigh of relief among the bog dwellers after he said, "The gods demand the firstborn of your First Man." They had not said, "Let Hobble be slain. We are spared, and she is lame." No, they parted, making way for my father, his drawn dagger, and then they drew theirs.

Fox bends onto one knee, then the other, his face weary, beaten.

"I don't deny the meaning of the fox," he says after a silent moment, head bowed. "I don't deny that the gods show us the price of their favor. I'm glad to know of my usefulness in securing the Romans' defeat." Fox lifts his chin and looks out at us. "You, too, should be glad and rejoice with me."

We wait, suspended, uncertain how to proceed, though we well know the sacred rites: First, the heels of our palms must go to our foreheads, as is our custom in exalting Protector. Then the ax must be lifted from the stone altar and a crushing blow struck. But this man, this Fox—prepared to give his life for his rebellion, even now unwavering in his belief—how unsteady he makes us. Daggers drop to sides.

"I've got a ewe waiting," Shepherd says. "A fine ewe. Twins most every Hope. I'll go fetch her." He nods and makes for the path leading to the clearing.

"Be still," Fox commands, and Shepherd freezes.

Fox closes his eyes, bows his head, awaiting the blow that does not come.

He lifts his face to my father. "Give me your blade."

My father hesitates for a moment, then tilts the handle of his dagger to Fox. He grasps it, holds it to his own throat. "You will do as I command, or I will cut my throat," Fox says, his voice steady. "You will honor me, honor our gods. You will follow the sacred rites as long have our people."

Fox bows his head. My father lifts the heel of his palm to his brow. We follow, and Fox waits for the blow my father finally delivers with the ax. Fox falls sideways onto black moss and lies there, unconscious, the whites of his eyes exposed, until Hunter and my father lift him onto the stone altar and put him on his back with the mistletoe wreath laid on his chest. We draw fingers across our throats, paying tribute to War Master. Hunter slips a length of sinew around Fox's neck, knots it in place, and then pulls it tighter by rotating a stick slid between sinew and skin. Still Fox's chest rises and falls. We touch our lips, the black earth, and Carpenter slides his dagger into the right side of Fox's neck, severing the vein so that blood drains onto the altar, spills onto the moss, sating Mother Earth. Hunter gives the stick a final twist. Breath ceases and Fox's head lolls to one side, his cheek meeting the blood pooling on the stone.

The men carry Fox's body to the bog—my father and Hunter at the shoulders, Carpenter and Shepherd at the feet, the rest of us solemnly trailing behind. I watch as my father peers down the path at each turn, as he catches sight of a splash of blue. I want to run to him as he slumps, realizing he has only mistaken a bed of forget-me-nots for a swatch of my mother's dress.

As we near the bog, the woodland opens to a brush of greenery not yet flowered. My father looks east, then west. He casts an eye over the causeway, and I know he feels the weight of Fox's body, the heaviness of the hanging mist that does not reveal my mother kneeling there.

At Begetter's wheel, the men set down Fox's body and run their hands sunwise over the old wood. Then the procession continues. Fox's head lolls. His mouth gapes open. His neck drips blood. I feel only relief as the body slides into the bog's pool. The men stand silent on the causeway, palms flattened against their chests in tribute to Begetter, as do the rest of us gathered on the shore.

The gruesome task accomplished, the body sinks, disappearing from view. Protector got his blow, War Master his garroting, Begetter his drowning. Mother Earth drank her fill. But to what end? So that the gods might be with the tribesmen as they raise their swords somewhere in the east? So that Fox might depart this world with his illusion of victorious rebellion intact?

"No bog dweller will march east," my father says. "None among us will be bludgeoned, garroted, drowned, nor drained of his blood. Hobble will go on as before, running like the wind. Let us remember some part of this day, though, our low feelings just now. Let us remember our uncertainty, the comfort that has not come, though we followed the command of a druid. Think on it," he says.

And I do. I think of Fox's insistence, his conviction that glory awaited on the battlefield. And yet we will go down in defeat. Druids are mere men—men with earthly needs and earthly desires, and with the earthly frailties that accompany fervent zeal, too. Fox will not be the last to urge men into violence, hatred, to proclaim righteousness, to assure triumph—assertions that only the less zealous can see as unsure.

Tanner brushes one hand against the other, as if to rid himself of the undertaking, and says, "It's almost like he never came to Black Lake."

With Fox departed to Otherworld, I will enter our roundhouse without dreading that I will find him inside. And I will lie on my pallet without stewing over his intentions; my father, too. But my mother will not lie beside him. It is not almost as if Fox had never come to Black Lake.

35.

DEVOUT

~~~

EVOUT HAD BEEN CAMPED IN the woodland bordering a river for almost a moon, surviving on greens and eggs. In the distance, the swath of paving stones leading first to Hill Fort and then to Viriconium cut across the land. As severe as vengeance, she had thought on first sighting the Roman road. It meant the market town was close, but she felt no triumph, only the burden of days that would stretch on without end. Without Hobble. Without Smith.

She had meant to push on to Hill Fort, but as she watched from a thicket, small groups of tribesmen trudged along the road in the direction of Hill Fort, some bloodied, some bruised, all heavy footed as yoked oxen. When finally she worked up the nerve to approach one of the travelers, she chose a lone youth hauling a handcart. As she drew close, she smelled rot. Closer still, she saw that his eye socket glistened blue red, that his handcart held stacked bodies. A severed head knocked the side rails, bobbing on a sinew loop drawn through punctured ears. "Boy," she said, "you have news about the rebellion?"

He said Camulodunum, Londinium, and Verulamium, those three largest Roman towns in Britannia, had been reduced to ash and their citizens wiped out, a massacre that tallied eighty thousand. His good eye avoided his cart, and he kept his voice buoyant as he continued. With those early successes, Boudicca's ranks had swelled to seventy thousand by the time they met the Roman army. He paused, and his chin trembled. Boudicca's rampaging horde had charged the Romans, spreading over the plain like milk over a tabletop. The Romans held still, their front line a wall of shields with swords protruding from the right-hand gaps. The boy wagged his head slowly, as though the air were thick as pitch. "We severely outnumbered them," he said, "but we never stood a chance."

He told of the defeat Hobble had prophesied—tribesmen falling, Romans pressing forward, trampling the toppled men.

"They were your kin?" she said, indicating the stacked bodies.

"Except the head. Belonged to a Roman." His voice broke as he said, "A trophy to remember my father by."

He was eager to press on. Even so, she made him wait as she gathered purple loosestrife, as she beat it with a stone and gently pressed the pulpy mash to his eye socket. She instructed him in preparing a new dressing and applying it twice each day. As he resumed his journey, his cart creaked under the weight of all it bore.

She retreated to the thicket, put her face in her hands a long while. Then she gathered the provisions she needed to set out the following morning. But when daybreak came, mounted Roman warriors appeared on the road, the madness of battle still clinging to them as they hooted and slashed their swords through the air and jabbed their heels into their horses. She settled back into the thicket.

She had kept to the woodland ever since, venturing to the river only to collect water. Great flocks of marching Roman warriors had begun to appear in the distance and the odd tribesman, scuttling along the border of the woodland. Twice, as she collected greens and eggs, she had come upon a tribesman's body—a boy with a severed arm, an old woman with her entrails spilt from her gut.

EARLY ONE MORNING, intent on filling her drinking skin, she paused at the oak that marked the edge of the woodland and peered from behind the trunk, surveying first the road and then the near bank of river. All appeared clear.

She lifted her drinking skin from her shoulder and crouched on the bank. But then, just as she lowered the skin toward the river, the water before her shifted, as though a sudden gust of wind had disturbed the surface. An area roughly the size and shape of a face took on the color of flesh, dark hollows emerging where one would expect eyes and mouth. The water around the face gleamed milky white. She fell onto her backside, then scrambled to her feet. She took a further backward step, and then Hobble's sweet voice rose from the river and whispered, "Wait." The next moment the water was as before, calm and reflecting the blue sky overhead.

Devout skittered behind the oak and then slid down the trunk to squat at its base. Her heart fluttered that Hobble, who had ducked from her arms, had somehow pierced the long distance from Black Lake to whisper an instruction. Had she softened toward her mother? Had Smith? The next moment, though, Devout remembered her exhaustion, and tilted her head against the trunk. How her mind played tricks.

Then the sound of splashing water came from beyond the oak,

and she peeked around the trunk. She gasped to see a Roman warrior kneeling not more than six strides away, bathing his forearm in the river. He leapt to his feet, drew his sword, held it in the direction of the oak, the gasp. She dropped her drinking skin as she scrambled to standing, the heel of her palm flying to her forehead, her lips mouthing the words *Hear me, Protector.* This was it, then? This was how she would meet her end?

He stepped closer, and his eyes widened. Recognition flickered in his face. "You," he breathed, and the point of his sword fell to the ground.

He was, in fact, familiar—unforgettable for the scar that extended from behind his ear to the base of his neck. He had been among the warriors who had come to Black Lake. "I tended an abscess," she said and touched behind her ear, indicating the spot.

"You reminded me of a girl I left in Italia." His shoulders rose, fell. "Your grace was the same."

He picked up her drinking skin, filled it at the river, and nudged it toward her, though she could not direct her hand to reach for it.

He tried again, and she took the skin, drank from it, and passed it back. He swallowed a mouthful, sat down, placed the skin on the dirt beside her.

Eventually, she shifted to sitting on the ground bedside him and told him that she was called Devout, that she was headed to Hill Fort but had been living in the woods. She had seen Roman warriors and knew by their yelping she should stay hidden.

"Still drunk on blood," he said.

She glanced at his forearm, the raised welts he had been bathing in the river. She went into the woods, came back with a handful of dock leaves, rolled them between her palms until they were bruised, and then placed them over the welts, telling him all the while how Crone had taught her, that her daughter—tears spilled as she said *Hobble*—knew Mother Earth's magic as well as she.

"You weep for your daughter?" he said.

She wiped her face with the back of her hand. "I was sent away from her."

"How so?"

"My mate's doing."

"The blacksmith," he said.

She lifted her eyes, struck that he had remembered Smith's trade. "It was his right."

The Roman stared at her for a long moment. Then, his eyes still fixed on her face, his hands moved to his neck, where he tugged on a length of gut and coaxed from beneath the neckline of his armor an amulet of gleaming silver. "I'm meant to return this."

He ducked his head, removed the length of gut, held it out to her, nodded certainty.

Perhaps she was not awake. Perhaps he had not lowered his sword but thrust it under her ribs. She blinked, then blinked again to see the Mother Earth's cross that Smith had crafted for her in their youth.

Impossible.

Incredible.

Slowly, feebly, as though she were an old woman who had lost steadiness of limb, she reached for her lips, the earth, and then the amulet. She held it in the bowl of one hand while the fingers of the other traced the raised intricacies of the cross, the smooth outer ring. "How?" she whispered.

"The evening you tended my abscess, your mate showed it to me. I threatened him with a dagger. I wanted it."

She remembered Smith following the band of Romans from the roundhouse into the black night. But still. She lifted her shoulders, bewildered that Smith had, for a time, possessed the amulet she had lost.

Eventually the Roman said, "This last moon—" and shook his head. "They say more than a hundred and fifty thousand are slain." He turned his solemn, searching face to hers. "I brush against stinging nettle, choose this spot to bathe my arm. You happen to appear, the same woman who tended my abscess. The woman who can at least right one wrong."

She threaded the gut loop through her fingers, felt the weight of the silver against her palm. He had thrust his sword into old men heaving stones, into young boys waving daggers. Then he had turned to pondering just what he had achieved in Britannia, what civilizing force he had delivered. He had wielded a dagger against a man who shared his beer, whose mate had nursed his wound. Then he stole the man's prize. It seemed, now, that he had linked that night to the smoldering tinder Britannia had become.

She held herself still, uncertain, pondering her own failings, how deception had kept her distant from Smith, unworthy of him. If she had been different, if she had let him bask in her love—a man so cherished as he—might his love have survived her deceit?

"His gaze didn't leave you all that evening by your fire," the Roman said. "He thrust his dagger into the tabletop with such force that I knew he meant to tell me he would not hesitate. He would give his life for you."

Her eyes glistened, damp.

The Roman cupped his hands beneath hers, and her gaze fell to the beauty, the grace resting on her palm. "To look at the amulet is to know his devotion, his steadfast love," he said.

He lifted the gut loop, held the amulet over her head. She dropped her chin, and he lowered the loop around her neck.

She sat, fingering the cross, drawing together this fragment, then that, of her life with Smith. She turned each fragment in her mind, pieced it into the patchwork of their story until a single hole remained in the assembled account—the part that had taken place at Black Lake after she stumbled from Sacred Grove.

IT IS THE FRAGMENT of my parents' story that I, Hobble, can describe with precision, without calling on imagination to fill the gaps. I could tell my mother that my father grieves, that he looks longingly toward the trackway coming from the southwest and wraps his arms around the pillow where once she rested her head. I could say I have softened, would not again duck from her embrace. Anger has slipped away as I construct, as my parents' story takes shape, as I decide I possess a gift that was not born of darkness but of love, a gift I can harness to bring her home—to my father, to me. I think how water vaporizes and collects and spills back onto the earth, how some droplet of the pool before me wends its way to the water my mother drinks.

DEVOUT CLOSED HER EYES, smoothed her fingers over the ridge of her eyebrows. She thought of Hobble whispering "Wait." She thought of herself retreated to the oak and then of the Roman appearing and lowering the gut loop so that she might wear an amulet crafted with steadfast love. She thought of her mate waiting, his hand on the place where she once lay beside him.

She lifted her face to boundless sky.

36

HOBBLE

≋

MY FATHER JAMS THE FLATTENED end of a bar beneath the end of a plank and begins the work of prying loose the walls that had boxed him inside the forge. He removes one plank and then another. As he begins a third, Carpenter appears and works a second bar, prying loose the opposite end of the plank. Hunter comes, helps with the next. Singer approaches and Old Man, Shepherd, and Tanner, too, then a dozen other men. Soon enough his forge is as it once was—low walled so that the heat might escape, so that my father might greet a passing bog dweller, so that he might look to me in the fields.

I bring mead into the clearing, and then Reddish and Hunter's mates do the same. The bog dwellers sit on stacked planks in late afternoon sunshine, laughing, enjoying mead, and saying that the wheat flourishes, that in two moons we will sharpen our scythes. Sliver combs my hair, fusses as she decides the position of a braid. Once my hair is braided, coiled, and pinned into place, Seconds sets aside the slingshot he has been whittling. "We'll go to the causeway today?" he says.

Usually, after we run its length, we sit together at its farthest reach, our feet dangling over the pool. Ever since my mother's banishment, I peer into the black depths as the sun creeps lower. At first I pondered the patchwork and then, once that patchwork was near complete, I turned to willing my way to my mother, to the water she drinks. Seconds whittles or sands the dozen tablets commissioned by my father or lies back, hands clasped behind his head. Ever patient, he watches damselflies dart and dodge, or dreams up an improved yoke, an improved plow.

I wave a hand to take in the basking bog dwellers and say to waiting Seconds, "I'm enjoying this."

His eyebrows lift. Am I certain?

I nod. Today the black cloud of my mother's absence is kept at bay.

"Good," he says and the lips I know to be soft—he has kissed me twice—lift into a smile.

At one point, my father stands, swallows the final gulp of mead from his mug, and proceeds to the entryway of the forge. He reaches overhead for the bronze serving platter, works it free of the brackets fastening it to a timber brace. He carries it back to the gathering, says, "I think it might fetch a pair of oxen. With a youthful pair, we could clear the woodland to the east of the fields. The earth drains better there. We'd increase our yield and have a field that better withstands too much rain."

Hunter nods, gets up from the makeshift bench of planks, crosses the clearing, returns with the skull that has long hung over his door. "I won't see you trade your platter, not unless you take this old skull."

My father touches the skull, the hole pierced by Old Hunter's spear. By accepting the gift, its meaning would shift. Anyone setting eyes on it would be inclined to think of alliance, even friendship. I look from face to face in the clearing, taking in warmth, softness, eyes not stirred from my father as we await the answer he will give Hunter.

"All right, then," my father says. "I'll take your skull."

I think how Fox saw the world as though looking through a length of hollow reed. Only a single outcome was possible, as far as he could see, and he would achieve that end. It did not matter that I had prophesied otherwise. It did not matter that a ragtag horde of tribesmen never stood a chance against the Romans, that any one of us, even without prophecy, knew that truth. History had not swayed him, neither our easy defeat seventeen years ago, nor our western highlands wiped clean of the last holdouts against Roman rule. He turned his mind from tempered blades and hinged armor and practiced skill in hurling spears, in rotating lines. We had witnessed zealotry blind a man, had watched as he bowed to the final blow he believed would secure his one possible outcome. I had heard Hunter say to my father that the druids' undoing was the way they clung to the past. My father had nodded, and I supposed it made sense that the Romans knew the druids schemed to take back supremacy, to return Britannia to an earlier time. "We'd do well to remember that," Hunter said.

How I want my mother to know the reflection such a man as Fox has awoken among the bog dwellers. How I want her to see the softness returned to my father, and budding in Hunter, too. How I want her to feel the togetherness, the goodwill stirred at Black Lake.

———

AT NIGHTFALL, we gather in Sacred Grove, that place where the words *I banish you* had fallen from my father's lips and slid into our ears and the carpet of black moss, the crevices of the ancient oak's bark, the recesses between stone and earthen floor. He passes a hand over moss, trunk, stone, earth. He licks his palm, gathering the collected words with his tongue. He swallows long and hard and holds up his hand so that the bog dwellers might see his empty palm. A hawfinch flies beyond the grove, returns to her chirping fledglings a dozen times, as my father passes from woman to man to child and puts his mouth against an ear. He pulls breath deep into his mouth and swallows, and each bog dweller says, "Gone. Gone. The words are gone."

He turns last to me, lays a hand on the back of my head. With his other, he holds my chin. His lower lip touches the lobe of my ear and his upper the ridge traversing the crest. He draws a great breath. He swallows bitterness, the words that once escaped his mouth, and then they are gone.

He touches his lips, then black moss, and stays on his knee a long moment, his head bowed.

I think of the Feast of Purification all those years ago when, for a brief time, an amulet hung from my mother's neck. I picture Fallow's cold, empty fields on that day, the slow thaw of Hope that had not yet arrived. Then I recall the vision that came to me as I endured my mother's final embrace here in Sacred Grove: As she touched the amulet resting at her throat, the field just beyond her was not marked by the bareness of Fallow but was awash in resplendent green—just as the fields are now.

I turn to my kneeling father, feverish to describe for him the truth soon to take shape alongside the flourishing wheat—my mother appearing as she had that last day in Sacred Grove, except that her blue dress has grown tatty and caked with dirt at the hem, except that she wears an amulet, except that her face brims with hope.

Acknowledgments

Written during a period of personal tumult, *Daughter of Black Lake* was eight years in the making and required extraordinary patience, faith, and skill from my agent, Dorian Karchmar; and my editors, Alison Fairbrother, Sarah McGrath, and Iris Tupholme. I am ever grateful for the grace and dedication of these women in bringing this book into the world.

I am grateful, too, for the boundless support offered by my steadfast friends (most particularly the Riverdale crew and Kelly Murumets) and my ever-loving family. Without you, *Daughter of Black Lake* would be a lesser book, or perhaps not a book at all. A heartfelt thank-you to my first reader, Ania Szado, for telling me, all those years ago, that she wanted Hobble to have a voice; to early reader Henry Krause for his keen eye and the heartening speed with which he polished off the book; to archaeologist Willie Rowbotham of Odyssey Adventures for arranging an insightful tour of the relevant museums and archeological sites in Great Britain and for expertly answering the thousand questions my sons and I asked along the route; and to archeologists Don Brothwell and Anne Ross for their exhaustive efforts to decipher the life and death of Lindow Man.

Many books were important in researching this novel, particularly Joan Alcock, *Life in Roman Britain*, Tempus Publishing, 2006; Don

ACKNOWLEDGMENTS

Brothwell, *The Bog Man and the Archaeology of People*, Harvard University Press, 1987; Alan Crosby, *A History of Cheshire*, Phillimore & Co., 1996; Barry Cunliffe, *Druids: A Very Short History*, Oxford University Press, 2010; P. V. Glob, *The Bog People: Iron Age Man Preserved*, Faber and Faber, 1969; Miranda Aldhouse Green, *Dying for the Gods: Human Sacrifice in the Iron Age & Roman Europe*, Tempus Publishing, 2002; Christina Hole, *Traditions and Customs of Cheshire*, Williams and Norgate, 1937; Ioná Opie and Moira Tatem, *A Dictionary of Superstitions*, Oxford University Press, 1989; Anne Ross, *Everyday Life of the Pagan Celts*, G. P. Putnam's Sons, 1970; Anne Ross, *Druids, Gods and Heroes From Celtic Mythology*, Douglas and McIntyre, 1986; Anne Ross and Don Robins, *The Life and Death of a Druid Prince*, Touchstone, 1991; M. J. Trow, *Boudicca: The Warrior Queen*, Sutton Publishing, 2003; George Patrick Welch, *Britannia: The Roman Conquest and Occupation of Britain*, Wesleyan University Press, 1963; Graham Webster, *The Cornovii*, Gerald Duckworth and Co., 1975. In addition, two ancient texts, Cassius Dio's *Roman History* (book 62:1 to 62:12) and Cornelius Tacitus's *The Annals* (book 14:29 to 14:37), were used extensively in researching this novel.

Fox's firepit sermonizing on the abuses of the Romans draws heavily on a speech Cassius Dio attributes to Boudicca in his *Roman History* (book 62:3 to 62:5). He asserts that she delivered it to her seething horde of tribesmen just prior to facing slaughter by the Roman army.